Logost

Kris Villarreal

ISBN-13: 978-0692284858
ISBN-10: 0692284850

DEDICATION

For Tyler Medler, for believing in me when I couldn't believe in myself.

ACKNOWLEDGMENTS

I would like to acknowledge all the survivors of sexual assault and abuse. This book is for the broken, the beaten, and the abused. This book is for the people who felt trapped, helpless, and who couldn't see past the hurt. To all my lost souls; this book is for you. You are not alone.

{1}

I've never been normal. When I was seven years old, I discovered I could fly. That dark fall morning, my brothers were playing on the fire escape behind our apartment building. Each one would race down to the last set of stairs, and then jump to the bottom. I watched them take turns as they pushed off their heels, landing with a sharp quickness on to the sidewalk below. When no one was watching, I ran down and jumped too, mimicking their movements.

But I was too little, and I jumped too soon.

My Mom screamed from our apartment window, as she envisioned my small body slamming in to the pavement. But it didn't. They watched me as I floated over them for a while, looping back up to our apartment window before cascading down and letting my toes caress the concrete.

Two years later, my Mom stood in our brown and white kitchen, assembling the ingredients for snicker doodles, her favorite cookie. She was having one of those days when tears would spout

1

from her eyes like a broken fire hydrant, off and on every few seconds. She shouted for one of my brothers to bring her a stool, so she could reach the mixer from the highest cabinet, but neither one came.

She leaned against the counter and hung her head in a silent sort of sadness. I wanted to help her. So I asked the mixer to come to her instead. The cabinet door opened as it had in my mind, and the mixer levitated in midair and sat down beside my Mom.

That day I learned that I could control any object that I wanted.

I've been reading minds for as long as I can remember. With practice, I taught myself to make the Earth move and the weather change, with just one thought.

'Unusual,' was the word my Mom used to describe me and my brilliant difference. But I liked thinking of myself as 'the other,' a phrase I'd created some time ago to remind myself that I would always be different, special, an anomaly that would never exist again.

That day was ordinary. Nothing felt special about it. I had no way of knowing that would be the day that I met him. I felt that same longing for greatness that I always did, and that longing usually led me finding myself alone, sitting in Fort Tryon Park near the Cloisters, an outdoor museum of medieval sculptures and humbly quiet gardens.

The park was a few blocks down from our apartment, and most days after school it would eventually occur to me that I was sitting there. When the final bell would ring, I would step out of the school, past the metal detectors and wire fences, and just start walking. Not really thinking about the direction my feet chose, but somehow I always ended up there. That lonesome park was the one place where I didn't have to fake it. Keeping up false pretenses and giving fake smiles wasn't a requirement because few people came there. So that's where I was that day, sitting on a damp park bench outside, next to the French Medieval Cloister, allowing the gentle rain to fall on my face.

My favorite spot was a small bench that overlooked the Hudson River. A willow tree hung over it, and in the warmer months I loved listening to the sound the leaves made when the wind tousled them. But it was November, and there were no leaves on the trees. The sky was cloudy and gray, and although it was so cold out that I could no longer feel my ears, I made no move towards my home. Even in winter the scenery was enough to make you stay – frozen water droplets coated the trees in such a way that seemed unlike the Earth. The barren gardens embedded themselves on the backs of my eyelids. This was my sanctuary. No one would judge me here. I didn't have to lie to the stone bridges or the leafless tree that hung over me in vain.

I sat there near the river, and watched as a father and his daughter stood inside one of the stone archways. The father picked up his daughter, and put her on his shoulders, reading her the origin of the French sculptures that depicted a distant time.

"How pretty," I heard the small child thinking, and she reached out her tiny hand.

I envied the girl. I had no father. My parents never married and my father had never been a part of our lives. My mother liked to pretend that he never had existed. She never entertained our questions about him. My brother Paris had a picture of him, though. He found it in our Mom's jewelry box one day, and kept it hidden from her in a drawer next to his bed. I caught him looking at it once, and he handed me the black and white faded picture of our Dad.

In the photo, our Dad stood near a willow tree in a field filled with dandelions. In the background was a stone cottage, covered in vines. He had black hair and gray eyes. There was certain wisdom about him in that photo, but it was hidden by a deep sadness that showed only in those gray eyes.

I wondered what if I would be a different person if both my Dad and my Mom were home waiting for me. I dreamed about that sometimes – about that perfect family with two parents in a home where there was enough money that we didn't have to sign up for free lunch at school. And where we didn't have to live in Inwood, we could live somewhere nicer, and safer, like Manhattan.

"Please don't hurt her," I heard the girl's father's train of thought change. And I watched through the father's eyes, as a man with a knife stood there whispering to him that if he just gave him his wallet he would not hurt either of them. The thief didn't want to hurt the man and his daughter. That much was clear in his mind. He was desperate for money, and he pictured a small boy in his head that would need food for dinner that night.

I wanted to stop the man from robbing them, but I worried

about the little boy who might go hungry. I thought about the man turning and leaving, and usually when I thought about something I wanted someone to do, it happened. But the man just stood there, holding the knife.

There was a sudden change in the atmosphere, and I sensed someone's eyes watching me. I searched for the mind, I searched for the person who was watching, but I couldn't feel them there. I wanted to leave, but my limbs were locked in place. There was someone else there, and I knew it. The caring thief turned his back to the man and his daughter, apologized, and retreated – no wallet in hand. But it wasn't me who had made it so. I looked up at once, and that was the first time that I saw him.

A man crouched atop the stone archway looking down at me. He wore a gray pin-striped suit and a collared shirt, with the top three buttons undone. His eyes were a dark green, but I could see gold swirling around the irises. The man's features were strikingly unreal. He looked like a glimmer, a fading image that only I could see. He locked eyes with me, and I found myself unable to look away. I walked toward him, no longer thinking of the child and her brave father. I thought only of him as he held my eyes for what seemed like days. I wanted to fly on top of that archway, and ask the man if he'd done that. If he could control minds like I could, but the instant I pictured my feet leaving the ground, he faded away.

I stood there for a second longer, and then I flew to the top of the archway and searched for traces of his thoughts. I found nothing. But I could hear someone laughing. The laughter was dark, unnerving and I could feel it taunting me. The wind blew past me, ruffling my hair, and I swore I heard it whispering my name. I sat on top of that archway, waiting to see if the man would return, but he didn't. And once the sun set, I walked home to my tiny apartment and my small family.

"Dinner's ready, Mina," my Mom announced as I walked through the door. She worked as a teller at the Inwood City Bank, and was always home before I was. My older brothers sat at our ragged dining table, which was given to us by one of her friends who pitied our misfortune. I told her I wasn't hungry, and that I needed to study, but really I just wanted to be alone.

"You never want to have dinner with us," Paris said from the dining room.

"So what," I replied heading towards my room.

"Paris is right, Mina," my Mom called out to me. "You have to stop all this loneliness! You can't keep acting as if you're the only person who matters." She pinched the rim of her nose and tilted her head back. Her job stressed her, her life stressed her, and I stressed her. My mother didn't understand me. No one did. I was alone, lost and waiting for something I wasn't sure I would ever find.

I wanted to hold on to the memory of that man. I needed to preserve his face in my mind, but no matter how hard I tried, he didn't seem real to me anymore. I kept picturing his face, and the gold swirls in his eyes that had bewitched me. That part must have been real. And the feeling he gave me when I looked in to his eyes, was one that I would never forget. It was a feeling of a complete loss of control, an utter and dooming vulnerability.

I pictured those eyes as I drifted off to sleep, and I dreamed of the man who was just like me. I went to the park every day after that, and searched for the strange man, with the strange eyes. There were some similar looking men there that lingered about, dressing as he had, but it never was him. I tried to forget, but I still dreamed of those eyes. Those eyes I would surely not forget.

{2}

A month passed, and I didn't see the strange man again. It was Monday and I sat alone, as usual, on my bench near the river. The wind blew in to me, and I felt it chill my bones. I had on my wool overcoat, scarf, and hat, but my nose was raw. Under my coat, I had on my comfort sweater. A sweater I wore when I was feeling less than exceptional, and Monday was a day for feeling rather unexceptional.

It was after school and I knew I should have been on my way home, because it was almost time for the street lights to click on. But I couldn't move myself in the direction of my family's small apartment. I've never been a huge fan of New York City's winter ugliness, but I knew home would be worse. My brothers were probably at their friend Chris' house in order to bypass the evening.

My Mom had planned a big dinner for her new boyfriend, Micah, who I had met before. But this dinner was supposed to be the breaking point to see if he could get along with me and my two brothers. I liked Micah. He played the guitar, and used big words like 'existentialism' and 'neo-liberalism.' He was well-groomed and always nice, a little boring, but I couldn't hold that against him. No, it wasn't that I didn't like him – it was just that I knew he would be gone soon.

My Mom went through boyfriends like you would tissue when your nose is running so bad that you have to sleep with your mouth open. So what was the point in me getting to know him? She never made up her mind about anything, least of all men.

I pictured her reaction to my lateness and wondered if I could freeze time, but was too afraid to try. I was afraid of most of my powers. I was afraid of flying too high and falling. I was afraid of reading someone's mind and having to hear something unpleasant. The sun could shine and the wind would stop if I decided to make it so, but things like that don't typically go unnoticed, and it was a goal of my Mom's to keep my abilities under the radar.

So instead, I sat on that bench near the river and concentrated on shifting the large boulders at the bottom. I wasn't always so indiscrete about using my powers, but I was bored that day, and my mind was set on prolonging that inevitable walk home. The boulders were harder to move when I couldn't see them so I was frustrated, and desperate for a quick peek at the river bed. I looked around to make sure that no one was watching, and no one was from what I could see.

I stood up on the park bench, closed my eyes and drew in a steady, slow breath. A current of electricity surged through every cell in my body as the winds blew in a gentle circle around me, singing my name. My eyes turned dark – and I couldn't see, but I pictured the water separating and moving further, and further apart.

"*How are you doing that?*" I heard someone whisper. I jolted back in to consciousness, having almost forgotten the time and place. I thought about running, but I backed away from the river's edge and focused on finding the body that held the mind of that voice. But I felt nothing. I opened my eyes and I saw nothing.

"*How did you do that?*" I heard the unknown ask again, but no one had spoken. The voice was only in my head. Their thought patterns were unrecognizable because I wasn't reading their mind – they were reading mine.

I sank to my knees as I felt a sharp, aching pain in my skull. I felt the urge to scream, but held back. I gritted my teeth and then it happened again. That same feeling of intense vulnerability overtook me. Whoever it was, they were determined to know everything about me. I was immobilized as I watched every memory and thought my mind held wash over me. The memories were tiny, like watching them in a dark room on an 8 inch television screen that's too far away.

"Are you alright?" This time the voice was definitely out loud. I rolled over on to the ground and on my back, staring up at the darkening sky. I thought I was dreaming when I looked in to those eyes again. A man's face peered over me in concern and what looked like anxiousness.

"I'm sorry," he said. "I didn't mean to hurt you. Can you hear me? Are you alright?" he asked again. The man was very thin and tall with dark hair. His eyes were that same dark green, his features angular – too straight and narrow. He reminded me of that distant memory, of a faded glimmer of a person, but there were no gold swirls in his eyes. It was hard to tell if he was the same man. He stared at me in astonishment, waiting for me to say something. But I couldn't stop staring in to his eyes. He looked so nervous, so worried. My limbs trembled under his close-watch.

"I'm fine," I admitted in embarrassment, staring at the crook in his nose. I had to look down. I couldn't watch him once he bore his eyes in to me.

"I *am* sorry," he apologized again, but his tone changed. I could hear the confidence behind his words, and all signs of his nervousness began to fade. His face was controlled, but he kept his jaw clenched. "I lost control when I saw what you were doing. You didn't answer me. I didn't know if you were dangerous."

"Why would you try to hurt me? I'm not dangerous," I said sitting up.

"I wasn't trying to hurt you," the strange man said. "I just didn't want you to hurt me. I needed to know how you could move the water like that. I've never seen anything like it. That's why I forced your mind to replay every memory you've had since birth."

"All of them?" I thought about the things I wouldn't want this peculiar man to see. The things I'd done in private, the things I wanted to keep secret. "Is it supposed to hurt like that?"

"No, it usually doesn't hurt. I shouldn't have done that. I didn't realize how young you are. I promise not to do it again," he said, but the look in his eyes was too honest.

"I didn't answer you because I was afraid. Can you help me up?" I asked as he grabbed my arms and pulled me from the cold ground. "How did you speak to me in my head like that?" As curious as he was about me, I was just as curious about him. He was the same man that I had been searching for. How odd that he would go around doing good deeds and disappearing, but when he'd nearly caused me to go into a seizure he lagged behind asking questions.

"That's one of my gifts," he said. "I can convince people to hear, see, and feel whatever I want." He smiled widely revealing his white, absolutely straight teeth. "I'm brilliant when it comes to manipulating the minds of those around me." He smirked again in dark satisfaction.

"You're like me, then?" I asked.

"In a way yes, but in other ways no, we're of the same kind, but I highly doubt we're very much alike. Tell me, how were you able to make the water move?"

"I asked it to, and then I pictured it in my head."

"That's all? You didn't have to do anything else?" I shook my head. "You're so young," he said scrutinizing my face and hands. "What else can you do?" He stared in to me then. And I felt as though he were searching for something inside me. I couldn't look away once the gold swirls around his irises returned. Without thinking, I asked the wind to blow. And it blew past the strange man, I asked it to circle him, and it did. The debris and fallen leaves that lay on the ground moved all around him. And he let go of my eyes.

"Amazing," he said. He put his finger under my chin and

tilted my head upward, looking down at me. Chill bumps covered my arms as he touched me. His face was so breathtakingly perfect. Despite my fear, I felt an unfamiliar longing to stare in to those eyes for all eternity.

"You're beautiful, extraordinary," he said and my breath hitched. No one had ever given me so much attention before. I didn't know how to react, and this man was intimidating. "Show me more," he said. "Show me all that you can do."

It was getting late and it was very unlikely that anyone would walk down near the Cloisters after nightfall. But I was still hesitant, and a little frightened by the fervor in his voice. I knew that I couldn't show him all that I could do, even if I wanted to.

"I'm not really supposed to," I said. "My Mom thinks it's risky. She doesn't want me to hurt myself. She wouldn't want me to be here. I should leave," I told him as I turned to walk away, but the strange man grabbed my arm.

"You can't leave. Please," he said, but I knew he wasn't asking me. "I won't force your will, but if you try to leave I'll just follow you, and you won't be able to outrun me."

"I'm not afraid of you," I lied. "Who are you?"

"Drew Elliot, but I'm sure my name means very little to you."

"I'm Mina, Mina Culvert. I would say it's nice to meet you, but this introduction hasn't been exactly pleasant." I rubbed the space on my skull that still ached.

"Please, Mina," he purred staring in to my soul. "I know you want to. I know that you've always had to hold back, so beautiful, but not brave, always so timid, always so afraid."

"I'm not timid." But I *was* afraid, and I didn't want him to know that. I hadn't ever seen the full extent of my abilities. I didn't know what it would look like. I wanted to see it though, and I was suddenly desperate for his approval. Frightening wasn't a word that I ever used to describe myself, but I wanted this man to be terrified of me.

I stepped away from him and back towards the river – my hands shaking in fear of the unknown. I sucked in another cold, deep breath, and closed my eyes. I let my feet leave the ground, and I promised myself not to crash down to the ground below. Flying was new to me, as I rarely did it, and I walked my feet over the river, instead of gliding. I flew further up in to the sky as I hovered above the water, and I called to the wind asking if it would comfort me. It blew past me with certain swiftness, and I felt it balancing my feet as it swirled around me stronger than it ever had before.

I summoned the clouds and the rain, and asked the lighting to shatter and break upon the water's surface. The water ran parallel with the wind and it whirled around me in a circular motion. Then my body plunged in to the river, separating it, and allowing me to drop straight to the bottom, without a drop of water touching me. I shot back up in to the sky, and I landed behind Drew, but not before flinging a boulder from the river directly at him. He dodged it, and flew up in to a tree, landing on the branch that hung over my bench.

A natural high overwhelmed me, and I felt like I could kill him only too easily if I wanted to. The strangest urge to hurt him, to watch him die shattered in to a dark corner of my mind. I couldn't control myself, and my laughter came out in a deep barrel and shook the ground. With each blink of my eyes I motioned for the tree to shake him loose. I made a move toward him, and he raced to meet me before I could take another step.

"Is that what you wanted?" I asked, but he was silent. I looked away once his eyes focused on mine. "What do you want?"

"I don't know yet," he said moving towards me. I made no move to protect myself. "You're stronger than I thought. I need time to think about you." I thought about causing him pain. I pictured his bones ripping out from his body, but he only smiled at me, unaffected. He forced me to look in to his eyes. "I don't want you to upset me. I don't want to see such power go to waste."

Not needing any further explanation, I ran down the paved walkway leading back to the street, and when I could no longer see him I flew in to the sky. Suddenly, he appeared beside me and pulled me back down to the ground.

"I want to help you Mina," Drew said. "I've come here because you need to know more about who you are. He placed both hands on my shoulders and whispered in my ear. "You're not stronger than me. I don't want to hurt you," he said comforting me with his lies. The ground started to shake and grumble beneath me as Drew called to the stone statues that stood in the French Medieval Cloister. "Come," he said with veracity and one of the statues walked towards us. The stature broke in to a run sprinting towards me, it lifted off the ground and its mouth opened in an earsplitting scream.

I turned my back to shield myself, covering my ears.

There was a booming blast and the pieces of the statue shattered over me.

"I should leave," I said.

"No, don't go. I'm sorry. I did come here for a reason. I came to help you, to save you. You don't belong here, Mina. You belong with me."

"Are you insane?" I asked completely baffled by his words. He looked confused. "I don't belong anywhere, and I certainly don't belong with you."

"You need my help."

"Just tell me who you are, please? Why are you saying these things? I just want to be left alone. I can't think clearly with you trying to get inside my head." I could feel him there, trying to convince me that I wasn't afraid of him, but I knew that I was. Images of me running from him were mixed with thoughts of kissing him and killing him. I couldn't trust what my mind was telling me with him in my presence. "Please, just let me leave. I have to go home."

"Fine," he laughed. "But aren't you always alone? Don't you want to know more about what you are, and why you have these powers? You don't have to answer. I already know that you do, and I know that you don't *really* want me to leave. You've been searching for me, dreaming about me at night. I've seen it all, Mina. And I'm here to help, I'm not lying."

"There's no chance I'll believe what you say," I said only to myself. It didn't matter what I said aloud, he could hear my thoughts. I felt naked standing there.

"I'm a teacher for people like us, Mina."

"They're more people like us?"

"You have a lot to learn, and you'll be killed without my help."

"Will you be the one to kill me?"

"I hope not, but only time will tell. I have no way of knowing what will come to fruition. I just know that I need to take you away from here. It's not safe for you or your family if you stay. Don't you want to keep your mother and brothers safe?"

"How do you know about my family?" I asked, and he didn't answer just as I'd foreseen. "What do you mean 'away from here,' this is my home? I have nowhere else to go."

"You could go with me if you'd like. The school where I teach is called Winchester, and you belong there, Mina. Where you can learn and be with people like me and you. Just stay here with me. There's more to be said."

I couldn't handle anything else he had to say, and my mind felt too fragile to be near him any longer. "I can't – my Mom's dinner," I said. "I have to leave."

"Can I come with you?" he asked. "I should speak to your mother. She should know that you belong at Winchester. You belong with me," he said again. "Would you please invite me to your mother's home for dinner?" His demeanor changed when he asked, and I knew that he was trying to be charming. I rolled my eyes at his ill attempt.

"You're welcome to come if you want," I said afraid to reject him. "But I doubt it will be tasty. My Mom isn't the best cook. And today's Meatless Monday. Besides, I'm sure you already know everything about me that there is to know anyway, so it would probably be best to just leave me alone."

"I don't think I can do that." Drew said quietly, and the intensity of his words frightened me even more. I said nothing, but I kept my mind focused on him as I was unaware as to what he may do next. I stared down at my feet as I led the way.

{3}

We walked the four blocks down the road to my apartment, where I hoped my two older brothers would be. Not a word was spoken between the two of us. I kept my pace a few feet ahead of him, but I felt him watching me. He was probably convinced that I would try to make a run for it, but really I was too afraid. I kept trying to force myself in to his consciousness, but was blocked at every turn. I wasn't use to having to guess what people were thinking. I hoped that he wasn't some serial killer, who had plans to murder us and eat us.

His powers were stronger than mine, probably because he was older, and I didn't know if I could stop him if he decided to hurt me and my family. I pushed the thought to the farthest corner of my mind, and broke the silence as a quick distraction.

"What are the others like?" I said. "The ones who are like us? Can they control objects too?"

"Everyone's powers work in different ways," Drew told me. "Some can do things that others cannot. It was a surprise to see you

19

controlling the water like that. I thought I knew of every Logost on this Earth." The strange word was overwhelmingly familiar, but still I couldn't place it.

"What's a Logost?" I asked.

"You and I are Logosts. We have an extreme mental capacity and can often control people and the objects around us with our thoughts. But you're something different, Mina. I've never seen anyone who can alter all the elements with their mind."

"Is that why I make you so nervous?" I guessed.

"Not nervous, just wary. You possess great power, perhaps even stronger than my own. You need to learn control. You'll have to be taught so that you don't hurt anyone, unintentionally."

I ignored the arrogant way that he hung on the word *unintentionally*. It was obviously some clue to his strange behavior, so I tucked it away to further examine later.

"And I suppose you'll be the one to teach me, Drew?" I guessed again, hoping those were his intentions. I'd never met anyone else quite like me, and I was desperate to spend more time with this eccentric and frightening man.

"Call me Mr. Elliot. And you'll need more than just me to hone your craft. Most students start at a younger age, but your gifts are extraordinary. The principal will be impressed that you're self-taught."

"I just started high school. There's no way I'm switching schools."

"You seem to be confused. You do not have a choice in the

matter. If you do not go to school then you will be killed. You are too great of a risk for me to allow you to live without training and a strong sense of responsibility."

"Why do you keep bringing up killing? You've killed people before, haven't you?" I asked and Drew grew quiet. He increased the protection around his thoughts. I didn't want to press him further, in fear that he may not say more.

"Can all Logosts read minds?" I asked, changing the subject.

"Very few are mind readers."

"But you can read minds?"

"Yes, we've already discussed that."

"I know. I'm just trying to figure you out, and why you would take such an interest in helping me." I smiled, trying to keep my mind empty.

"Like I said before, I've never met anyone who could control the elements, although I've been trying myself for several years..." He stopped and faced me.

"Why would you want to control the elements?"

"I don't need to answer that. You're clever enough to figure it out without my help." He gave me another fake smile. His eyebrows almost touched his hairline.

I would tuck that away for later too. "What else can you tell me about this school?"

"It's small. We house around 150 students and the numbers haven't changed in years. It's a rare occasion when a Logost is born. Everyone in the community is notified. That's another reason why I was so shocked earlier. It just didn't make any sense that you would exist. We're all required to register ourselves with the Informants, our government. Where's your father?" He asked me unexpectedly.

"Why do you care where my father is?"

"The only memory you have of him is an old photograph. Your mother isn't a Logost, so your father must have been. Do you know anything about him? It surprises me that he would take such a great risk by hiding you. Do you know where he is now?"

"No, I've never met my father. My Mom doesn't talk about him." Any mention of him tended to make her very sad. The thought of my Dad made me feel unwanted. I didn't want to talk about this anymore. "What's the school called again?"

"Winchester Academy, it's disguised as a boarding school for wealthy children in the French Alps. Logosts from all over the world come there to be trained."

It was about 45 minutes passed dinner time once we reached my apartment building. We walked the four flights of stairs, and I knocked instead of just waltzing in. I didn't know what my Mom's reaction to this man would be, so I thought it best to prepare her.

"Who is it?" She said politely. Micah was still there, I could hear the quiet murmur of his thoughts near our kitchen.

"Ma, it's me Mina!" I shouted rudely on purpose, just because I wanted Micah to see the actual level of politeness that was reached in our home.

"Did you forget your key again?" She asked, sounding irritated before even getting a confirmation. I always forgot my key, and it got under her skin.

"No, there's someone here with me," I said hoping that she would just open the door and stop asking questions.

"Mina, who is this?" My Mom opened the front door just enough for her face to peer through.

"This is Drew Elliot. I met him at the park."

"Nice to meet you, Drew," she said in her fakest tone of voice. "I'm Olivia, Mina's mother. You'll have to forgive me but this isn't the best time for company. Why are you here? *And why did you bring him here, Mina?*" She asked me in her head.

"Because he told me to, it wasn't my idea," I replied knowing that Drew could hear her thoughts anyway.

"I'm here to discuss your daughter's special gifts." Drew said eyeing Micah who sat in the corner at our small dining table. "But I think we should talk in private."

"Private?" My Mom asked.

"Yes, if you could please ask him to leave I'll explain," Drew said still standing in the doorway. If my Mom hadn't invited him in yet, it was doubtful that she would.

"Ask *him* to leave?" she said and I could see her short temper flaring. Whenever my Mom's top lip disappeared, I knew she was about to explode. "I think *you* should leave before I call the police. There's nothing to explain as I am fully aware of my daughter's gifts. She is none of your business, and neither is my home. I don't care what you have to say. Leave, before I lose my temper."

"You have no idea how much she is capable of. I'm only

trying to help. Please, just listen."

But I knew she wouldn't. She wasn't interested in learning more about me or what I could do. She wanted to pretend that I was just like everyone else.

"Get out now. Stay away from my daughter." She screamed, emphasizing each word.

The expression on Drew's face didn't change. I wanted to say something, but I couldn't think of anything that would keep me out of the line of fire with my Mom. Contradicting her in front of strangers was a death sentence. But I couldn't let Drew leave.

"No, don't go," I said to Drew. "Please Mom, just listen, he's told me so much already. He's the only connection I have to myself. I know this is weird, but please try to understand."

"Mina, I don't think you understand how much danger you put yourself in today by being alone with this man," she said. "You don't know him. I'm sorry but he has to leave."

Drew faced me and then stalked off towards the empty stairwell.

"Just because you don't care about what I am doesn't mean I don't," I said to my Mom as I pushed past her in to the apartment. "You just want me to hide."

"I don't want you to hide. I just want you to be happy. I want you to be normal."

"Was Dad like me?" I asked, and her face turned to hardened stone, the look she gave me when she was trying to keep me from reading her mind. I knew she wouldn't say more. I knew that she couldn't. It would hurt her too much to try. I walked over to the window to see if Drew would fly away in to the cloudy night sky, and he did. I wanted to leave with him. I pictured myself soaring by his side, and the idea of ever being that free gave me a feeling that I had never had before.

{4}

That night I couldn't sleep, and my eyes were swollen shut from exhaustion the next day at school. Every time I closed them, Drew's face was in my mind, mouthing words I couldn't hear. I felt a weight bearing down on me that next morning, and the more I tried to remember the dream the foggier the details became. Drew seemed different in it – intimidating and more frightening than I wanted to admit. I still hoped that he would come looking for me. I needed to know more about Logosts.

After two hours of staring at my alarm clock, waiting for it to scream at me, I decided to get up early. I spent more time than usual getting ready. Lingering in the shower, and putting fancy makeup on my eyes in an attempt to stand out from the other girls at school. Getting attention was like breathing to me. I wanted people to notice me. And I wanted to look older, but I usually failed at it. My small chest and narrow hips were two of the few things that made my confidence falter. Even though I was pretty, all of the guys at school seemed to be after the curvier girls, the ones who acted older and looked more mature. But the idea of dating any of the boys at my school was horrific.

I didn't want them. I just wanted them to want me.

"Oh my God," Carter screamed. "Mina! Hurry up and get out of the damn bathroom!" He said banging on the door. "If you're not out of there in five minutes I'm taking the hinges off this stupid door and throwing you out into the cold."

I took one last look in the mirror, deciding that my hair was hopeless. I leaned against the bathroom door to see if I could hear Carter on the other side. I waited until his back was resting on the door, and I flung it open with such force that he tumbled over in to the hall.

Carter got up and elbowed me in the stomach. I reached back and smacked him on the head as hard as I could, and ran for my bedroom. I got dressed quick, throwing on a gray, knit sweater dress with leggings and tan boots, then went to the kitchen to grab a piece of fruit for breakfast. My Mom sat in the living room with a wool blanket wrapped around her shoulders. She was usually dressed before we were, but she sat there in her pajamas, her hair disheveled.

"Mina," she said, and her voice was tired as if she hadn't slept last night either. "Why don't you come sit with me, we need to talk." I didn't feel like talking. I just wanted to forget the whole thing. Micah had been thrown off by the dramatics of the night, and left early without any explanation. When my brothers got home she told them what happened, but blamed me as usual. I didn't want to hear what any of them had to say so I stalked off to my room, and pretended to sleep to avoid their accusations.

"We really don't have to, Mom. I need to leave, anyway. I don't want to be late."

"Just give me a second to explain myself. I know you want to know more about why you're so different. And I know I haven't been much help. But I need you to understand that some things are just better left unsaid for now. I promise that there will be a day when things will become clearer. I just hope that you won't stray from me, Mina. And the values I've instilled in you."

"Why would I ever? You know I try hard to do what you ask."

"I know, but you're young. You shouldn't have trusted that man yesterday. I want you to promise me that you won't do anything like that again. And if he ever finds you again you won't go near him."

I didn't know if I could promise her that, but the look in her eyes was so scared and helpless, as if she felt there was nothing she could do. And really there wasn't. If Drew came back, I wouldn't be able to stay away from him, but I lied and said I would. I hated to lie, but I knew it was best, for her sake anyway. I gave her a hug that lasted longer than it should have, kissed her cheek, donned my winter gear, and rushed out the door, grabbing my books on the way.

"Wait for your brothers," My Mom shouted. "I don't want you walking to school alone. It's bad enough you go to that park all by yourself, if you come home again when the street lights are on, you're dead." I don't know why she worried. It's not like anyone could hurt me. I had a knack for sensing danger, and being able to manipulate the minds of others put me at a slight advantage over almost any attacker.

It wasn't long before Carter and Paris emerged from the main door of our building. I sat on the steps looking at a fashion magazine when they stepped out.

"Finally," I groaned getting up from the top step.

"Why would you try to walk to school alone, anyway?" Carter said. "Did you forget where we live? This isn't Manhattan," he said eyeing my magazine. I stowed it away inside my Algebra book.

"I'm capable of handling myself," I said. "I don't need you two trying to baby me."

"You may not need us babying you," Paris butted in. "But you definitely need some sense knocked in to you. What were you thinking yesterday? I mean honestly, doing your freaky shit in public was stupid to begin with. Why don't you just quit it, and try to stay away from grown men while you're at it. You don't want me and Carter to catch a murder case, do you?"

"I can't quit it," I argued. "That's like me telling you to stop being so smart or telling Carter to stop scoring touch downs."

"That's different," Paris said. "It's just weird, ok? I bet if you stopped for a while you'd be able to forget you can even do that stuff."

His words hurt me, and all my little insecurities started to eat away at me. I hated to feel like an outsider, but I always did. I was on mute for the rest of the walk to school. I couldn't even look at Paris.

Paris was taller than me and unusually shy. His light brown hair and blue eyes stood out in our family. He was only a year and a few months older than me, but he was a junior, and the girls in his grade swooned over him as if he were some kind of king.

Carter was older than Paris and I, a senior in high school who would graduate in the spring. His short, stocky frame and dark curly hair matched his temperament.

I was the sophomore, the youngest, the least coordinated, but by far the best looking. I was an average height for my age, skinny, and well-kept. My hair was long, dark, and wavy. My face was round, a perfect setting for my huge and childlike, light-brown eyes.

I had never been stellar at academics or any extracurricular activities like Carter who was good at football, or Paris who always made the principal's list for his awesome grades. I was rash, mean at times, and too boyish in most ways. I floated, drifted through life. I could be passionate about one thing for a few weeks at the most, and then I typically moved on to the next. I never felt the need to excel at anything because I already knew I was special. It would have been nice to know that I was the only one who could control things with my mind. It irked me that Drew had similar abilities.

"Mina?" Paris said. I didn't respond. My eyes stared down at my feet. I wanted to fly away and go anywhere, be anyone, but me. No, that wasn't it. I wanted to live in a world where I didn't have to lie about who I was, where I could be proud of my gifts like Paris and Carter were. Where my Mom would beam with pride when I got recognized for my talents, and where I didn't have to feel like my main goal in life was just to blend in. Blending in was weak, a light shade of gray, neither black nor white but muddled, and lost in between the two contrasting colors.

"I must have hurt her feelings," I heard Paris thinking. *"I just wish she could be normal, that's all. I'm not asking her to change."*

He didn't get it. He didn't understand why I could never be normal, and why I would never want to be. And that by asking me to stop using my gifts, was asking me to change.

School felt like burning for all eternity that day. I couldn't stop thinking about Drew, and that just made me anxious to leave this dismal school with its remedial students. I was still in a slump because of what Paris said that morning, and that made things even worse.

High school sucked in general, but it was harder for me because I couldn't walk through the halls without everyone shouting their most intimate thoughts at me. I had to concentrate to keep the murmurs out, but some still slipped through.

"I wonder if Ian noticed me at breakfast this morning. He's so hot. If I could just get him to look at me. Maybe I'll try sitting next to him at lunch, or dropping my pen near him in English." Some tall, blonde girl thought loudly as she stood by her locker.

We arrived early to school that day, and that meant sitting in the school cafeteria until the first bell rang. When we walked in, a few of Carter's friends from the football team motioned for him to come and sit down. A lot of older brothers wouldn't want their younger siblings hanging around their friends, but Carter was different. He was very protective of us both, and he always wanted us around. Despite our occasional bickering and rough housing, we all genuinely liked one another.

We sat down at the very back of the cafeteria with Carter's four friends. I sat between Carter and Paris just like always, and pretended not to notice the menacing looks the other boys gave Carter for allowing me to sit there. It was common knowledge that sophomores didn't sit with seniors, even in the morning.

"Nice dress, Mina," said Theo, the only one of Carter's friends who ever acknowledged my presence. "Too bad it would look better on someone who didn't have the body of a nine-year-old boy." He said with laughter caught in his throat.

"Thanks, Theo," I said pretending to be clueless. "I didn't realize you had such a strong attraction to nine year old boys." Theo's mouth hung open for a bit, and Carter punched him in the shoulder signaling him to leave me alone. I pulled out my fashion magazine and flipped through the pages as if I were reading it for the first time. I didn't want anyone else to talk to me, and if I pretended to be busy they were less likely to annoy me.

"Paris," said Dana. We all turned around to watch her walk up to the table. Dana was tall, curvy, brown-skinned and by far one of the prettiest girls in school. She always made me nervous. She'd been after Paris for what seemed like months now, but as far as I knew they were still just friends.

Dana slid in at our table next to Paris and started playing with his unkempt hair. I hated being subjected to this, but I didn't dare complain in front of her.

"Cute dress," she said to me and I could feel my adrenaline

racing. She spoke to me, and I needed to say something back, but I was silent for several moments in search of the perfect phrase to prove my awesomeness.

"Mina, stop being so rude, didn't you hear Dana speaking to you?" Paris said.

"Thanks, yours is a lot prettier though," I said, chewing on my fingernail. Then I dropped my magazine like the clumsy creep that always submerged, no matter how hard I tried to keep it at bay.

"You look very pretty today," Paris said to her. Dana leaned in to him and they started making out right there in the cafeteria, in front of everyone. I felt my breakfast rise to my throat and I had to swallow back bile to keep from vomiting. Our table went silent and all eyes were on Dana and Paris. But my eyes shot to Theo, and I saw what he was thinking before he had a chance to make it happen.

"Damn, Dana! You look too good to mess around with Paris. You and me need to hook up," said Theo and he reached his hand back to slap Dana's bottom. I concentrated on Theo falling backward before he was able to go through with his intended action. He stumbled and fell on to the floor. The cafeteria roared in obnoxious laughter.

"Thanks Theo," said Dana. "But I prefer guys who can talk *and* stand at the same time."

"Did you do that Mina?" Paris asked. I smiled at him. *"Thanks,"* he thought. *"I'm sorry about this morning. I guess you do have your moments."*

{5}

The first bell rang, and I parted ways with my older brothers and dashed off to homeroom, where I knew my closest friends, Beau and Samantha would be waiting for me. Beau and Samantha were good friends, but we weren't close. I had to keep my distance from most people because I had to lie about almost everything.

They were both kind of mean, but so was I, so I didn't really mind it. We tended to pick on a lot of the other kids, mainly because we were all so insecure. Beau and Samantha usually did whatever I said – they were kind of like my back-up dancers. They knew I was different, but they fawned over me anyway because they both thought I was pretty.

I nodded my head upward, greeting them as I sat behind Beau and next to Samantha. "And how are you two lovely ladies doing this morning?" I said. Neither of them responded, and they kept their heads facing towards the front of the class.

"I do not want to be here today," Sam sighed. "I wish I could leave, this is going to be the longest day ever."

"Why?" I asked.

"Because Ian won't stop stalking her," Beau said. "If you just agree to go out with him, he'll leave you alone," he said to her.

"Gross, I would never go out with that overly-masculine, cocky idiot," Sam said. "He can't even spell the word 'resign.'"

"How do you know that?" I asked.

"Because I stupidly agreed to help tutor him in English, and now I wish I hadn't. He thinks I like him."

"Let's skip today," I said not really asking, but telling. "I can't be here today, either."

"Yeah, fuck this place," Beau said. As bad as school was for me, I knew it was much harder for Beau. When you're one of the few openly gay kids in school, people tend to watch you like you might sporadically combust, or just do something really gay like sing show tunes down the hall. But Beau wasn't like that, he wasn't a stereotype. He was just Beau. He didn't care about trying hard to be straight or gay. I really don't think he knew how to be either. He liked guys, and I don't think that fact comes with a written personality script.

"I'm down, but not yet," Sam said. "We've already checked in to homeroom, if we leave now they'll know we skipped because our teachers would mark absences for the rest of our classes. Let's wait until lunch."

I didn't know how I felt about Sam. We'd been friends since second grade and I just got used to having her around. One day at the park, some mean boy had made her cry, so I asked all of the butterflies to come down and cheer her up. She'd been fascinated by me ever since. Sam was pretty, but she was dull. She was perfect in every possible way and that annoyed me, and bored me at the same time. I would never try so hard to be perfect. It just made you uninteresting, flaws added character, something that Sam was severely lacking.

When the homeroom bell rang, we merged with the swimming crowd of puffed up coats and headed for Gym, the only period besides lunch that we all had together. Sam and I walked in to the girl's locker room and changed our clothes. I noticed the same tall, blonde girl from earlier that morning. I wondered what she was doing there. I'd never seen her in Gym with us before. Once Sam and I were finished changing, we stood in line to enter the gym and the tall, blonde walked over to us.

"Excuse me," the tall girl said with too much attitude. "Is your name Sam?"

"Yes, it is." Sam said, looking her up and down.

Then the tall girl did something without thinking, so there was nothing I could do to stop her. She reached her fist back and punched Sam in the face.

"Ian's mine," she said. "I don't care if he likes you too. Stay away from him."

Likes you too? Why didn't this girl get her facts straight before physically assaulting someone she doesn't even know? Blondie walked out and everyone ran over to Sam, comforting her. I asked her if she wanted me to walk her to the nurse's office, but she insisted she was fine. Her thoughts stayed calm, it worried me, but I respected her privacy by not listening. I could tell she was ashamed even though it wasn't her fault. She didn't even like Ian, and now she just took a punch for him.

"She punched you?" Beau said as he balled over with laughter once we were inside the gym. "That is awesome! I would have paid to see that." I mouthed for him to stop because I could see how upset he was making Sam.

In Gym, we just sat in the bleachers and watched as the other kids participated. Most of the girls sat on the sidelines while the guys played basketball on rainy, cold days like these. Sam kept her eyes on Ian as we all watched the guys play another round.

"I don't get it," she said. "How does he make girls act so crazy?" Sam said rubbing her jaw. I looked at Ian and I couldn't see it either. He looked like any other boy to me. He was taller than most, but his face didn't stand out.

"You two are idiots," Beau said. "He ignores them and that's why they like him. And he's good looking too, even if you two can't see it, everyone else does."

His words made me feel like I was lagging behind. Everyone else seemed to have a crush or a date. Everyone except for me, Sam and Beau. I was glad not to be completely alone.

"How was last night?" Sam asked Beau, and he shifted his weight from one foot to the other.

"It was fine," Beau replied.

"What happened last night?" I asked. Sam said that Beau went out on a date with some older guy who owned several fancy restaurants downtown. The fact that he hadn't told me about his date bruised my ego just a little.

"Was it weird going out with someone so much older?" I said.

"A little," Beau admitted. "He makes me nervous and I always try to be more adult around him. He's unlike any of the guys here, but that's why I like him. Why do you care anyway, Mina? We all know you're asexual."

More than half the school was convinced that I wasn't attracted to either sex, but that wasn't true. The boys at school were average. They were immature. I was too different, and I could never really be myself with any of them. Sexuality wasn't something I dwelled on, anyway. I didn't feel like a boy or a girl and I hated having to choose a side. If I would have been able to, I would have liked describing myself as a *girly boy*, but I knew that sort of thing wasn't allowed.

The rest of the day wasn't as bad as it could have been, and lunch time came around before my stomach even started growling. As soon as the bell rang, we all met in the hall by my locker and made a run for it. We didn't live in the richest neighborhood, so our school was really overcrowded. If we wasted anytime we never would have been able to make it through the traffic jam of bodies to even get to the cafeteria.

We walked in, and sat at a table near the closest exit. Once the cafeteria was full, we ducked down and huddled our way outside.

We walked past the gym and headed down the road to a local pizza place on the corner of 5th and Maple Street.

"Let's not go in there," Sam said, before we reached the corner. "Cops love to eat here. If they catch us they'll send us back to school and call our parents."

"Oh my God, shut up." Beau said. "Who cares? Surprise, we're not perfect. It's not like anyone will really be shocked." He opened the heavy door to the restaurant, allowing the cold wintry air to rush in.

I felt something strange as I walked in – a familiar presence, an erratic and urgent longing that I couldn't place. But as we neared the counter to order, I saw him there. His hair tidy, his suit pressed, as he sat in a booth all alone, shredding napkins and balling them into tiny pieces. Drew impatiently waited for me.

"Some creep is staring at you, Mina," Beau said gazing at Drew. I thought about ignoring him, but the dull memory of the pain I felt the evening before hummed in my mind, and I walked over to sit with him. Sam grabbed me before I could get close.

"What are you doing?" Sam said, but once she saw the look in my eyes she dropped her hand. "Do you know him?" I was silent. I knew it was strange.

"Oh shit," Beau said. "She does know him. He's beautiful," he whispered.

"He looks older, though," Sam said, and she craned her head around the line of customers, trying to get a better look at him.

I imagined the structure of his face, and those piercing green eyes. I stared at his lips and thought about how soft they might feel. I had only kissed one other person, Sam, and it had hardly been romantic. She thought it would be good to practice with one another first before embarrassing ourselves with actual boys. I really didn't see the point in practicing at all as I had very little interest in boys, and they showed very little interest in me. But Drew wasn't a boy. What could he possibly want with me? I was kidding myself, grown men don't chase after little girls.

I looked down at my body self-consciously. Nope, I didn't have a shot, but that didn't mean we couldn't be friends, after all I wouldn't have to fake things with Drew. He was different, just like me.

"Mina," Drew breathed my name in anxious anticipation as I walked up to the black and tan booth where he sat. He pulled the shredded napkins together in to a pile, and brushed them away to hide his twitchy behavior.

"How long have you been waiting?" I said.

"Not long. I knew you would be here. I just wasn't sure when. I couldn't stay away. I wanted to leave, but here I am hoping you'll listen to what I have to say." His words made my pulse quicken, and I felt the urge to run. This was happening so fast, but I knew that I felt differently about him. I just didn't know how to explain the way he made me feel. It was as if he would take all my worries on as his own, and I wouldn't have to think about them anymore.

"I feel like I've been waiting my whole life for you, Mina," Drew said. "What you showed me yesterday in the park... I've never met another Logost like you. I heard stories of those who can control the elements and I wasn't sure if they were real. Your power beckons me to you in a way I can't explain. I didn't realize how entranced by you I could become because I was being so neurotic yesterday — trying to convince myself that you would be my undoing. But I haven't slept. I've only thought of you. I should have known by the feeling I got yesterday when you mentioned leaving. I couldn't bare it."

"How could I be your undoing?" I asked, and Drew looked away from me.

"Your powers are strong. I couldn't stop thinking that you would be the one to kill me, the only one powerful enough to finally end things for me." He took a deep breath and turned to look at me again. "I called to you in your mind last night. I wanted you to come to me. I wanted to kill you. I'm sorry for thinking that." It was stupid to trust him. He only wanted to kill me, but I couldn't get past the look of remorse in his eyes. If he really wanted to wouldn't I be dead already?

"What stopped you?" I said and exhaled. Fear rose in my throat, but I hid it from him because I worried he would be offended.

"The thought of you dying saddened me in a way I thought was impossible," he said. "I've killed so many others before, and I thought your death would mean nothing. When I envisioned you coming to me last night, I knew I wouldn't be able to go through with it. It would have been like killing a small piece of me. I need you, Mina. There's so much that I need to learn about you, and so much that I can teach you. I want us to stay together as one. But I'll have to train you. You have to leave with me and go to Winchester."

"Mina," Sam said as she walked over to us, leaving Beau to stand in line. She broke me from Drew's spell. *Was he manipulating me?* I couldn't be sure because the yearning to snuggle close to him returned when my eyes met his gaze. "We should probably leave," Sam said to me.

"No," Drew said. "You and your friend should be in school. Mina will stay with me."

"Do you want to stay with him?" Sam asked. I nodded, and sat next to Drew in the booth. He pulled me close to him and kissed my hair. Sam motioned to Beau and told him they were leaving. He gawked at me in astonishment.

"I thought Mina was smarter than that," I heard him thinking as they both turned to leave. I faced Drew and he stroked my cheek.

"I'm so confused," I whispered to him. "I just don't understand what it is you want with me. This whole thing seems wrong." How could I sit here in a booth with a man who had fantasized about my death? My mother was going to kill me, she'd been right. I should stay away from him, but I didn't want to. His voice, his smell, I wanted to breathe all of him in to my soul. I knew I wanted nothing more than to be near him – to know him.

"Was it you I saw in the park that day? Why did you help that girl and her father?"

"I hoped to gain more of your trust before telling you this, but I've been watching you for some time, Mina. I saw what you were thinking. That you wanted to help the man and his daughter, and I wanted you to trust me. But I needed to know more about your first, so I kept myself hidden, but I've always been here watching you. I couldn't help myself. Very few Logosts exhibit the desire to help anyone but themselves."

"How can I believe you?" I said. "How do I know you won't still try to kill me?" I asked speaking in to his shoulder. I looked up at his eyes, waiting for him to answer.

"I love you too much to ever hurt you, or to ever desire it again," he said. "Leave with me. I know your greatest dreams and your smallest fears. I can make all of them come true or none of them if you'd like. You can be yourself with me, Mina. I'll always take care of you. You won't ever have to hide or be afraid. I promise you, my love." I opened my mouth to speak, but found myself only staring in to his eyes, trying to find the truth in his words. I couldn't see it at first, but there it was — a small golden twinkle around his irises that comforted me.

I nodded my head again, and lay it on his shoulder. I nuzzled deep in to the space and inhaled his scent — only it burned in my nostrils. I wanted to stay this way forever, but I knew that I couldn't. I didn't want to leave my family, but I wanted to go wherever Drew would be. I convinced myself that he would always protect me.

Being that close to Drew made me nervous. I was no good at this. I didn't know how to be romantic with anyone, and I was sure Drew would realize that fact, and want someone older. He would want someone who didn't have the body of a nine-year-old boy, and who was more mature. I still laughed whenever anyone said the word 'penis.' I wanted to know what I was dealing with.

"How old are you?" I asked.

"Age shouldn't matter, Mina. What we have will be so much stronger. We'll be together forever, and it won't matter once you're older. But I will be one of your teachers once you've enrolled at Winchester. The other teachers wouldn't understand the way I feel about you. You shouldn't tell anyone there."

"Should I tell my Mom?" He laughed at me and I felt like I shrank two inches.

"You won't have to. Your mother is very intuitive. In fact, I'm sure she saw this coming. She didn't want me there last night, and I can see her point of view. She thinks I'm too old, but she's wrong. She doesn't realize how mature you are," he said and leaned in to me kissing my hair. It made me feel safe. "I will take care of you Mina, for as long as you want me around. I believe that I could quite possibly love you forever, if you'll have me." He laughed and I knew that I felt the same. It was strange because I barely knew him. I only knew that he was a Logost, and I wanted to be like him.

"I need to go," I told him. "I should go find Beau and Samantha," I said and I stood up to leave. I knew how I felt about Drew, but everything was still so new. I needed time to process things, away from him where I could think. I turned my back to him, and I felt his heart breaking as I walked out the restaurant to find Beau and Samantha.

I didn't have to look far. They were a few blocks up the street, sitting on a stoop near the Cloisters. I walked up to them in silence and sat down. I already felt self-conscious enough without the two of them gaping at me with their mouths open.

"Who the hell was that?" Beau asked.

"He's just a friend," I said. "I met him yesterday at the park and things have been a little awkward since then."

"Well, I think that's great Mina," Sam said. "I'm glad that you've met someone." But I could hear the indifference in her voice. Of course she would be jealous. "I just wish that he were closer to our age," she said. "Honestly Mina, you have no idea what his intentions are. He's a grown man."

"Don't be such a hypocrite, Sam. You were all flustered earlier when Beau was telling his story about that older guy. Why is it so different because it's me?"

"Because Beau knows how to handle guys, Mina. I'm not trying to be mean, but you really don't. And neither do I, I'm not pretending I do. I just want you to think this through. That man seemed so intense. It was weird. He made me feel cold. I'm not the only one. He gave Beau a bad feeling too." I glared at Beau for a confirmation and he dropped his head to avoid the intensity of my gaze.

"Do what you want, Mina," he said. "I know that whatever we say won't make a difference. I can see that you've already made up your mind." Beau was right. I wanted to be with Drew, but their cautiousness about him made me falter. I didn't know if I should reconsider.

"What is it about him that bothers you?" I said, looking only at

Sam.

She shrugged her shoulders and stared at me with guilty eyes. "The way he watches you and stares at you makes me nervous. It's almost like he's hoping you'll do whatever he asks. I've never seen you so easily swept up in anything, and I'm just worried you're making a mistake."

"I'm not happy, Sam," I said being honest for once. "You know that I'm different. Drew is more like me. He's different too," was all I said. I hadn't cleared up anything, and now I was going against what my closest friends were telling me.

"I understand Mina," Beau finally said. "I'm not happy either. But I think that's just a part of being young, being young means being melodramatic. I trust you though, and if you like that guy then who are we to judge?"

I wasn't sure about anything, and I didn't want to think about the decision I was making. It seemed wrong to be attracted to Drew, and I knew it was wrong for him to admit being attracted to me.

The school day was over, and Beau and Samantha went home in hopes that their parents would not be suspicious about us skipping. I wandered around the park for another hour or so and then I went home to my mother and brothers.

{6}

When I walked up to the entry way of our apartment building, I saw Drew standing there. "Mina," he said, and I found the way he hung on every syllable of my name irresistible. "I don't want you to be upset, but I just couldn't stay away." And he hung his head in unnecessary shame. I ran up to him and he embraced me.

"You knew I wouldn't be upset. You knew I would want you here," I whispered to him. He leaned in to me and kissed my forehead, sending a fear-filled quake down my spine. I pulled away from him. "How dangerous are you?" I said my voice shaking.

"Dangerous enough to keep you safe," he said smiling darkly again. "But perhaps not as dangerous as you." He winked at me, and pulled me close. We stayed like that for a while – standing there, just holding one another until I told him he needed to leave. My brothers would be home soon. He asked if it was alright to come see me again tomorrow. I told him it was fine.

And he waited for me every day after that, by the park bench that was no longer mine, but ours. Drew cared about the little things that went on in my life, like what the boys thought of me at school, or if any of them liked me. I told him they were stupid, that none of them were worthy of me, and he agreed. I admitted to him that I'd never had a boyfriend, nor had I ever been kissed by anyone besides Sam. He thought that was funny.

He wanted to hear about the girls at school that were jealous of me and Sam. And about how Beau was one of the meanest sons of bitches I'd ever met, but I loved him anyway. But more than anything else he wanted to know about my powers. Drew was entranced by me. He wouldn't blink when I would ask the rain to fall, or hold a tiny seed in my hand and persuade it to bloom, despite the cold.

Drew believed I was amazing, but he never talked about himself. I knew so little of his hopes, dreams and desires while he knew every thought that had ever crossed my mind. I assumed it was because he recognized my arrogance, and wanted to fuel my ego. He told me that I was the most beautiful, and that not a single creature on this earth could ever compare. He comforted me and I loved watching how powerful he could be. Drew could do no wrong in my eyes. He was frighteningly perfect.

No man would ever match up to his eloquence, intelligence, or the strength of his control. He told me that he could move mountains, and showed me in the park that he was able to control numerous objects and people all at once. I was mesmerized, and being near him was like a drug. Any time I spent away from him got me down. When he flew back to Winchester, it made me crabby and irritable. I believed that he was my happy, that he was everything that I would ever need. He flew back to Winchester each night when we parted and would come back for me when the school day was done.

But one day he left without a word.

Coincidentally, it was the same day as our first kiss. We hung over the bridge near the river in the Cloisters, making ripples and small gentle waves. He kept forcing the fish to jump out of the river and splash the freezing water on my face. I started to get upset, and stalked off to a tree garden nearby. He raced after me and pinned me to a tree, laughing at my annoyance as he leaned in and pressed his lips to mine. The feeling was unlike any other, and in a matter of moments I found myself drunk with passion and desire from the way he touched me. His breath felt quick and urgent, and it frightened me.

I pushed him away and told him to stop. "You don't really want me to stop." Drew said trying to manipulate me again. I shouted that I did, and my anger blew him five feet across the garden. I walked towards him, but he flew away without a word. I called out to him in vain. He stayed away for three days, and I cried every night hoping that he could sense my yearning for him.

That was when the nightmares began. Sometimes they were different, sometimes they were the same. Drew was there always and I was always afraid of him. When I woke, I couldn't remember the dreams, only the look in his eyes and my fear.

I didn't dwell on the nightmares. I thought they were just a result of my being attracted to and afraid of Drew at the same time. When he returned he told me he was sorry, but I'd hurt him. He explained that Logosts are always rash, that their emotions change quickly and are so much stronger than they can control. I understood because I felt that way too sometimes.

The nightmares came in spells after that, but they never went away. Images of me struggling with myself in the dark floated in and out of my mind. Things went back to the way they'd been before, but Drew never stopped asking me to leave with him. He wanted to convince me that I didn't belong in New York. And although I wanted to be with him always, I never agreed to go to Winchester. A part of me wanted to go, but the unknown had never been easy for me.

Weeks had passed since that day at the pizza place, and Drew had finally stopped pestering me about going to Winchester. I'd told him that the only teacher I needed was him. His hands cupped my face and I stared in to his alluring green eyes as we sat on our bench.

"I can't keep coming back here," Drew told me. The other teachers were suspicious of his constant absences. And there was no way he could keep this up much longer. "I need you, Mina. It hurts me to be away from you. But I want you near me always. It drives me crazy knowing that someone might try to hurt you, and I wouldn't be around to protect you."

"I can protect myself," I said and he knew that I could. There was no human on this Earth that could harm me. "I'm not ready to leave. My Mom needs me."

"Your mother is more selfless than you realize. She knows that other people need you, too. You need to be with Logosts Mina, with your own kind. You don't belong in your mother's world. You belong with me." He kissed my hair and I laid my head on his shoulder, looking up at him. He leaned his head down and kissed me softly at first, but his lips moved in a more urgent and rough way. He pulled me closer and the intensity of the kiss increased. I pushed him away and moved further down on the bench.

"I'm not sorry," he said. "This isn't fair what you're doing. You know I love you, please just be with me. Leave with me, please?" I was silent knowing that I couldn't say yes even though I wanted to.

"You know I can't. I love you too. But it's just not the right time."

"I'm done waiting for the right time. I think its best I leave you." He couldn't be serious. He knew what leaving would do to me. He knew that I couldn't bare it.

"Don't leave. You'd only hurt us both," I said as I kissed his lips. "I can't imagine ever being without you now that I know you exist." But he didn't say anything else. He wouldn't even look at me. The time had come. He'd had enough of my games. I knew I had to make a choice between my life here, and the new life that I wanted with Drew. I sighed, finally realizing that I wanted nothing more than to leave this place. I was finally ready for the necessary change.

"I'll leave with you," I told him. "But I'm not telling my Mom alone. You'll have to come with me."

"We should tell her you're leaving now, but I think we should wait to tell her about us. It might be too much all at once." I knew that he was right, but it didn't make me any less nervous. She would see right through me the second I walked through the door. There was no way I could hide from her.

"What should I say?"

"Just tell her that you love her, but this is what's best for you. She knows I'm with you. I'm not sure how, but I think she can sense my presence."

I used my key to open the door this time, not wanting to give her a forewarning of what was to come. When Drew and I walked in my mother and brothers were sitting in the living room, waiting for us.

"It's good to see you again, Olivia," Drew greeted my Mom as we walked in.

"I wish I could say the same," she looked at me, then turned her head in disappointment. Paris and Carter were silent, but the looks on their faces made it easy to tell what they were thinking. They wanted to tear Drew from limb to limb. I hoped they wouldn't try.

"You should leave, you fucking pervert," Carter shouted as he stood up from the couch. "I should fucking kill you for even going near her."

"Carter, don't," my Mom pleaded. "Sit down. Mina has something to say."

"I'm sorry, Mom," I said trying to meet her gaze, but she wouldn't look at me. "I know I said I would stay away from Drew. But being around him is one of the few things that make me happy. I need to be with other people like me. I won't be happy if I stay here."

"Listen, Olivia," Drew said. "I know this all comes as a bit of a shock, but I have no intention of hurting your daughter. I only wish to protect her and teach her control."

"You're not here to protect her," my Mom said. "You just want to take her away from me. I don't know you and I don't trust you."

"Mina trusts me," Drew argued back.

"Mina doesn't know who she trusts. She's just a child."

"You're right she is a child, but she cannot stay here with you any longer. You know our world Olivia, and you know what will happen to Mina if she does not attend a Logost school. The Informants – our government will put a price on her head and then they will kill all of you. I'm risking my own life by trying to bring her there. This is who she was meant to be. You knew this day would come, Olivia. Don't fight this. Mina belongs at Winchester where she can be taught by me and other Logosts. You've done her a great disservice by keeping her hidden so long."

"I've kept her safe, and that's all that matters," and then she was silent for some time, dwelling on some small detail that she didn't want to admit. "I know she's not happy. I feel like I've failed you, Mina," she said finally looking at me. "If I'd made things right, you wouldn't have any desire to be near this man."

"It's not like that, Mom. I promise not to stray from you. You know I won't ever really leave this place. This is my home."

"This is what you want? This is what will make you happy, to go to Winchester?"

"Yes, I believe it will."

"I honestly don't know much about it," she admitted. "I know that your father went to school there and that's it. I hope you'll be happy there like he was." Paris and Carter froze at the mention of the word, 'father.' It made us all uncomfortable, but at least now I knew. My father had been a Logost. He'd gone to Winchester just like I would. I hoped to be happy there too, just as he had been.

{7}

My Mom let Drew stay until the sun went down. He talked for what seemed like hours about Winchester, and how much I would love France and the people there. I could tell that he wanted to paint a picture for my Mom, of what my new life would be like. He wanted to comfort her, and let her know that I would be happy. I knew she wouldn't visit, but I hoped for it anyway.

Drew told my small family that I would have to leave for a flight first thing in the morning, so I wouldn't miss any more school. I wouldn't even get a chance to say goodbye to Beau and Samantha, but I wasn't worried. I had plans to come back and visit at holidays.

I woke early that Wednesday morning, so I could pack my clothes and belongings. Even though the leave wasn't permanent, it still left me with a troubled feeling, like I wouldn't see any of them again.

Once my things were packed, there was still an hour left before Drew would be here. Sitting in my room and staring at the clock made me anxious, so I decided to walk down to Fort Tryon Park. I walked along the river, lost in thought. I believed this was what I wanted. That leaving to start over was what I needed, but I felt my park calling out to me, asking me to stay. I sat down on my bench and stared at the water. I was motionless for several moments until I sensed Paris' presence. I recognized the loud, then suddenly quiet train of his thoughts. He was sad and angry, and I understood why.

Paris walked over to my bench and sat down. "So you're leaving us?"

"Don't think of it that way. I'm going where I belong, and I won't be gone forever."

"I know. It's just that things won't be the same without you here. Who will stop me and Carter from killing one another? Who will take care of us when Mom has her sad days?"

"You'll figure it out," I said. "We're not little anymore. Carter's leaving to start college in the fall anyway. Things were already going to change," I reminded him. "You will come visit me right, even if Mom doesn't?"

"Of course, you really think I would miss seeing what a school full of little freaks looks like." Paris laughed. We were both quiet for a while, sitting there enjoying one another's company. "Take care of yourself, Mina. I don't want to see you get hurt," Paris said. I knew he was referring to Drew, but he didn't want to say it out loud. He didn't want to admit even to himself that I was with someone so much older. "Just remember that things aren't always how they seem, and nothing is permanent. You can always change your path." Paris certainly was the wisest out of the three of us. I don't think he ever intended to be as philosophical as he was sometimes. I smiled at him, and stood up to give him a hug.

"I won't be gone forever," I said again, and we walked back to the small apartment together for the last time, where I knew Drew would be waiting.

My Mom sobbed in the doorway to our apartment building, burying her face in to Carter's shoulder. She told me that she loved me, and that she hoped I would do great things. She said she hoped that I would always try my best to be a good person. And do to the right thing, even when those around me faltered. I told her that I loved her and I asked her to be happy, to just try for me. No more crying, I told her. Those days were gone.

Drew loaded my suitcases in to the trunk of the taxi. I said goodbye, and we climbed inside. I leaned my head against the taxicab's window and cried silently. I let the tears fall, but I kept my face turned away from Drew. I wanted him to think I was more mature than that. I didn't want him to see me cry like a baby for her Mom, but that's exactly what I was, a baby, and he knew it.

The flight from New York to France was about eight hours, and it would be my first time on a plane. Winchester was on the outskirts of Chamonix, a small town near Mont Blanc, the highest peak inside the French Alps. I imagined it would be cold, but I figured that living in New York all my life had prepared me, it hadn't.

When we arrived in France, we took another taxi through

Chamonix to get to Winchester. Chamonix was unlike anything I'd ever seen. The city reminded me of the ballet the Nutcracker. A small river runs through the town that's paved with cobblestones and uneven walkways. Tiny shops and restaurants littered the streets. The houses and buildings looked like chateaus and nestled close together, snow lay over every inch of the toy-like town. Drew told me that I would meet the school's principal as soon as we arrived. Her name was Wilma Whorton, and he said she was an extraordinarily powerful and brilliant Logost.

Wilma Whorton was not a forgiving person, he told me. She would expect me to live up to the expectation that Drew gave her about me. I asked him why we needed to take a cab and why we couldn't just fly together. He explained to me that it was necessary to keep our powers secret. He told me that I was only allowed to fly at night and to use my powers in the most discrete way possible.

"We don't want a witch hunt on our hands," he laughed. I thought about what a real witch hunt would look like, and I didn't find it even the least bit amusing. I was beginning to see that Drew had a very dark sense of humor.

It was dinner time when we got to Winchester, and all the students and teachers ate together in a large dining hall near the school. The school rested on a hill near the mountains. Snow covered the space like a sheet of sparkling sequence. Wherever you went, whether it was in the city or at the school, you could always see the mountains. The waves of white ocean and stone followed me at every turn. A tiny little roadway led us up to the school and a stone moss covered sign indicated that we had arrived.

Winchester had three buildings. The largest one stood in the center, and Wilma told me that was where they ate their meals and held classes. The other two housed the students. The buildings looked like cabins, except for the one in the center. It looked more like a government building – square, gray, and with very few windows. The natural scenery of the campus looked like a painting, like someone had created all of it. The air smelled crisp and clean, the water was always pure. Several snow covered courtyards and frozen fountains enclosed the school's campus. And I'd never seen snow like that before. Snow in New York turned muddy after a while from the dirt in the streets. It would get dirtier and slushier as the days passed. But the snow here fell frequently and somehow managed to stay pristine.

Wilma greeted us at the front door and handed me a pile of starched and pressed clothing.

"What's this?" I asked.

"That's your uniform, Ms. Culvert." Wilma smiled at me with uncaring eyes. "I'm so glad you're finally here. You will be a great asset to the school. But you must study hard and practice. Diligence, perseverance, and learning to control your emotions are the keys to success in this life." Wilma's frame was tall and slender. She had long straight, dark brown hair and blue eyes. The contrast in the two tones was alluring, and the pinkness in her skin made her seem human, even though her beauty was unworldly. Her fingers were long and bony, and I couldn't stop myself from staring at them.

She opened her mouth wide when she spoke, and paused for too long in between sentences. I knew that she was someone who loved the sound of her own voice. She brushed me off, and told me my room was in the farthest building to the right. She warned me about going to the building to the left and told me that it was the boy's dormitory. Ms. Whorton gave me my room assignment and told me that dinner was over, but she would be sure to have someone in the kitchen send something up for me to eat.

The girl's dormitory looked like a large cottage. An enormous common space with a colossal stone fireplace, a tiny kitchen, and several emerald-colored couches and chairs scattered throughout took up the first half of the cottage. The front door was made of gold plated metal and green colored class. To my right was a long wooden coat rack, which had been nailed to the wall with tiny little owls carved in to the wood.

Past the common room, a large hallway jutted out with several others leading from it, and there were two doors labeled as bathrooms. I walked down several halls until I found a wooden door with my name on it.

The room was small, and there were two twin canopy beds pushed in to each corner of the room. Above each head board was a wooden plaque, one with my name, and over the other bed was the name Lily. I didn't really see any need to put on the uniform that Ms. Whorton had given me, the day was done, and everyone would more than likely stay here for the rest of the night. There was a dresser for each of us and two small closets. I put the pressed uniforms down on the bed and started unpacking all of my things. Once I finished, I walked back in to the common room and sat down near the fire. A bowl of clam chowder and a warm baked potato sat on a rectangular coffee table with a folded note beside it. My name was written on it, so I ate the small meal.

The girls who I would live with for the next three years, chatted outside the front door. I turned around as they piled in to the entry way of the cottage. They all stood there staring, waiting for me to speak.

"Hi, I'm Mina," I said as politely as I could manage. I wanted to make a good impression. "I just came here from New York." They stayed silent, but I noticed some movement near the back of the crowd. A short and pale, red-haired girl pushed her way to the front. Her lips were red and chapped from the cold, so I stared at them without thinking. The girls all wore the same uniform, a white blouse and a plaid skirt with tights, but she wore black platform stilettos with hers, her skirt was hiked up much higher than the other girls, and her blouse plunged lower, as she'd undone too many buttons.

"I'm Cassandra," the red-haired girl said. "You're the one who can control the elements?" She asked in an elegant and soft French accent. The sound of her voice was melodic. I nodded, and watched her as she walked towards me with an intrigued glint in her eye. She held my eyes for only a second, and then everything went blank. I could only see darkness. My heard started to spin and it felt like I was being ripped in half. I could hear someone screaming and a loud cackling at the same time. Then the pain was gone, and I opened my eyes only to realize I'd been lying on the floor screaming and writhing in pain in front of all of them.

The cackling laughter came from Cassandra. She stood over me with the same intrigued glint in her eyes, but now a satisfied frown hung from her rounded features.

"You better learn to protect yourself," she said to me. "Or you can expect much worse, and not just from me," she laughed, the sound was like metal dropping to the floor, then she walked away. The other girls laughed too, but it was hardly as obnoxious, and they all stepped over me and went off to their rooms as I lay on the floor disoriented. I got the feeling that I wouldn't be as popular here as I had been in New York. I made a move to get up and noticed a pair of dark-brown eyes staring down at me. The girl was shorter and more petite than I was.

"I'm sorry," she said to me as she helped me up. "Cassandra can be a real bitch sometimes, but she's not that bad once you get to know her." She smiled with a warmth in her eyes that I'd never seen before. She had long, jet black, curly hair, light brown skin, and the longest lashes I'd ever seen. "I'm Lily Andrews you're roommate," she said looking down at the ground. "Were you able to find the room?" She asked as we walked down the hall.

"Yeah, I already unpacked."

"What time did you get here?" Lily asked.

"Only a few minutes before you all came back." I sat down on my bed. "How was dinner?"

"It was fine, a little lonesome, but I'm sure that will change now that you're here. It was awful being the only one without a roommate."

"I'm sure you'll miss the quiet now," I said knowing that people always want the opposite of what they have. "How long have you been a student here?"

"Since I was twelve, but most Logosts start training at thirteen. I had to come here earlier because I got caught. Some boy saw me flying in our neighborhood. Once the Informants found out, they sent me here. My Mom was ecstatic though, she's a Logost too, but my Dad isn't."

"What about your brothers and sisters?"

"Nope, none of them are, just me. Out of seven, I'm the only one," she said smiling. I could tell that she valued her difference just as much as I did.

"How did you learn to control the elements?"

"It was kind of an accident," I said. "When I was little I had a glass doll that my Mom told me belonged to my father's mother. It was old and really fragile. My older brother and I got in to a fight, and he grabbed the doll and threw it on the ground outside. I started crying and I couldn't stop because I was so sad about the doll. And then it just started raining. But not normal rain, it came down in heavy drops that left welts on my arms. When I stopped crying, the rain stopped. I practiced a little at a time after that with small stuff like making the wind blow, or the sunset earlier. I can move the Earth too," I told her and wondered if she could hear the insolence in my voice.

But Lily's eyes just widened in astonishment. "That's amazing," she said. "You have to show me tomorrow during free period. We'd better make sure that Cassandra isn't around, though." I asked her why. "If she's this jealous of you already she might try to kill you if she found out you can move the Earth too."

"It would really upset her that much?"

"At first. I mean, you know how Logosts are, we can't control our emotions. Especially the heavy ones like greed, jealousy, and anger. We're power whores," Lily laughed. Did everyone here have such a dark sense of humor?

We chatted for a little while longer, and I told her about the Cloisters in New York and my friends Beau and Samantha. Lily was from California and grew up outside of San Francisco. She missed the big city, but loved how beautiful France was. She told me that I would love it here too. I just needed tougher skin, and to learn how to put barriers up around my mind. Lily could read minds, but had mastered the art of keeping out the thoughts of others. She told me to try hard not to think about things that I would want to keep private, or else the few students who were mind readers would know my secrets.

Lily fell asleep, but I just lay there all night, nervous and a little scared. The room was decorated in green and gold, and our comforters were dark green, velvet. My eyes memorized the location of the furniture in the dark, and I thought about how different it was at Winchester than I imagined. I thought about Lily's advice. I would have to learn quickly if I wanted to stay alive.

{8}

That morning, an earsplitting screech woke us. It felt like your ears were ringing because the sound was only in our heads, but it sounded more like the noise a car's brakes make when the driver is screeching towards their death. At some point in the night I fell asleep, and was so startled that I fell out of my bed and onto the floor. Lily told me that's how Ms. Whorton woke them every morning, and that it meant we had 30 minutes to shower, dress, and line up outside to meet her.

"Thirty minutes is all we have?"

"I told you to shower last night," she said. "You'll just have to skip it now, and you'd better hurry up or she'll embarrass you in front of everyone during line-up."

I didn't wait to hear what else Lily had to say. I threw on my uniform, a starched white button up shirt, a navy blue, green, and gold plaid skirt with pleating, and then ran to the bathroom with my bag of toiletries. The strong odor of too many different perfumes and fragranced body washes filled the bathroom. Sinks lined the front and back walls, with stalls in the middle and showers on either side. No one was showering, though. Apparently, they all knew better then to wait until the morning. I had to elbow my way through a crowd of girls just to make it to a sink.

Once I was finished, I stormed out of the bathroom and went to go line up outside in the snow. The temperature was below ten degrees. I breathed a sigh of relief when I noticed Ms. Whorton wasn't there yet, and I went over to stand in line with Lily who was saving a spot for me.

"Where's your coat?" She asked. It hadn't taken me long to realize I wasn't wearing one, as it was freezing outside, but I knew it would take too long to go back and grab it. So I stood there shivering, when Ms. Whorton walked up to us all. The line was split straight down the middle, with girls on one side and boys on the other. The boys wore similar white shirts, but theirs had long sleeves that they wore with navy blue slacks and a navy blue and green tie.

"Good morning to you all," Ms. Whorton said greeting everyone that stood there. Six other teachers stood behind her, and I noticed Drew at her side. He winked at me without her noticing, and I smiled. Everyone grumbled 'good morning' back at her in sleepy voices. "I don't think I heard that. I said, good morning to you all," she shouted.

Everyone shouted back, "Good morning, Ms. Whorton," in unison.

Ms. Whorton opened her mouth wide to speak again, so wide in fact that I could see several gold fillings on her bicuspids. She stopped short though, and her eyes wandered over to the far left building, our left, her right, and everyone's heads turned to follow her eyes. Mine did too, and I watched with everyone else as a tall, dark-haired boy with dark brown eyes, and olive toned skin stumbled out of the boy's cottage and into the snow. I'd never seen anyone so intriguing, so commanding, yet out of step. He was beautifully uncoordinated. His shirt was un-tucked, his tie lay around his shirt collar, and his hair was flattened from having slept on it. I noticed I had stepped out of line, in my curiosity to get a better look at the beautiful boy who was late. Ms. Whorton glared at me, and my feet suddenly took two steps back to be in line with the other girls.

"Lucas," Ms. Whorton called to the boy who was late. "I was beginning to think we might not see you at all." She looked down at the skinny gold watch on her wrist. "Two minutes late. Do you think we're all stupid, Mr. Ramos?" She asked as he walked up towards her. "Don't you think we all deserve the respect of your punctuality?"

Lucas nodded, and I could tell that no matter what he said she was going to embarrass him. She'd made up her mind and there was nothing he could do. "What do you all think?" She said facing us. "Does Mr. Ramos deserve to be punished for the mismanagement of his time?"

Everyone was silent until Cassandra shouted 'punished,' and the corners of Ms. Whorton's face turned up slowly in to the most contemptible smile I'd ever seen. Then they all said it, laughing and taunting. I could hear the word popping up all around me as if someone were sticking needles inside of at least 100 balloons. The beautiful boy called Lucas screamed in agony as everyone focused their mind on torturing him. Even Drew stood there, grinning with dark satisfaction. I would never be like them. I would not hurt others to give myself an advantage. I still didn't even understand what exactly it was that everyone was vying for, but I was certain I would find out in due time.

Lily looked at me, and shook her head, knowing what I was planning before I even started acting. I wanted to listen to her, but there was no way I was going to stand by while that poor boy was tortured to death. I didn't want to see anyone die, ever. I ran over to him and put his head in my lap. He shook uncontrollably, I couldn't see the pupils of his eyes.

"You're killing him!" I said. "Stop, please stop!" But they all kept laughing at the boy's torture and my horror-stricken expression. I grew angry, and found myself losing control. I wanted to kill everyone that stood there. I wanted them to scream out in pain and beg for death. The cold wind whipped around me, awakening me from the thoughts of my murderous killing spree. I stared up in to the snowy mountains that lay just behind the school, and I shot up in to the sky, letting go of my fear of flying. The wind came out in gasps, and blew the snow off from the mountains, covering the crowd below.

"Stop!" I shouted, but they already had. They all lay on the ground motionless, except for the teachers who were strong enough to keep me out of their minds. Ms. Whorton glared at me in a cheerful way, and I felt myself sinking further, and further down to the ground, until I crashed on to the snow next to the boy who was now sitting upright. He looked at me in confused amazement.

"That was brilliant," the boy called Lucas whispered. "Stupid, but brilliant," he said, making no sense whatsoever. "You certainly don't belong here. No one who would endanger themselves to save someone else, could ever belong here."

"Well, at least I wasn't stupid enough to arrive late," I said. "You shouldn't antagonize someone who just saved your life." He smiled at me, and his dark eyes sparkled. He shrugged as if endangering his own life was a regular occurrence, and exhaled a breath of idiotic confidence.

"What a wonderful introduction you've given yourself," Ms. Whorton said to me. "Far better than anything I had planned. But let this be your first warning. I had no intention of killing Mr. Ramos, and if you ever interfere with the way that I, or any other teacher at this school punishes our students then you will be killed." I saw the truth in her words and I stood up, not wanting to cause more trouble. "This is Mina Culvert," she said addressing the other students. "Mr. Elliot has told me that she is the most powerful Logost that any of us have ever seen. Today is her first day, so let's all be sure to give her a warm welcome." She gave me another hardened smiled, and dismissed us to start the day.

At Winchester, our core classes consisted of Levitation, Manipulation, and Blocking, which I was desperate to learn. I wanted to learn blocking because I didn't want anyone inside my head, manipulating me or placing false images in to my consciousness. My favorite class was Levitation. The room was always filled with dozens of objects that floated and bumped in to one another. I learned that I could cause things to sporadically combust just like most of the students there. Everyone possessed a higher degree of intelligence and spoke with carefully chosen words. All Logosts were able to use a larger amount of their brain than most humans, and I wasn't afraid to be smart here.

The rest of our time was split between learning Philosophy and practicing our skill. Ms. Whorton was a strong believer in studying the classics, and bore Aristotle, and Plato in to our minds. Our free period was practice, and Ms. Whorton thought it was ideal for the more advanced students to attack the less-experienced ones. Being new meant that I was a usual target. "It helps teach you to block Mina," she said and told me that she meant no harm to any of the students. I wasn't sure I believed her.

It turned out that Lucas was fine the whole time. He thanked me later but told me that he was faking. "If they think you're dying they give up easier," he said. I had a few classes with Lucas, and Lily was in nearly all of them except Manipulation, the class that Drew taught.

In class, Drew treated me like he would any other student, and it bothered me. I hadn't anticipated receiving special treatment from him, but I didn't expect to be downright ignored. If I knew the answer to a question, he would act as if he didn't see my hand raised and call on another student. But I knew that he loved me. He told me I was the only one who mattered.

Every night, once all the others fell asleep he would come to me in my dreams. He would say that he only wanted me, then he would wake me up and have me come outside to him. We wandered through the mountains and the trees, trying to frighten one another with our power, but we always ended in a chilling embrace. I didn't think I could ever love anyone as much as I loved him. He was always so patient with me, and I felt he understood me better than anyone I'd ever met. Drew had my trust and my undying affection. The memory of his touch – his kiss, the texture of his voice was like silk as he caressed each word he ever spoke, and his erratic presence and neurotic behavior attracted me to him in ways I could not explain – not ever. He was always so in control, so nervously confident and edgy. I thought I wanted him for always, and in all ways, until the day would come when I would exhale my final breath. I prayed that the exhale would carry his name. I was his.

With Drew I was happy, and I eventually adjusted to my new environment. I stayed on the sidelines for the most part, while undertaking as much as I could to advance my strength. Classes didn't bother me, and it helped having Lily there. She was nothing like Beau or Samantha. Lily was selfless and kind, and she always stood up for me.

If she was busy and I needed her help, she always stopped whatever she was doing to tend to me. She was immature and innocent in too many ways, but it didn't bother me. She had never had a boyfriend or kissed anyone, and she showed so little interest in boys that it often intimidated me. Gaining knowledge and strength were her number one priorities, she told me. But she was becoming my best friend and I found that I always needed her around to explain something or to help me.

Lily Andrews stood out in her own way, and was the smartest person I'd ever met. She could remember an entire book word, for word after only spending an hour with it. She could recall dates and days without a calendar. Lily was like a human computer, but her social skills were weak. Most of the time she would shout out random facts about animals that didn't pertain to any part of our conversation, but I found that enduring. She was clever and cunning and she enthralled me and surprised me at nearly every turn. We listened to one another, and through her I learned to value things like tenacity and intelligence.

We all had our own unique talents, and Lily's was speaking to animals. She could control them, but she never would, she loved them too much. Lucas spent a lot of time with us after my first day. He admired me for trying to save him, even though he thought it was a foolish thing to do. Lucas and Lily were already close, so when they added me in to their group I wasn't going to complain. No one else wanted me around. They all felt I was too different.

One evening, after classes I hiked through the mountains to practice flying on my own. Cassandra loved to follow me. She usually watched me whenever I didn't want to be watched. I didn't want to be her enemy, but I never had a choice. My flight was deep in to the night sky and I practiced getting used to the altitude. I sensed Cassandra's presence below. My body jerked back and forth, between the night sky and stars. She caused my mind to go blank and I felt myself falling.

"Say hello to the angels, Mina." Cassandra thought and placed the words in my mind. Someone caught me before I crashed to my death. I looked up and Lucas was cradling me in his arms. He flew like lightning and traced the mountaintops.

"We're even now," he said.

Lucas was the best at flying. He was faster than anything I'd ever seen. His assurance in his own sense of self was a mystery to me. His freedom came naturally. He wasn't as smart as Lily, but he came from a wealthy family in Colombia and spoke three different languages – English, French, and Spanish. He charmed me often without meaning to, and I admired how he always stayed true to who he was, and went against the grain. I think he got a thrill out of breaking the rules.

Lucas provoked the other students by starting Levitation fights with them during free period, and he always talked back to Whorton. He impersonated her behind her back, and she caught him a time or two. He told her that she should be pleased, and that he only did it because he admired her, but she knew that was total crap. Lucas picked at Drew too.

We had Manipulation together, and he always made fun of how nervous Drew was. Drew made himself an easy target, though. Sweat rolled across his brow whenever he stood in the front of the class. He smiled awkwardly and stuttered often. Lucas wasn't as powerful as Drew, me, or even Lily. But he was in his own mind.

Lucas, Lily and I leaned on one another and we had too, because the other students got a kick out of listening to our screams – especially Cassandra.

Cassandra's special talent was mind control, Manipulation, like Drew. She could make people believe they were seeing anything she wanted. She could convince us of anything, but usually she just liked tricking us in to thinking we were in pain. Cassandra never grew to like me, and neither did her flunkies Amy and Sasha. They thought they were better because they loved watching the fear in someone's eyes. I kept the fact that I was able to move the Earth a secret from Cassandra, but she still tortured me every chance she got. I was getting better at Blocking, and I knew she wouldn't be able to for much longer. I thought about trying to get back at her, but I knew that it wasn't worth it. Ms. Whorton fawned over her above all the other students. She thought Cassandra was her best student, and the greatest asset to the school. I could tell that Ms. Whorton wanted to like me, but she didn't.

It wasn't long before I learned what everyone was vying for because it was one of the simplest things you could ever imagine: power. Everyone wanted to control everything and that included one another. The most powerful Logost was the most deadly, and for the time being I was the most powerful among the students, but certainly not the most deadly. Whenever I was punished or tortured during practice, I never fought back and they thought I was weak, but I knew I wasn't. It took strength to control my anger, and I would learn to be stronger than all of them. They would not defeat me. I refused to allow them to control my emotions. I refused to be broken.

{9}

Four weeks had passed since I came to Winchester, and though things weren't always pleasant, I'd learned not to complain. Complaining was useless. It only hindered. It never helped. If I dwelled on the bad it only made me unhappy, and I was set on convincing Drew that I was strong enough for this life, even though I wasn't too convinced of that myself. With Lily's help I was doing well in all of my classes.

At night, Drew was teaching me to control fire. He was so mesmerized at the sight that he wasn't able to keep his hands off me for days. But we wouldn't take our relationship to the next level. I wasn't interested in sex with Drew, and I knew I wasn't ready. He said he wanted to wait until I was older, anyway. He said it would mean more that way.

The date was February 27. It was my sixteenth birthday, and the only people I told were Lily and Lucas. Back home, my Mom made a big deal of my birthday no matter how little money we had. One year, she worked nights at the post office every day for a week, after working 8 hours as a teller at the Inwood City Bank. She did all that to buy me an expensive pair of Italian leather boots, and to take me to a nice restaurant in Manhattan. I didn't know what people did for birthdays at Winchester, but as far as I could tell they were ignored.

When I woke that morning, I ate, went to class, ate again, and went to more classes. The monotony of the days was nearly unbearable, but the dark days made me stronger. There was a school dance that Friday and the students were in a buzz about it. The dance didn't mean a thing to me because no one would ask me. As invisible as I was to the boys back home, I was even more invisible here.

You would think that my being the most powerful would mean everyone would compete for my friendship and attention. But it meant just the opposite. They all wanted to forget that I existed. They wanted me to give up and go back home. And that just fueled my desire to outdo them further. I would show them, they weren't better than me. Besides, Drew was my partner, and it wasn't like he could take me to a school dance or even on a date.

It shouldn't have mattered, but I was heartbroken about not being able to celebrate my birthday. When classes were done that day, I returned to my dorm room to find Lily gone. She must have forgotten all about my birthday. I planned on asking her to go in to the city with me, so I could buy something nice for myself. I didn't have much money – but it was my birthday, so splurging a little couldn't hurt. But I didn't want to go alone. I assumed Lily was off studying somewhere, and I plopped down on my bed and rolled over, thinking that all I wanted was to nap the rest of the day away. Sleep seemed to be my only escape from this dreadful hell hole.

"Mina," someone said knocking on my room door. "The phones for you," spoke a curly, blonde haired girl who everyone called 'Frizz.' She poked her head through the door. "It's your mother."

My Mom hadn't called me once. My second day at school, I had been the one to phone her, to let her know I had arrived safely. She was indifferent over the phone, and only talked about herself and my brothers. She was uninterested in my life here. I wanted to know why she felt like I abandoned her, but I was too afraid to ask. My family tended to glaze over unpleasant conversations. I jumped up, and ran to answer the phone in a small booth housed inside the common room.

"Mom," I asked waiting for her confirmation.

"Happy Birthday, Mina," she beamed with false excitement. "How does it feel to be sixteen? I wish I was there to see how much you've grown."

"I haven't grown much. I still look the same."

"But do you feel any different?" She said, and I thought about what she wanted to say, but wouldn't. My Mom wasn't as clueless as she pretended to be, and I wasn't as naïve as she thought I was either. It was clear to me now that she'd known all along that Logosts were volatile creatures. It wasn't that she didn't want me to be happy. She just wanted me to be a good person, and I was learning first-hand that being a Logost and being a good person was no easy feat.

"No, Mom," I said. "I haven't changed, if anything this place has made me more humble."

"Well, I'm glad to hear that. I won't keep you long. I just wanted to wish you a happy birthday and make sure you got the package I sent." The day before a care package filled with body washes, makeup, and perfume had arrived. Everything looked expensive, but I didn't want to think about all the sacrifices she made for me, even in my absence.

"I got it this morning," I lied, not wanting to admit that I hadn't called immediately to thank her. "Thanks so much. I really mean it. Thanks for everything." I said hoping she could hear the double meaning in my words.

"I love you, and I know just how tough you are. You'll make it through this, Mina, and you'll come out on top. I just know it."

She had too much faith in me. But I was her only daughter, and she wanted me to be just as strong as she'd always been. Being a single mom in New York was a death sentence. It was impossible for her to keep up with bills, work, and managing her children's lives. I admired her more than she would ever know. I didn't think I could ever be as strong she was, but I always hoped for it.

"I love you too," I breathed. She hung up the phone before I could say another word. My Mom was flighty. It was hard to keep up with her emotions sometimes. She was the only person back home who knew how to keep me from reading their minds. I assumed it was because she'd been with my father. She probably never let him know what she was thinking. If she could be that good at Blocking, surely I would have an equally easy time at it.

Sleeping wasn't really what I wanted, so I decided to go look for Lily. I walked back to our room to grab my coat from the bed, when I noticed she'd left a note for me saying she was studying late, and to come find her if I wanted company.

I headed towards the school feeling unreasonably sorry for myself. I was still having the nightmares that I couldn't explain and they left me feeling sad and numb. It was after classes, and the school was dark. I was never one to fear a lightless moment, but I felt unsafe. I couldn't tell if there was someone else lurking in the building, and my instincts felt raw. Footsteps trailed behind me. I turned another corner, and pushed open the door to the only lit classroom.

"Happy Birthday, Mina!" Lily and Lucas shouted. They stood under a birthday banner, and a large French crepe sat on the desk between them with the number sixteen drizzled on it in powdered sugar. My happiness overwhelmed me. Even this far from my home there were still people who cared about me.

"Were you surprised?" Lily asked in excitement. I told her I wasn't expecting any kind of celebration and that I was glad to have made such considerate friends.

"We could tell you wanted something special to happen," Lucas said and placed a stiff arm around my shoulders. "There's something else. We also made reservations for three at *Atmosphere*, a fine dining place in downtown Chamonix. Lily said you like eating at fancy restaurants, but it was my idea."

"Well, don't sell yourself short." Lily said, peeved by Lucas' attempt to hog all the glory.

The restaurant was nice, but not as nice as the ones in Manhattan. It was dimly lit with white table clothes and white walls. The dark mahogany tables, and the lighting fixtures that hung from the walls like works of art, added to its elegance. A waitress seated us at a round table in a corner near the back of the restaurant.

Atmosphere' was known for its vintage French wine selection but none of us were old enough to drink. We goofed around the whole time, picking at the fancy food, and making rude comments, trying to make the other guests feel uncomfortable. When I was with Lily and Lucas, I was able to convince myself that I didn't care what other people thought, just as they didn't. Hopefully, the lie would eventually turn to truth.

It was getting late and the restaurant was closing in an hour. Lily said she needed to get back to study for her private lessons test the next day. Wilma Whorton taught Lily individually in the ways of animal persuasion. Lucas and I made a move to leave, but she urged us both to stay and enjoy ourselves. She got up from the table, and I watched her tiny silhouette as she floated out the door. I turned back to look at Lucas, and he stared at me with curious eyes.

"Sorry," he apologized in his Colombian accent, when I raised my brow at him. "I didn't mean to stare. You're very pretty, I'm sure you've heard that before," he muttered. I didn't know what to say, but my silence egged him on. "I like being around you, Mina.

I've never known anyone as uncommon as you."

"I could say the same about you," I said, teasing him. "You're actually fun to be around when you're not being so bossy." I laughed trying to lighten the mood.

"Has anyone asked you to the dance?" I shook my head, and explained that I was too much of anomaly for anyone to want to ask, and he scoffed at me.

"Are you kidding?" he said. "All the boys here are crazy about you. A few are obsessed, but most are just intimidated. They think I'm brave to have the gall to even speak to you without zoning out. I wouldn't admit this to them, but I zone out a lot when I look at you," he said with a hint of reservation in his tone. I didn't believe him. I knew he was just trying to flatter me.

Lucas seemed more nervous than usual. I was used to seeing him at ease, and my mind wandered, contemplating the cause. I stared out the window of the restaurant, and saw Drew outside chatting with a short, older French woman. He caught me staring, and I turned back to face Lucas whose face was leaned in to my own. I thought about what this might look like. The door opened, but I didn't turn my head to watch Drew walk through it. Lucas didn't notice Drew's entrance, and he opened his mouth to speak. Drew walked up to our table, and I would never forget the expression on his face.

"Good evening, Mr. Ramos, Ms. Culvert," Drew said without even glancing at me, his eyes honed in on Lucas. "Might I ask why the two of you think it appropriate to sit here all alone, at this late hour? If I didn't know better I would suspect you were up to no good, Mr. Ramos."

"We haven't broken curfew," Lucas said. "We were just about to leave, anyway."

"You should leave Mr. Ramos before I get upset. I'll walk Mina back to her dorm." Lucas gave me a confused look, like he was worried for my safety. I mouthed to him that it was fine, and that I would see him tomorrow at lunch. I smiled at him, and he walked out in to the cold, his eyes never leaving mine.

"Well, that was rude," I said looking up at Drew. "Haven't you wrecked things enough? You do realize that today is my birthday, don't you?" I said. He had forgotten all about it, and now he had ruined my evening.

"Get up, now." He said, commanding me without raising his voice. My eyes fell to his and they were a new shade of light green. I had never been more frightened of him, and I regretted every word. This was not the time to antagonize him. "I said, get up."

Drew grabbed my arm and pulled me from the table. He handed me my coat, and motioned for me to take his hand. He wouldn't look at me as we walked down the small streets of Chamonix, so I stared at the shops and cottage-shaped architecture. My hands were cold from the snow and I wanted to put them inside my pockets, but I was worried about what Drew would think if I let go of his hand. I didn't want to make him any angrier. I decided that I didn't care what he thought. I was still mad. I dropped his hand, and he stepped in front of me.

"Have your feelings changed?" Drew said, demanding an answer. My feelings hadn't changed, but I was still upset with him. This was a side of Drew I wished never surfaced, but I always did something to upset him.

"No," was all I could muster to say. I was trying to hide my fear – trying to pretend that I wasn't afraid. I kept my thoughts blocked, even though I knew that would only upset him. I didn't want him to know how afraid I was. His eyes turned chilling again – that same lethal shade of light green and I swore he looked as if he wanted to kill me.

"Do you want to be with that boy? Not once have you ever looked at me that way. Are you trying to kill me with this pain? Do you get some divine pleasure out of watching me suffer?" He wanted me to look at him, but I just stared down at the snow, too afraid to say anything. He was being unpredictable, and I knew he was on the verge of losing control.

"Don't be jealous," I whispered. "It hurts when you're upset with me. I promise I'm not trying to hurt you. Lily and Lucas took me there for dinner. Lily left early to study, and Lucas and I were just talking. We're just friends, I swear. I'm sorry for what it looked like." He took a deep breath, and turned away from me to gather his thoughts.

"You promise you're telling the truth?" he said. "You wouldn't lie to me, would you?"

I shook my head, and fell in to him, wrapping my arms around his waist. He kept his arms pinned to his side at first, then placed them firmly on my shoulders, staring down at me. I stared in to his eyes and watched as the golden swirls turned.

"Stay away from that boy, Mina. His intentions with you are no good. He cares for you as more than a friend, and his powers are insignificant. He's not worthy of you like I am, my love. He'll only sully your true potential."

"He's one of my only friends. I don't want to stay away from him." My anger surfaced. "You can't ask me to do something like that. I'm not under your control." He grabbed for me, but I ran, fast enough that he couldn't catch me. When no one else was in sight, I dove into the sky and flew to the girl's dorm, where I knew Drew wouldn't follow.

That night, the nightmares returned and were the worst they had ever been.

I woke up in a fearful sweat from images I couldn't replay. My room was dark, and Lily wasn't sleeping in her bed. I could hear something pounding. Then, I saw him there, standing in the corner of my room near Lily's vanity. Drew walked towards me without saying a word. I tried apologizing to him again, but he just stared at me.

When he looked at me, I wanted to scream, but I didn't. He grabbed the back of my neck pulling me in to a kiss. I went numb as he reached his hands under my nightgown. He'd never done this before. I wanted him to stop, but I still couldn't speak, no matter how hard I tried. Finally, the smallest part of me pushed him away, and he laughed. He pushed me down on the bed and put his hand over my mouth. He pulled up my nightgown, and wrapped his other hand around my throat.

None of what had passed the night before seemed real anymore. I couldn't really remember anything about it, and it was just a nightmare. I'd been having nightmares like that ever since I met Drew, and I wasn't sure what they meant. I knew I couldn't tell anyone about them, and I was not going to ask Drew about them. That would upset him. If he knew that my subconscious had painted such an ugly picture of him, he'd feel hurt. I was still upset with him for trying to control me, but I wouldn't hurt him deliberately. I just wanted to avoid him until I could clear my head.

{10}

Lucas avoided me during lunch the next day. Lily was in a good mood because her private lessons test with Ms. Whorton went well, and a mousy-haired boy with glasses, named Darius had asked her to the dance. I acted happy for her as I stared down at my uneaten sandwich, but I was worried about Drew. The dream haunted me. They had never been so vivid before. I skipped Manipulation that morning so I wouldn't have to see him, and the rest of classes were canceled for the day because of the dance.

We decided to practice in a courtyard near the mountains before the dance. Lily said she would meet us there, but Lucas was being weird and I was worried about being alone with him. I stood to leave as soon as Lily did, making an excuse about needing to call my brothers. I walked out of the dining hall and past several classrooms, when I saw Drew.

His eyes met mine and he walked over to me. I turned around and headed in the other direction. I wasn't ready to talk to him, but he was behind me before I knew it.

"So you're avoiding me now?" Drew said. I didn't respond. I just looked up at him, searching for the kindness in his eyes. I was still upset about his controlling behavior. He wouldn't get to make all my decisions for me. I refused to allow that to happen. He pulled me in to a nearby classroom and shut the door. "Stop this childish behavior, Mina. You're only making the situation worse."

"Stop acting as if you know what's best for me."

"But I do know what's best for you," he whispered. "I just want to take care of you. I love you, so much. I can't risk losing you. I need you, Mina."

"I need you too, but Lucas and I are friends. You're just going to have to get used to it."

"I know. I was jealous yesterday, that's all. The way he looked at you made me want to kill him. But I promise to be good now. I won't get in the way of your friendships. I'm more mature than that." He picked me up and sat me on top of his desk. He leaned in to me and pressed his lips to mine. "Tell me you love me."

"I love you," I said breathing heavily.

He kissed me again, making my head spin. "Tell me that boy means nothing to you," he said looking me in the eyes. It was hard for me to think when he looked at me that way, it made it hard for me to make sense of anything.

"He means nothing," I said without a thought. He stopped kissing me and leaned in to me, blinding me with his terrifying smile. It was so wide it almost curled in to the corners of his ears.

"Good, we should leave. I'll see you tonight at the dance. I'll be there chaperoning."

"I'm not going. What's the point? I can't go with who I really want. I'd rather not go at all."

"Just go, Mina. We don't want anyone getting suspicious." Drew walked out of the classroom, and I stayed there for several minutes so that no one saw us leaving together. I walked back to meet Lucas and Lily in a nearby courtyard enclosed by enormous pine trees and a cement walkway. When I approached the courtyard, Lily sat in the snow with several dark-haired squirrels surrounding her, and her back turned towards the snowy mountaintops.

"Where's Lucas?" Lily asked. Before I could answer, Lucas sauntered up without making eye contact with either of us. He lifted his head to face me. I turned away from him, not quite sure what he was accusing me of, but I could see the accusation in his eyes.

"Mina, can I speak to you alone?" Lucas said. I looked at Lily and she shrugged, obviously just as clueless as I was about what was going on in his head. We walked away together, far enough away so that Lily wouldn't overhear. I put barriers around us, even though I was sure she wouldn't eavesdrop.

"What happened last night when I left?" Lucas asked as if he knew the answer. He was making me more nervous than I'd anticipated.

"What do you mean?" I said. "Nothing happened. Drew – I mean Mr. Elliot walked me back to the dorms."

"I know you're lying. I saw you with him today in Ms. Callaway's classroom."

He knew. Damn it, he knew. I couldn't think of a way out of this.

"What did you see?" I asked turning around so I didn't have to face him. I couldn't look him in the eyes when I knew I would have to lie. When he knew I had been lying all along.

"I saw you kissing him, Mina. You know what I saw." Lucas was older than me and Lily, but not by much. He was seventeen and had been in relationships with girls before. I didn't understand why he was upset. What I did with my partner was my own business. I thought he would understand that.

"So what if you saw us?" I argued. "It's none of your business anyway. What are you going to do now, tell Ms. Whorton?" I said angrier than I should have allowed. I was in his corner now. He knew my secret.

"That's exactly what I should do. This is sick. He's too old for you. And he's your teacher. Don't you think he might be taking advantage of you?"

"Drew loves me. We were meant to be together. He can't help how he feels about me. And I'm glad he can't. I love him too."

"How do you know what love is? You're way too young to talk like this. You need to stay away from that pervert," Lucas said. "But I won't decide for you. I'm not going to say anything, not even to Lily. Do what you want, Mina. It's your mistake, not mine. I just hope you don't regret this too much." I knew I would never regret loving Drew. Lucas asked me about the dance again, and told me he had a date but hoped I would save him a dance. I promised him I would.

We practiced for a while together. I made sleet fall, and Lucas focused on dodging the frozen drops of precipitation. Lily sat there persuading the squirrels to build a log cabin out of twigs, but it kept falling over. She asked me if Lucas knew that I could make the Earth move.

"Let us see it," Lucas challenged. I was apprehensive, but I wanted to redeem myself with Lucas.

"Don't get scared," I told him, and he laughed. I sucked in air and floated over them, holding my arms out at my sides.

Snow circled around my motionless figure and the ground shook. A lonely sound echoed through the mountains, and I lost myself with a feeling of power. Before I took things too far, my body slammed in to the ground. I still couldn't see, and I tried getting up, but couldn't. I sensed someone else.

"Who's there?" Lily said. "Let her go."

My body convulsed. It felt like I was being burned alive. Every inch of my body was covered in flames that no one could see. I could hear Cassandra laughing. I sensed her feelings of superiority haunted by jealousy.

"Stop it Cassandra." Lucas knew she was there too. "You don't have to be such a jealous bitch all the time," Lucas said. Cassandra stepped away from the tree she was hiding behind. Her smirk wasn't as gratified as I imagined.

"Sorry, Lucas," she said, venom oozing from her tone. "I wasn't going to hurt her. I was just having fun."

Cassandra leaned in to Lucas, and kissed his lips. My heart fell past the ground. *How could he kiss her?* She was the devil in a plaid, uniform skirt. I wanted to make fun of him, but he hadn't given me too much of a hard time about Drew, so I let it go. Maybe they were just good friends, the type of friends who always kissed when they parted. The lie comforted me.

"Crazy girl," Lucas said to her. "I'll see you later." Cassandra walked off, staring back at Lucas. We all headed back to the dorms to get ready for the dance.

When I opened the doors to my closet, I couldn't decide what to wear. I settled on a light blue, satin cocktail dress that my Mom bought me for me Christmas last year. I stared at myself in the mirror. My skin was pale and my cheeks were red from the cold. I put dark purple shadow on my lids and silver pumps on my feet. I walked back to our room and saw Lily wearing a lavender, floor-length evening gown.

She looked absolutely perfect. I couldn't stop staring at her as she leaned her head over, fluffing her curls before she left. I figured my dress was too short for the occasion, but I decided I didn't care. I wanted to stand out anyway. Lily told me that Darius was already there waiting. She asked me if I wanted to walk down with them, but I declined. I sat there on the bed for a while, trying to build up the courage to leave the room. I didn't know why I was so nervous. I had been to plenty of school dances in Inwood, but I had a bad feeling about this one.

The teachers set up a large heated tent outside to house the dance. When I walked in, I knew this dance would be different than the ones back home. There were actual decorations, not just paper streamers, and there were crystal centerpieces on the tables. The lighting gave the room an ice-blue hue, and it complemented my dress. I saw Lily sitting at a table with Darius and his friends, and I walked over to join them.

"It's beautiful," I said to Lily as I pulled up a white, covered chair.

"What's beautiful?" Lily said, "The tent? I guess I'm just used to it. They use the same decorations for every dance."

Lucas stood near a large rectangular table where the refreshments were. I waved to him, and he waved back. He walked over to our table with none only than Cassandra. I couldn't believe he brought her. I wondered if they were dating, but it wasn't any of my business. I wanted him to hate her just as much as I did, but that was selfish. When she looked at me, I felt the strangest urge to kill her. I glared back at her with hateful, resentful eyes and a low growl escaped my chest.

"Are you alright, Mina?" Darius asked. Both my hands were locked to the table. Things couldn't go on like this, I had to stop letting my anger get the best of me. I threw on a fake smile, and pretended that I was overjoyed to see them together.

"You look beautiful Cassandra," I said once they were close enough. "I'm so jealous," I lied. She was taken aback by my unexpected kindness.

"You look nice too," she stuttered. And I watched Lucas walk away from me, with his arm around her. It shouldn't have bothered me, but it did. I tried not to think about the way he felt about her, or what could have possessed him to choose her.

That night, I didn't dance with anyone. I sat at the table alone, making myself miserable with thoughts of insecurity and worthlessness. Every so often a brave boy would walk nervously towards the table where I sat, and ask me to dance. For the sake of adhering to social norms, I cordially declined every invitation. Boys my age seemed distant. All I could focus on were thoughts of Drew, and when I would get the chance to feel his arms around me, protecting me from this place.

Darius and Lily grew tired of my depressed speech and pessimistic choice of conversation. They turned away from me, and talked to the other couples at our table. I thought that I could be myself here. That this place would put me in touch with who I was meant to be, but I felt more lost than I ever.

I watched Lucas spin Cassandra around the dance floor, and had to look away. Drew stood near the tent's entrance with Ms. Whorton, refusing to make eye contact with me. When I could no longer bare the night, I got up to leave, but someone placed their hand on my shoulder.

"You can't leave without giving me the dance you promised," Lucas said. He took my hand and spun me around once, then a second time, and pulled me close.

"I can't." I said pulling away. "I don't know how to waltz. Just go back to Cassandra." He knew I was jealous, but he didn't say anything.

"It's not hard, just try, please?" He said smiling, exposing a few crooked teeth. And I did try. I let him lead me around the space while I did my best to keep from falling in my too-high heels. Our dance wasn't graceful, we swayed back and forth like a couple of middle school kids. Cassandra sat down with Sasha, Amy, and Lucas' friend Elijah. They laughed at my limited dancing skills. I was embarrassed to have everyone watching, but discovered that I didn't care. Lucas didn't, so why should I?

We danced to Fur Elise and I would never forget the song. I wished that I had been more graceful. I wished that I'd paid more attention to the way his eyes bore in to me, searching for something that wasn't there yet. But I couldn't. I couldn't keep my eyes from searching for Drew. He was missing, and his absence was all that I could think about. Lucas frowned, and I tried to hide my uneasiness.

"Looking for him?" Lucas said.

"No, just enjoying the ambiance and the good company," I smiled in regret when I looked in to his rejected eyes. The music stopped, and I felt cold as the space between our bodies grew. Cassandra walked over, grabbed Lucas' hand and pulled him away from me. I tried not to think about how satisfying it would feel to hear her gasp her last breath at my hands. I shook the thought from my head and stormed out of the tent – forgetting my coat yet again. I was ashamed to walk back for it, but I knew I needed to say goodbye to Lily.

Lily and Darius huddled close at the same table, their lips

locked together. I rocked back on my heels and spun around, not wanting them to see my sudden return. I grabbed my coat and headed for the door. The night was quiet and silver. The snow glistened in the moonlight, and I felt the darkness that lay in the shadows behind the mountains, whispering to me. I wrapped my coat around my waist and kicked off my shoes, preparing to fly to the nearest mountain. I stopped short when I sensed Drew's erratic presence.

It was dark and I couldn't see him there, but I knew better than to call out to him. The sounds of hushed voices and false promises made me shiver, as I stood there. I could hear him whispering, and I followed the tone of his persuasive voice. I froze when I saw them there. He leaned in to her the same way he leaned in to me, but their embrace was different. He didn't kiss her hair and cradle her in his arms like a child. He wasn't the one leading – she was in control. He kissed her, and I screamed in fury and rage.

My limbs shook with the force of my anger, and the Earth faltered beneath me, but I couldn't stop myself. The swirling winds came out in gusts, and blew the tent in to the mountains. The Earth quaked violently under the weight from my tantrum. My voice rang deep, as the wind swirled around the unsuspecting students. The snowy tornado moved closer to Drew and Ms. Whorton, who stood there in awe at the strength of my emotions. Whorton called to me, and I sank to the ground. I made no move to resist her control. I put up no barriers to protect myself. I would let her win. I wouldn't fight once she decided my punishment.

{11}

I lay there ice cold in the snow, staring at Ms. Whorton's bright red pumps, unable to feel any part of my body. My eyes wouldn't blink. I tried moving my fingers and toes, but they wouldn't budge either. Whorton looked in to my eyes and I tried to read her mind – desperate to know what she had planned for me. Pity and fear filled her eyes. She looked back at Drew and said something, but I couldn't hear what was being said. I think her words were in French, but my mind was too numb to be sure.

Whorton kneeled beside me. "You stupid girl," she laughed. "All of that over a meaningless crush on a teacher. My God," she spoke in utter amazement. "You nearly killed us all."

She released my mind and body from her control, and I let out a deep gasp. My throat burned from my wailing and I sat upright, trying to calm down, trying to suppress my anger. Everyone at the dance had been disoriented by my temper tantrum, but once I gave up control, they came over to stare at the irrational freak, who had continuously shown that she would always act with her heart, rather than her head. Ms. Whorton took me by the hand, and led me to her office with Drew following close behind. It was housed in the main building of the school.

The office was lit by a fireplace that was nearly flushed with my own height. I walked towards it, staring at the strange etches carved in to the stone – they were little owls, just like the markings on the coat rack in our dorm. Every wall and every corner of the room housed a shelf, and the shelves were filled with an endless amount of books – books about race, gender, class, and philosophical entitlements. I stood there reading the titles, when Wilma asked me to have a seat. She was silent and motionless for some time, and that only added to my fury. I wanted to lunge at her and rip her hair out. But I kept my composure. If she was convinced that it was nothing more than a crush, maybe that's all it had been.

I turned my head when Drew walked in, and shut the door behind him. I didn't look up at him, deciding that he was no longer worthy of my glances. I wanted them both dead. I crossed my arms to my shoulders, trying not to go through with my suddenly deepest fantasies.

"Mina," Wilma said finally addressing me. I stopped her before she could say another word.

"I'm sorry," I said. "I lost control. It was stupid to get so upset over an unreciprocated crush on a teacher," I repeated Drew's words, no longer sure if they were a lie. "Please don't hurt me," the tears were streaming down my face before I noticed them there. I buried my face in to my hands, not wanting to look at either one of them. I was humiliated by my own actions. How could I be so emotional? I was taking everything personally, and that just wasn't how things worked here. Lily was right, I did need tougher skin, and now it seemed I could never acquire it.

"Stop crying! No one is going to hurt you!" Drew shouted. But he looked at Wilma with uncertainty.

"I should be upset," Wilma said. "But I'm not. I've never seen anything like that. No other student has ever shown such power." My mood shifted as her words sunk in. I'd finally impressed her.

"Yet, so much lack of control," she finished her sentence and her expression wavered. "You are very powerful, Ms. Culvert. But you cannot seem to control yourself, and over something as small as this. I'm afraid that Winchester isn't the place for you. You're far more dangerous than I expected, and your lack of training for the past few years is discernible." She sighed. "We'll have to send you to the Informants. I'm afraid this problem is too grave for me to handle. I'm only a school principal, and your powers are simply beyond me."

None of what she'd said made sense. I'd never had any outbursts like that prior to coming here. It was this place that was making me crazy. I wasn't dangerous.

"The Informants?" Drew said. "No, Wilma, don't do this. She's just a girl. We need her here. We need her on our side. They'll use her to gain more power, and then discard her as if she were nothing. Don't let this power go to waste. This will end badly, the Five Leaders cannot be controlled. I'll train Mina myself, away from the other students, so she can't hurt them. Please, just don't – they will kill her."

"I swear this won't happen again," I butted in. "Nothing like this has ever happened before. I can learn control. I can. I've already learned so much. Please don't send me away." I never dreamed that I would beg to stay at Winchester, but anything was worse than death.

"How do you know she can even be trained?" Ms. Whorton asked Drew.

"She can," he said. "She's just stubborn. I have an extra period. I can set up a private lessons course for her."

"You don't know how to control the elements, Drew. What could you possibly offer this girl in that aspect of her powers? None of us do. She has to go."

"I know more about controlling the elements than I've lead on. I can help her and she'll be greater than any Logost that has ever lived – even more powerful than Sophia." And his eyes turned to the painting that hung above Ms. Whorton's desk. The painting depicted a blue-eyed girl with long, wavy blonde hair. The wind was painted in gusts of smoke, as it lingered behind her fueling a fire that had existed long ago. "And her alliance will be with us. To our school and all that we stand for. Knowledge is power, Wilma. I beg you to sleep on this. Don't make your decision now."

Whorton took a deep breath and peered at me through narrowed eyes. She decided to wait until Monday morning to discuss the matter further. But she told me to not be so hopeful, and to be on my best behavior, because if there were a repeat in my actions she would end things herself. She dismissed me, and I walked back to the girl's dormitory where Lily was still awake, waiting for me.

"Thank God. You're still alive," she said embracing me. "I was worried. I didn't think she'd let you live. You almost murdered the whole school."

The night had been disastrous and I only wanted to sleep. I wasn't ready to talk. She was right. I did almost kill the whole school, and her reminding me right now was the last thing I needed. I climbed in to bed – not even bothering to remove the expensive cocktail dress or makeup, pulled the covers over my head and closed my eyes.

"I'm sorry Lily, but I just don't feel like talking right now. I need to sleep."

I closed my eyes and thought of cool lakes and open fields. I wouldn't think about Drew or Ms. Whorton. I wouldn't think about the Informants or Lucas and Cassandra. I needed to protect myself and stop worrying about everyone else. I closed my eyes and fell fast asleep. Drew never did call to me that night. I think he knew better than that.

When I woke that morning, Lily was sitting up in her canopy bed, staring at me. When my eyes met hers, I rolled over and put the pillow over my head.

"What is it you want Lily?" I grumbled at her. She sighed and stared up at the ceiling.

"I'm just worried about you, Mina. You were screaming in your sleep. I haven't slept. You kept me up all night." My mind had been blank when I drifted off to sleep. What could I possibly have been screaming about?

"I'm sorry, Lily. I didn't mean to frighten you."

"Are you coming to breakfast? You haven't been eating much lately." I was too nervous to eat. The whole weekend had to pass before I would find out my fate. I wished for my Mom. I wished that she would storm in to the room to take me home, and yell at everyone who'd made me sad. But I knew that couldn't happen. I would have to handle all of this on my own.

An anxious and raw feeling rumbled in my stomach whenever I thought about Drew kissing Whorton. Did he love her? Did he want to be with her more than he wanted to be with me? I wanted to pretend I didn't care, but I was so jealous I couldn't stand it.

"No, I'm not going," I said. "You go, I'm just going to sleep."

"Do you want to talk about what happened?" Lily asked. "I know you're hurt, you might as well just let it all out. I'm not here to judge you. I love you. You're my best friend."

Why did she have to be so caring and understanding? It was driving me insane. I hated feeling vulnerable. I hated talking about my feelings. At my house that was something that never happened. If I tried talking about my feelings with my Mom or my brothers, they just slunk away, and pretended to be busy.

"I want to tell you, but I can't," I said. "It's complicated. And I don't want to bring you in to the mess I'm in. You're better off."

"But are *you* better off? This isn't about me. We're talking about you and what happened last night." Lily paused. "Why did you come here, Mina?"

"Because I'm a Logost, why wouldn't I come here?"

"I don't want to pry, and it wasn't something you mentioned, but it's odd that your parents didn't register you with the Informants. And it's even more bizarre that you would start training at Winchester when you're sixteen years old."

"I told you Lily, I don't know where my Dad is, and my Mom doesn't know anything about being a Logost. I don't think she even wants me to be one. I think she hoped that none of us would turn out like my Dad." My existence reminded her so much of him, and I hated myself for that. The difference I had always thought would lead to great things, had only led me to a deep mistrust for myself and my own choices.

"And then you met Mr. Elliot and he brought you here?"

"Yes," I replied.

"But how did he know where to find you? Why was he in New York when he should have been here?"

I didn't have an answer to that question. It wasn't something I had ever considered. I just assumed we were connected, and Drew had always been searching for me, waiting for me. But everything was so muddled now, I couldn't see the beginning or the end. The future I'd envisioned for the past few months had been drawn solely around Drew and our love. If there was no love, what was my future?

"I don't know, Lily. I just know that I don't belong here. I should leave. I just want to go home."

"Why did you want to come here in the first place?"

The main reason had been Drew. But there was something else – an ever-present longing to prove my greatness, to be with people who were just as unique, to be with people who I thought were like me. But I wasn't really a Logost, and I wasn't really human. I was the Logost who had been raised by a human, so where did I fit in?

"Drew convinced me that I would be happy here," I blurted out. "He told me he loved me, and that I would never have to be afraid. He said he would always protect me. But just look at how exposed he's left me. I might as well have the words 'fool me' stenciled across my forehead." I looked at Lily when I realized I was talking out loud. "I should have told you, Lily."

"Mina, you honestly think that I haven't known this whole time? You were horrible at blocking when you first got here. You thoughts were so loud that every time I drifted off to sleep I was jolted awake by your *fantasies*."

"Why didn't you say anything? Why did you let me think that I was actually keeping this a secret from you?"

"You know how I am. I try not to be a bother. I figured if it was something you wanted to talk about, then you would. And when you didn't, I just left it alone. It wasn't my secret."

"And you haven't told anyone?"

"Of course not, do you think I want to see Ms. Whorton hang you? Besides, everyone already knows about your 'crush' on Mr. Elliot, or at least that's all they think is going on."

"Stop Lily, I can't talk about this anymore. I should just go back home."

"I need you here, Mina. Lucas is a good friend, but he's a guy. There are a lot of things about Mr. Elliot that you haven't considered. I think you need to talk to him. He needs to give you straight answers, and don't let him distract you with his good looks and soft lips."

She had definitely seen too much. I pulled the covers over my head to hide from my thoughts.

"I can't right now. I don't even want to look at him. I'm so embarrassed."

"You're right. You need time to gather your thoughts, and think about what to say, and then predict his reaction in case he tries to outsmart you again."

"He hasn't outsmarted me."

Lily rolled her eyes.

"Whatever you say, Mina, I'm going to eat some breakfast. I'll bring you back a banana. Try not to blow up anything while I'm gone."

"Just get out." I sighed and watched her walk out of our dorm room. I tried sleeping some more but that was a useless attempt. My mind was whirring like an overheated laptop. Why had Drew been in New York, if this is where he belonged? And why was he so set on gaining my trust in the beginning, if he really didn't love me? He must care for me in some way, or he wouldn't have brought me here, and he wouldn't have stood up for me in front of Whorton last night. The more I thought, the more I was able to convince myself that he did love me. His eyes, his voice, his touch had always been so passionate, and filled with infatuation.

I grabbed my toiletry bag and treaded to the hall bathroom. The dorm was empty. Everyone was off enjoying their Saturday. After my shower, I threw on a pair of old jeans, boots, and a sweater, then decided to go for a walk. My initial thought was to head towards the courtyard, where I was certain Lily and Lucas would be. But I wanted to be alone, and I didn't want anyone to follow me. With each step, I asked the wind to blow over the tracks of my boots so that no one could trace me, but really if Drew wanted to find me there was nothing I could do. It seemed he would always get what he wanted. I felt powerless. He would always be stronger.

I shot up in to the mountains, and drifted down to an encasing nestled deep among the smaller mountaintops. I sat down in the snow, leaning my back against a rock. My knees curled in to my chest, and I started sobbing. The tears were uncontrollable as my sadness crippled me. My breath came out in deep gasps and the wind blew harder. The rain fell in ice cold drops, and I shivered, but I still couldn't stop crying.

"Mina," he whispered my name, but I knew he was there before he spoke. Recognizing his erratic presence was becoming so natural, like the rising and falling of your chest with each breath. I knew that I would always sense him there.

Drew stood over me, leaning down to touch his finger to my chin. He tilted my head upward, forcing me to stare in to his eyes. I turned away, and stopped the rain from falling. I didn't want him to see me cry over him. He moved, and I felt him sit beside me. He pulled me close and kissed my hair. I still couldn't look at him. I was too afraid of what I might see – that his love for Wilma Whorton would stare back at me through his eyes. The thought brought back a wave of panic and despair. I laid my head on his shoulder and cried until my eyes ran dry and red.

"Are you finished?" he asked pulling me closer, consoling me from the pain he had caused. I mourned the death of our love as I felt it escape me.

"For now," I said. "But it really depends on what you came here to say. I'm sure you realize how much it hurt to see that, to have to watch you kiss someone else. Why hurt me like this? Don't you love me?"

"You silly girl, you know that I love you. There's nothing on this Earth that I desire more than your presence. You know that. You've seen it in my eyes."

"Why did you want me to come here," I asked. "Why not just let me stay with my family?"

"Because I'm selfish," was all he said. "And I thought it would be good for you. I knew you weren't happy with your family. Even though you're different, I thought it would bring you joy to be with others of our kind. But I can see that it's only saddened you, and I know I've hurt you more than anyone else has, or ever will. I'm sorry, Mina."

"Could you be so selfish that you would think you could have us both, to think that I would be content sharing you with anyone else?

Do you love her?"

"Not the way that I love you. Wilma means something to me, but that feeling is only temporary. I'm doing this for us. She must not be suspicious that these feelings aren't mutual. We need her on our side, or else we have no chance at winning."

"At winning what, is this a game to you? You said the same thing to her last night that the two of you need me on *your* side. Who's side on your on Drew? You can't play us both. You can't *have* us both. I know you're lying. I'm done with this. I refuse to allow you to cause me any more pain. I refuse to let you think you can control me. I will stay here for my own selfish reasons, but I want you stay away from me Drew. Don't call to me anymore, please. Being with you is a hindrance to my growth. Be with her. I don't want you anymore."

It was a lie, but it was a good lie. I kept my mind blocked and my heart rate even. There was no inflection in my voice; he would hear it as the truth. I knew I had hurt him once I spoke, but I didn't care. However much he was hurting, paled in comparison to my own pain. He opened his mouth to persuade me with more lies.

"Just go, Drew. I don't want to see you anymore."

"So this is what you want? You won't even hear what I have to say?"

I shook my head and stared up at the sky. If I pretended he wasn't there anymore, maybe he would get the hint and leave.

"Please, Mina don't do this. I know I hurt you, but I love you. I'm sorry. I swear this is for us. I want nothing more than to be with you forever, my love. You are my special angel sent from above. We were meant to conquer this place, together. All of it will be ours, but you must be patient. We must put up with Wilma, and you must practice. No one will be able to stop us, not even the Informants once you're strong enough. I have a plan for us, a plan for true happiness. Don't do this, please."

He kneeled beside me, and I couldn't stop my eyes from looking at him, even though I'd promised myself that I wouldn't, that I couldn't. I didn't want to give in to him. I didn't want him to have his way. But there were tears in his eyes. He grabbed my hand and sobbed all over it. I bit my lip, and pictured him touching her, him kissing her. I couldn't forgive him. I couldn't trust him, either.

"I suppose I'm not privy to this plan you have that is *my* future?" He was silent. "Just leave. Leave now," I screamed and the mountains shook from the severity of my words. He looked up at me in perplexity, but I turned my head.

"I won't ever stop loving you. I can't stop trying to make this right. I hope that you will forgive me, Mina."

Drew walked away from me, and I watched his figure trace the clouds until I could no longer see him. There was only me in my plan now, even though I didn't have a plan. So I sat there and continued my sobbing alone until I could cry no more. Then I too flew back to the school. But I didn't go searching for Lily and Lucas like I wanted to. I didn't want them to see me this way, especially Lucas. I'd done enough damage already. So I resigned to my bedroom where Lily was missing, and I slept the rest of that Saturday away. Drew called out to me, but when I drifted off to sleep, I dreamed only of myself with no others by my side.

{12}

The sun warmed my bed, and awakened me the next morning. The sky was no longer a pale shade of gray, caused by the ever present clouds of snow, but a lighted blue enhanced by the sun's rays. I rolled over to see if Lily was still sleeping, but she'd already come and gone. My stomach growled, and I threw something on so that I could go to the dining hall for breakfast. On Sundays they had cheesecake and a chocolate fountain, and I needed junk food to trick my brain in to state of euphoria.

Lily and Lucas were sitting at a table together. They glanced up at me as I sat down with my plate of junk food. Lucas was reading a textbook, while Lily mulled over a crossword puzzle. Neither one of them had food in front of them. I wondered how long they'd been sitting here.

"You really should eat something substantial," Lily said, enviously eyeing the cinnamon roll I'd dipped in chocolate. "You've hardly eaten anything, lately. The last thing you need is sugar pumping through your veins." I ignored her advice and dug in, not caring enough to even shut my mouth to chew. Everything tasted so good and I wanted to savor each morsel.

"So what happened with Darius?" I asked Lily.

"She hates him," Lucas answered for her.

"What happened?" I said. "The last I saw, the two of you couldn't keep your tongues out of each other's mouths."

"Smarty wasn't smart enough for her," Lucas laughed.

"He's just not my type, besides I have enough to worry about without adding someone else's thoughts and feelings in to the mix. Love just isn't what I need right now." I nodded in understanding. Her words were also meant for me. I grabbed my glass of orange juice and finished it all at once. I burped loudly, and they both laughed at me. I discovered that I felt well enough to laugh at myself. It was hard to stay sad with them around.

"Did you talk to him?" Lily asked.

"Talk to who?" Lucas asked. Lily and I ignored him.

"Yeah, it's over," I said to Lily. "We're done." She gave me a suspicious glance, and I shrugged my shoulders. "Love just isn't what I need right now."

"It isn't what any of us need," Lucas chimed in.

We stayed there until Lucas felt confident enough in his hour long study session. Lily tried to convince him to go over a few more notes, but he refused, so we all went to the nearest courtyard to practice. I didn't really want to practice. But I knew I needed too. I wanted to become strong without Drew, but with the help of my friends, the people who really cared about my thoughts and feelings.

"So you're really done with him?" Lily asked while we practiced blocking each other's attacks. "What did he say?"

"That he's not going to give up. But he will if I ignore him completely. Besides, he's got Ms. Whorton to entertain him now." I regretted my words instantly, as the pain ripped through me again. He was hers now, no longer mine. My eyes burned, but there was no way I was going to cry over Drew in front of Lily and Lucas.

"Well, I'm glad it's over," Lucas said. "He's too old, and he's creepy. I mean seriously what grown man gets that obsessed over a teenager. He has issues. He and Whorton belong together. And now you can focus on guys your own age."

"There won't be any more guys in my life for some time," I said. "I have had my fill of feeling this vulnerable. It just doesn't seem worth the trouble."

"It can be with the right person," Lucas said.

"And who's the right person for you," Lily asked. "Cassandra?" she giggled. Lucas shot a suffocating image of darkness at her mind, and she blocked it.

"You two just haven't gotten a chance to know her," Lucas said. "She's fascinating."

"I think by fascinating you mean slutty." Lily said. "You've already had sex with her and you've only been on two dates." I thought Lucas was a virgin just like me and Lily. I wasn't jealous of Cassandra anymore, but that didn't mean I wanted to hear about him having sex with her. It seemed odd to me now that I was jealous in the first place. Lucas wasn't mine. But I knew he didn't belong with

Cassandra either, he was too good for her. I wanted to say something, but I kept my mouth shut about him and Cassandra, and changed the subject.

"I can handle Drew. It's Ms. Whorton I'm worried about. After the dance she threatened to send me to the Informants. Tomorrow, she'll decide whether I can stay at Winchester," I told them.

"Sounds like an empty threat," Lucas said. "She wouldn't really send you there. Whorton loves to gloat, and with you here she can gloat even more."

"What exactly did she say?" Lily asked, taking Whorton's words more seriously.

"She said she can't control me, and she thinks I can't control myself either."

"If she sends you to them, there's little chance you'll survive," Lily said. "They'll use you to destroy their enemies and then kill you."

"Why would they kill me? I haven't done anything wrong. No one was hurt. Why would our government murder innocent people?"

"Because they do whatever they want," Lucas said. "They're powerful and they're good at scaring people in to doing what they say. Manipulation is their core strength, and they're masters at the divide and conquer tactic. Most of us think that killing is bad, but we realize it does happen sometimes in the heat of the moment. We need them to punish the Logosts who perform mass killings. Every once and a while a Logost grows darker and kills everyone in sight. If we didn't have them, who would keep us in line?"

"What are they like?" I asked.

"There are five of them," Lily said. "Their home is an underground castle in the Netherlands. I've never been there, but my Mom's told me it's the most disturbingly, beautiful place she's ever seen. No one can walk through the gates without a feeling of sadness and hopelessness choking you. The oldest leader is Sophia," she said and Lucas cringed at the name. "She's the only female. She's the most powerful, but she's ancient. She used to be the principal here before Ms. Whorton."

"How do the five of them govern together?" I asked.

"They have lines of command. After Sophia, Narc's second to the throne. He's the most vengeful. Narc will have you executed just for looking at him wrong. Louis is next, and Andres and Chance were the last to join as leaders. Andres and Chance are younger, but they're strong, and volatile. Sophia controls fire that's why she's in charge. She was actually a good Logost before she joined the Informants. But once you start having to murder people, you lose any ounce of remorse."

"They came for Lily's roommate last year." Lucas said and put his arm around her. "It's what they do," Lucas said. "They like watching pain, they like torture and they only steal things that can't be replaced, like loved ones."

"Maria didn't want to be a Logost. She was brilliant, but she wasn't happy here. She tried to kill Wilma Whorton and they came for her," Lily whispered.

"What happened to her?" I said.

"She stayed with them for a while," Lily said. "But she didn't want to hurt people. They killed her four months later. You can't stay here if Ms. Whorton decides to have them take you away. You'll have to leave. You have to hide from them."

"And where will she go?" Lucas asked. "If they find out she can't be controlled then it's over, you know that, Lily."

"Don't be so dramatic," Lily said. "There's always hope, we can always try."

"We have to stop this at the onset," said Lucas. "We have to stop Whorton from telling them by any means. If Mina does what she says and plays nice. She won't say anything to them. And if Whorton still decides to rat her out," he sighed. "I have another plan. It's dangerous, but it will work."

Neither Lily, nor I asked about Lucas' plan. The distressed look on his face made it impossible to muster the courage. They loved me, but I didn't want either of them risking their lives for me. That night in Wilma's office, Drew mentioned that I could be more powerful than Sophia, if I could get strong enough then I could defeat her. I could kill any Logost that stood in my way, and I would keep my friends safe.

{13}

"I can't go see her alone!" I shouted at Lily during breakfast.

"You don't have to see her until after lunch," she said. "Just calm down, you know I can't go with you. It will be fine, and if she decides to send you to the Five Leaders, call to me in your mind. I'll be in Levitation but I should get the signal. Your thought patterns are more distinguishable now. Are you going to Manipulation?"

"I don't want to, but I have to."

"Well, you better hurry. You know how Mr. Elliot is about tardiness." I glanced up at the owl shaped clock that hung on the wall over the only kitchen window. I was already late, I'd been trying to delay seeing him and now he'd have to notice me when I walked in. Why couldn't I learn to think things through ahead of time?

"Don't call him Mr. Elliot in front of me. It sounds creepy."

"Well, then I should call him that in front of you. You need a dose of reality. He is your teacher, stop pretending that he isn't, and maybe getting over him will be easier."

I ignored her, stuffed another piece of toast in my mouth, and ran off to Drew's classroom. Manipulation was one of the few classes that Lucas and I had together. He always saved me a seat, and it made me feel kind of special. Even though Lucas and I were just friends, I wasn't oblivious to all the attention he received from every other girl. I mean he was charming enough, and I guess the accent added to his intrigue. It was unfair that anyone could be so beautiful, and yet so awkwardly confident at the same time. I stared at him sometimes. He noticed whenever I did, but he never would embarrass me about it. His face was so amazing it was hard not to stare. So that's what I would do when I walked through the door – I would make eye contact with no one else, but Lucas.

When I reached Drew's classroom, the door was already shut so that meant I would have to disturb his class by opening it. I thought about running back to the dorm and hanging out until the next bell rang, but I was no punk, I could be brave, even though it took far too much effort. I sucked in a deep breath, pushed the door open, and dragged my feet across the floor to the empty seat beside Lucas.

"Ms. Culvert you're ten minutes late," Drew said to me as I sat down. I didn't turn to look at him. I kept my focus on Lucas' dark brown eyes. They sparkled whenever he smiled.

"Ms. Culvert?" he asked and I was still silent, still refusing to meet his eyes.

"Damn it, Mina! Look at me!" he was starting to sweat. This plan was working out better than I imagined.

"Yes, Mr. Elliot," I kept my voice soft and mellow as I spoke, hoping to further infuriate him.

"See me after class."

"So that's what you want is it Mr. Elliot, to be alone with me?" There was a smile in my tone but not one on my face. Lucas was visibly uncomfortable by our heated interaction. "Sorry, but I don't trust teachers who prey on little girls. Why don't you just send me to Ms. Whorton since you can't seem to handle some teenager?" His demeanor changed after I said that. He seemed slightly amused by the way I was acting. I think he could tell I was trying to get back at him.

"Ms. Culvert, I'm sorry if I've hurt your feelings, but entertaining a childish crush isn't something a teacher does. If you cannot control your emotions then please leave my class." I wanted to scream at him, but that would just satisfy him further. "You should leave too Mr. Ramos since the two of you seem so distracted by one another." Lucas looked upset, but he got up to leave with me, and I slammed the door as we walked out.

"What are you doing?" Lucas said once we were alone in the hallway. "I thought you were over him."

"Don't be stupid," I said. "Of course I'm not over him. I just know things are done."

"Does he know that? Because it seems to me like he's fucking crazy." Of course he was crazy, but who wanted someone sane? Sanity was boring. Drew always held my interest because he was so unpredictable. His control, and lack thereof, always lured me in. "Did you have sex with him," Lucas asked, catching me off guard. What was going on in his head?

"We are not having this conversation," I said, turning my back to him. "It's none of your business."

"Oh my God, you did. You let that sleaze touch you. I swear to God if he ever comes near you again..."

"I'm not Cassandra!" I shouted. "Some people have more respect for themselves. And I don't need you to do anything if he comes near me. I can handle him myself."

"Yeah sure, you've been doing an ace job of it thus far, Mina. This whole thing is getting out of hand, and I don't want to be involved in your drama-filled romance. Just keep me out of it. I don't want his craziness coming after me too."

The bell rang and I left Lucas standing there. I was done talking to him. The rest of that day didn't drag like I'd intended it to, and I was sitting on the wooden bench outside of Ms. Whorton's office before I even had a chance to contemplate a nervous state of being. I could hear her whispering with Ms. Callaway as I waited. Their hushed voices made me curious. Even though I wasn't usually so nosy, I was convinced they were talking about me. I hovered above the linoleum floor, trying to get a look inside, in hopes that I could at least read their lips. But when I was high enough to look through the dingy, square-shaped glass, they both turned to me. I dropped down to the floor, and it was there that I sat when Ms. Callaway opened the door.

"Hello Ms. Culvert," Ms. Callaway said in an icy tone. They

had been talking about me.

"Come in Ms. Culvert," Ms. Whorton called to me. Ms. Callaway shuffled past, and I walked in and sat in one of the chairs positioned in front of the principal's desk. I huffed as I sat down, and Ms. Whorton looked embarrassed for me. My sense of tact and appropriateness needed some sharpening. I knew I wasn't very ladylike, but it had never really bothered me before this moment, as she sat across from me the absolute epitome of all things feminine. But that was her, that wasn't me. I couldn't be envious of something that was just a part of her personality.

Wilma and I stood in stark contrast with one another. What could Drew possibly see in the both of us? Maybe it was that obvious thing again – power. We both had power that he wanted to possess. He attempted to hide his staunch desire to control all things and all beings. I'd seen it in his eyes, but I always hoped that part of him wasn't as dominant as the parts of him that I liked.

"What's going on with you, Ms. Culvert?" Ms. Whorton asked sounding genuinely concerned about what was going on in my life. Did she really expect me to sit here and confess everything to her? I wasn't that stupid. But she intimidated me so I shrugged my shoulders.

"Not much," I said knowing that the words didn't really mean anything. It was a phrase that my generation used, not hers. They were filler words that allowed the person being asked to not have to reveal any real details. But they also were a way to spark curiosity in the person asking the question. If she really cared, she would ask again.

"Are you happy here? Do you want to go back to New York?"

Of course I did. But if I stayed here I could only benefit, and I could only grow stronger. Signs of unhappiness were a certain way to be sent off to the Informants, Lucas had told me that much. But I couldn't lie to her, she scared me too much.

"I'm not *unhappy*," I said. "I'm glad to be learning, and to be with others of my kind. This place is good for me. It's helping me grow. You have to experience discomfort at some point. You never develop if things stay the same." She was impressed by my unintended revelation. She pursed his lips and opened her mouth wide, pausing before speaking again.

"I don't like you, Mina. I won't pretend that I do. You think you're better than other Logosts, and that bothers me. You're not strong enough and yet you have so much doubt in your own abilities. You need the confirmation of others to feel confident, and that makes me want to shake you until your blood runs cold. But unlike you, I know how to control my emotions. I know how to leave my personal feelings about someone at home where contemplation is allowed."

"So this is a school where contemplation is discouraged?" I said.

"You see, this is what I'm talking about. That kind of tone, that kind of conviction, coming from someone so new to our world angers me in an indescribable way. You'll never reach your full potential. You're convinced that you already have."

"I know I haven't reached my full potential. But I know I can be strong. Mr. Elliot said himself that I was the most powerful, that I could be even more powerful than Sophia." I glanced at the painting hanging above Ms. Whorton's desk. The clouds of smoke looked as if they were moving. I could see the power and control in Sophia's eyes. I would have to learn so much more restraint if I would ever be comparable to her.

"Sophia is the archetype by which I lead my life. She is stoic – completely in control at all times. She cares nothing for anyone but herself – such self-discipline. And to think she never had any formal training. No, you'll never be like her," she shook her head. "Mr. Elliot has put too much stock in your abilities. He's convinced himself that you will be the key to our undoing of the Five Leaders. He doesn't want you sent to them." I was motionless, thinking that she would soon announce my fate. "You would serve a greater purpose with them. Your life wouldn't be as pointless as it is now. They would value your gifts." I called out to Lily in my mind, hoping she and Lucas would storm in to the room and kill Whorton. But who knew where they were? Anxiety gripped my chest. I rubbed the space where it ached, but I knew it would do no good. The pain was only mental.

"But I know that this is where you belong," Whorton finished. "I would rather have you on our side than theirs, and I think with the right training you will be a great asset to this school, maybe even more than Cassandra."

"Can I stay then?"

"You can." She said, but I could still hear her apprehension.

"But please understand my reason for despising you. You're too much like I was at your age. Arrogant and frighteningly beautiful, entirely unaware of the affect you have on those around you. Mesmerizing some while shunning others, it isn't fair to treat people that way."

"I haven't shunned anyone."

"Cassandra's told me all about how you and your friend, Lily Andrews mistreat her." How could anyone mistreat Cassandra? She would kill them before her feelings were even slightly damaged.

"Mina, I know how you are because I was you," Ms. Whorton said. "I never had such a strong infatuation with any of my teachers. But I always believed that I was better than those around me. The only difference is I found a way for it to actually be the truth. I trained until no one could touch me, until I was able to kill someone by only concentrating on the beat of their heart faltering." She laughed and the sound was filled with the excitement over what she considered an accomplishment. "I was a lonely girl like you too. I kept myself in a state of isolation, and was convinced that no one cared for me and that human life didn't matter. I grew up with no one. I was an orphan who never felt she belonged," she opened her mouth wide again and I could smell what she'd eaten for lunch – liver and onions.

"Before I came to Winchester I'd been obsessed with ending lives. Each death was like a medal and I would collect trophies that belonged to every one of them. I was fascinated by the books they'd read and the lives they'd lead. With each killing I stole a book, to peer in to their thinking. It was so exhilarating. But I went too far," my eyes fell upon the walls lined with books. I'd thought she just liked to read. "I don't want to see you fall down the same path that I did, Mina. You're more dangerous than I ever was, and I'm concerned for how many will die at your hand. I just hope they are humans and not Logosts. I have never killed a Logost and I hope that it will remain that you can say the same."

"I hope so," I said and I opened my mouth to say more, but she cut me off.

"I hope so too. I've decided to let Drew train you. You'll have a private lessons course with him at the end of each day, and at the end of the term you'll be required to prove your progress to me and the other teachers. I want you to take this seriously, Mina. And I don't want you to think that just because I'm allowing you to stay that I like you. I hope that you will keep your feelings for Mr. Elliot at bay, and come to the realization that your relationship will always be strictly platonic."

She stopped short – her mouth hanging open as we both turned our heads to the door of her office. There was a shuffling noise outside, the sound of someone running, then the door flung open. Lily and Lucas stood there, panting.

"Is everything alright?" Whorton asked them.

Lily searched my eyes, and I nodded my head in her direction, letting her know I was staying at Winchester.

"We were just looking for, Mina," Lily said. Lucas nodded in agreement. "Sorry to interrupt."

"We were just finishing up, Ms. Andrews. Actually, would you go find Mr. Elliot for me? This discussion concerns him as well."

"Yes, Ms. Whorton," Lily said.

"But not you Mr. Ramos, you go to class. You of all people should be studying."

Lily was only absent for a few minutes before she reappeared with Drew at her side. He winked at me; Lily must have told him I was staying. Whorton explained the private lessons to Drew, and said she hoped he would further his strength in the ways of controlling the elements. Naturally, I hoped he wouldn't. Controlling the elements was my thing, and he was already so good at manipulation. He couldn't have both.

"Your lessons will start tomorrow, Ms. Culvert," Whorton said. "I urge you to learn control. Maybe you will be great, in your own way at least." She smiled coldly and waved her hand, signaling me to leave.

{14}

I was not overjoyed by the fact that I was staying, but I was glad to be alive and in control of my own mind. A feeling of loneliness pecked at my eyes, leaving them red and sore. I cried a lot at night, and hid my sadness in the day. I missed my family. I missed my Mom's comforting words, her encouragement, and her never faltering faith in my own greatness.

Who cared what Wilma Whorton thought? What did she know? She didn't know me, although she seemed to think she had my personality pegged along with all my hopes, wishes, and desires. But I was a contradiction, utterly unpredictable. No one would ever know me, and that fact elated me and saddened me in an inexplicable way. I didn't really know myself. But I hoped that with time I would get to know me, that my own mind would be less of a maze. That I would see the potential outcome of things, before I acted. That I would focus on my future and not only the present, but it was hard to do so.

I knew I couldn't worry about the past, because I had no

control over it. But I also knew that I really had no control over the future. I wanted to stay away from Drew, but the feat was nearly impossible now that I would have private lessons with him. I believed he saw this coming. He knew there would come a time when I would want to stay away from him. It seemed he'd planned everything in an immaculate way. But I would be just as clever one day. I just needed to grow up first.

I rubbed my palms on my skirt, trying not to focus on their sweatiness as I sat in Ms. Callaway's Philosophy class. But the uniform tweed left wool particles on my hands, and that made the fact that I was nervous inescapable in my mind. Ms. Callaway babbled on about St. Augustine and his search for truth. Who knew what truth was anyway? Could it be possible that there would be such a thing when all of our minds had been so thoroughly muddled by modern societal standards, and expectations that haunted our every action?

The final bell rang, and all others rushed out, ready to enjoy their evening and their freedom, while I was confined to this stupid square prison. I would have to impress Drew. I wanted him to be jealous of my power. I wanted him to covet my abilities, then I would stomp all over him and laugh maniacally. I smirked as I pictured his sharp features scrunched in agony. Then, when he was thoroughly depressed and ruined, I would kill Whorton, and that I would enjoy more than anything. Once I graduated, I would come back for her, and watch her beg for death as I laughed maniacally again. My thoughts were suddenly interrupted. And I glanced up to see Lucas standing over me, as I sat at a desk in an empty classroom. Had I been laughing out loud?

"You are such a weirdo," Lucas said. "But I guess that's why I like you so much," his eyes sparkling with a smile that was only on the inside. "Who sits all alone in a classroom laughing to themselves like some evil villain in a cartoon?" I stared down at my scuffed ballet flats. Who told him to stand around so motionless and quiet anyway? I thought I was alone. "Are you looking forward to seeing Mr. Elliot?" he asked without meeting my eyes.

"You know I'm not. I'm visibly sweating bullets." He ran his finger across a drop of sweat that lingered on my forehead.

"Stop worrying, Mina," he said. "It won't get you anywhere, I hope you know that." Of course I knew that. Why did he have to be such a know-it-all? I knew he was older. I didn't need him making me feel any more immature than I already did. I got up to leave with Lucas still standing there, looking as if he needed to speak to me.

"Don't you want me to walk with you?" he said.

"I thought you met Cassandra for dinner after classes?" He shrugged at me and made his expression look innocent. He wasn't fooling me though. Lucas wasn't the best at blocking, and I watched him as he pictured her walking away from him with a tall boy called Matt who was closer to his age.

"She dumped you?" I asked.

"No," he said. "We weren't ever really together. We were just hooking up, that's all." I rolled my eyes at him. He'd only put up with her for sex. How unbearable.

"You can come along if you want, but I thought you were trying to avoid all the drama surrounding me and Drew?"

"I figure you're worth a little bit of trouble. Your presence brings me so much joy," he said looking away from me again. I wished he could be more confident when we had these discussions, but considering his age it was really all that I could expect from him. He wasn't Drew. We treaded off to Drew's classroom, which was on the far left side of the building. I was grateful for his company. I would need all the support I could get when Drew's eyes met my own.

"I just don't get it, Mina," Lucas said as we walked. "What do you see in him? He's a bigger power whore than all of us combined, even more than Ms. Whorton. It's obvious what he really wants with you. He probably doesn't love you at all."

"Just stop, Lucas. Stop trying to figure us out. You never will."

"Seriously, Mina. You're the only Logost who can control all the elements, and he shows up one day and announces he loves you. You have to admit that sounds odd." It did sound odd, but I didn't want to give Lucas the satisfaction of being right.

"It's over, so you can stop worrying about it," I snapped. "Why do you care so much anyway?"

He stopped walking. "You couldn't possibly be this oblivious, Mina! You know I care for you more than I should, more than a friend." I knew that he did, but this conversation was making me uncomfortable. I wasn't sure how I felt about Lucas. Of course, I had been jealous when I'd seen him with Cassandra, but that was a natural feeling. He dropped his eyes when I didn't respond to this planned confession. "You don't feel the same," he assumed. "You care too much for him still. Lily's told me that you call out to him in your sleep." I did? I was going to kill Lily for telling him that. Why torture him?

We stood in front of Drew's class, and he flung open the door looking angry, as usual.

"You two can't seem to get enough of one another, can you?" Drew sounded evil as he spoke, like a *real* villain out of a cartoon. He hid behind his polite demeanor, but I could tell he was trying to intimidate Lucas. He must have been listening to our conversation. I wished Lucas was better at blocking. If he would just try then things like this could stop happening.

"Ms. Culvert has a private lessons course with me, Mr. Ramos," Drew said. "And I'm sure you're well aware that other students are not permitted."

Lucas glared at Drew and a low growl escaped his chest. I saw the gold swirls around Drew's irises turn, and Lucas walked away from us. He whispered to me to be careful.

"There's no need to be careful," Drew shouted at Lucas as he walked away. "What greatness ever came from caution?"

Drew motioned for me to step inside, but I found myself unmoving. I was afraid, his demeanor felt threatening, as if he wanted to kill me just as much as he wanted to kill Lucas. I didn't want to be alone with him, but I didn't have a choice. I would have to prove to Whorton that I could be an asset to this school. Without breathing, I followed him inside.

"You seem quite taken with Mr. Ramos. Are you his now?"

"What?" I asked with bewildering eyes.

"Are you with him," he said. "Have you been with him? He follows you around like a dog does his master. Is that the kind of man you want? One who is beneath you rather than an equal who can stand at your side?"

"Don't act like you know me or what I want."

He looked angry for a moment, but then composed himself. His was expression solemn when he spoke again.

"I do know you, Mina. I know you better than anyone on this earth. Don't fall in to his arms because of the hurt I've caused. It would be unbearable for me to see you with him. I already have to endure seeing the two of you laugh at me in my class. Don't listen to that boy. He spews nothing but misconceptions and ill advice."

"So you heard what he said? That you never loved me and you only want me because I can control the elements."

"That's not true. You know that. In some ways that is what pulled me to you initially, but you know that I love you. You know that I would kill for you." He cupped my chin in his hand. "Kiss me," he said and I pushed his hand away.

"You have Whorton now, I'm sure you wouldn't want her to forsake you as I have. Just teach me like you're supposed to, and leave your feelings at the door."

I loved watching his expression change whenever I surprised him with my cleverness. But when I looked up at him he looked angry again. He pushed his body against mine and grabbed my breast hard. It hurt, and he'd never done anything like this before. I smacked his hand away and he pushed me in to the door to his classroom. I felt his hands grabbing at the bottom of my skirt, and I kept trying to move them. He grabbed my shoulders, and I started to cry. He had so much hatred and fear in his eyes.

"Stop it, please," I said, reaching for his hands. "You're hurting me. You're scaring me."

He dropped his hands down to his sides and stood back, staring at me. I was breathless.

"I didn't mean to hurt you," he said and his tone changed back to an alluring one, a charming one. "I'm sorry. I lost control. You know I would never hurt you. I promise not to do it again," he smiled. I was confused by what he'd just done. But maybe it really was an accident.

"Let's just get this over with. I need to study." And I wanted to be away from him as quickly as possible.

"We need to go outside, anyway. We can't practice controlling the elements in this space. Ms. Whorton is worried you'll harm the other students."

Stars filled the night, and the moon lit our path as we walked towards the shadows nestled deep in the mountain tops. Drew grabbed my hand and we flew in to the darkness. He pulled me close, cradling me in his arms, shielding me from the wind. He kissed my hair, and I looked up at him so innocent, so surprised. I loved him still.

We landed in the snow and Drew pulled up the sleeves of his collared shirt. I watched him as he pulled the night sky in different directions. He picked up a small stone from the ground and hollowed it out with his mind. He swept his hand back and held it in front of him, calling to a star that hung in the distance. He pulled it in, and held the star in his hands. He put it inside the stone and took a piece of string from his pocket. I walked over to him and he tied the star-filled stone around my neck. It hung low close to my chest, close to my heart. I held it in my hands and watched as the star changed from soft lavender to a neutral pink. It seemed to be in tune with me, in tune with my own feelings and insecurities.

"Don't ever forget how much I love you, Mina," he leaned down to whisper in my ear. "That will never change, no matter how much you despise me."

I knew that I wouldn't forget, that he would never *allow* me to forget. He pulled me close and kissed my hair again. "You are everything to me, my love," he said. "We'll be together again one day, but I'm afraid it will never be the way that I once wished. Your friend's interference will always be present. I don't want him to tear you away from me, but I'm afraid that he will. Don't let him, Mina. Don't let him take you from me." I stared in to his dark green eyes and I nodded. He seemed so sad. I didn't want to hurt him more than I already had. But I knew that I couldn't be his.

"You know that things can't change until you devote yourself to me. It's not me that's causing you this pain. It's only you and your selfish desire to control everything and everyone. If you gave that up then you could have me, but that desire is stronger than anything else."

"I shouldn't have to change my desire for power – one day your desires will mirror my own, and we'll be inseparable. Nothing will stand in our way, not fate or time – nothing."

I would never desire power the way that Drew did. My desire was greatness, not control. I told him that I didn't love him anymore and that his feelings weren't mutual. He knew I was lying, but he respected the way that I felt, at least for that moment.

My dinner went uneaten that night. Drew and I stayed there for hours, while he watched me manipulate the night sky and the winds at my command. Drew said that I would have to move beyond things like having the weather change in tangent with how I was feeling. It must always be conscious. That I must always stay focused no matter how I was feeling, or I would kill without thinking.

He felt the Earth move when he asked me to, and I did my best to impress him with all that I could do, but I knew that I could do more. And he knew it too.

{15}

The next morning I sat up in my bed, motionless with fear. Someone was in our room. There was a feeling of deep sadness and anguish that wasn't coming from me or Lily. I was afraid to roll over and look at Lily. I lay there thinking of the best course of action, trying to map out a plan for who could be there, and what I would need to do to kill them before they could harm me. But when I rolled over, slowly preparing for the act of murder, it was Lily who I saw leaning over me breathing heavily, focusing on something that was invisible to me.

"Lily?" I asked, my voice shaking. "Is something wrong?" She was freaking me out. Her eyes were dead. There was no emotion behind them. Her lips curled up in a murderous smile. But it wasn't her smile. I'd never seen Lily look that way.

"I have to kill you, Mina," she whispered to me. "You're too powerful," her face remained emotionless. It wasn't Lily speaking, someone was controlling her. Someone was asking her to kill me, and she was fighting their control.

Lily leaned down, hovering over me and wrapped her small hands around my throat.

I couldn't breathe. I couldn't focus.

She was going to kill me.

Her eyes darted back and forth, in search for a way out of this undying fate. I focused on freeing her mind. I focused on whoever was there occupying it, leaving. I shook the Earth and the wind beat at our bedroom window. Lily's eyes glossed over and then she blinked. She released her hands from my throat, stretching her fingers as she stared down at her hands. She sat down on her bed, not looking away from her hands.

"I almost killed you, Mina," she said, gasping for air. Tears fell down her face in to the corner of her mouth. "I would never hurt you. You know that, right?" she asked not really wanting me to answer, but trying more to console herself. "I don't know what happened. All I could think about was choking you to death. I'm sorry."

"It's not your fault. Someone else was in your mind."

"I can't trust myself."

"You can Lily," I said, moving towards her. "Whoever it was I think they know better than to try again. Did their manipulation leave any traces?"

"No, I'm not sure who would do this."

From then on, Lily and I put up barriers above our room each night.

Classes ended, but I couldn't stop worrying about who would

want to kill me. Lily racked her brain as well, in search for the truth. I think she worried that I believed she really wanted to kill me. But I knew that wasn't true. Lily loved me, she was my best friend.

Lily met me after my private lessons with Drew, and as always he continuously begged for my forgiveness. He was visibly distressed, and seemed to be getting more and more frustrated with me with each lesson. There was nothing I could do to comfort him, so Lily and I walked to the dining hall in silence. It was hard for things to be as they had before, but I hoped we would fall back in to the natural state of adoring one another. Lucas met up with us, and we sat together in the dining hall just as we always did. Lily and I were unusually quiet from the stress of that morning. We didn't tell Lucas. We didn't want to worry him. He had enough on his plate – his roommate and friend, Elijah had been behaving strangely.

Elijah was weak and easily corruptible. He tortured the other students with mind control, and loved listening to their screams. Why Lucas cared for him so much, I would never understand. Lucas said Elijah grew sadder as each day passed, and told Lucas that there was no point to this life. Elijah was convinced that all people were worthless, including himself. He screamed out at night, about wanting to leave Winchester, about wishing that he was not a Logost, because then he would never have to hurt anyone. Elijah didn't understand that he didn't have to be bad. But he was too impressionable and his values swayed like a frail woman in the wind. He wasn't as much of an individual as Lucas, and he didn't trust himself. Lily and I consoled Lucas as best we could, but we didn't know Elijah, and we really didn't like him. He was too much like Cassandra, too drunk with power, too convinced that he had to act as everyone else wanted him to, and not the way he wanted to himself.

We listened to Lucas' grief, and I hated having to hear him in such great despair. I wanted to fix his problems for him. But Elijah wasn't broken. He just needed to see past this school, past life as it was in this moment. All things are temporary, even feelings of self-loathing.

I told Lucas to be supportive, and to listen whenever Elijah wanted to talk, but not to press him when he didn't. Lucas said he wasn't hungry, and that he needed check on Elijah. Lucas didn't like leaving Elijah alone with his own thoughts for too long. Lily and I sat in silence for a little while longer, still unable to look one another in the eye.

When we got back to our dorm, Lily left to go shower and prepare for the next day. We all had white boards on our room doors to leave messages for one another like, 'hey stop using up all the hot water' or 'someone came by looking for you.' When I glanced at my door, someone had written that my brother had called, but hadn't bothered to give a name. I knew Carter wouldn't call. He was the type that you always had to make the first move with, to keep those lines of communication open. It was definitely Paris, we were the closest, and he undoubtedly missed my being there. I walked to the common room to use the phone. I was nervous as I dialed the familiar number, hoping that my Mom wouldn't be the one to answer. I'd been avoiding her calls, not wanting her to hear the stress and strain that was always present in my voice.

"Hello," Paris always answered the phone in a polite but commanding tone.

"Hey there buddy, it's me Mina," I said relieved at the sound of his voice. I missed him so much – the wise one, the shy one, the contemplative one.

"Hey sis, I miss you man," he said in a barely audible way, as he munched on some food cooked by our Mom that I wasn't there to share with him.

"I miss you too," I admitted. "I miss you all more than you can imagine."

"Then why haven't you called? It's been weeks since any of us have heard anything. I would have called sooner, but you know how stubborn Mom is. She's convinced herself that you don't love us anymore."

"That woman," I muttered.

"Yeah, I know," he said understanding without me really having to say anything. "I'm just so pumped about coming out there next weekend. I can't wait to see France and you of course." I was silent as he finished his sentence. I didn't know what to say. I was a horrible sister. How could I have been so preoccupied? "You forgot, didn't you?" he said. "I knew you would. I knew that was why you hadn't called."

"I'm sorry. It's not that I forgot. I just didn't think you were serious. I didn't think you would be able to come up with enough money."

"Why exude such small amounts of faith in me, little sister?" Paris said. "I said what I meant, and I meant what I said. I entered a few writing contests out here and I won first place, a whopping sum of around $2,000, proud?"

"That's amazing," I said pleased with his success. "Of course I'm proud, but shouldn't you use that money for something else, like college?" I could feel him shrugging his shoulders even though I couldn't see him.

"I'll cross that bridge when I get to it. I'll let future Paris handle that adult stuff. He'll do a better job of it. Right now, all I can think about is seeing your dirt smudged little face."

"I'm not little anymore," I laughed. "No more mud pies for me."

"Well, yeah, I know," was all he said, but I could hear him wishing that I was still his little sister. That I was still at home with him, and that things hadn't changed. We let a moment of silence pass, not knowing what else to say.

"Well, I'll see you soon sis, don't forget again, okay?"

"I won't," I promised him and waited to hear the click of the receiver. I was glad he was visiting. I needed a small piece of home with me. I just wondered if he would want to take me back with him as soon as he saw the state of things. Well, that part was inevitable. I just hoped that he wouldn't tell my Mom how bad it was. He seemed happy though, and that made me feel better.

***

"Is Elijah doing any better?" I asked Lucas that Saturday

afternoon, as we walked around the outside of the tiny campus. I stared at his hands, they were trembling. I tried to meet his eyes, but he kept his head turned away from me as we walked. I wanted him to look at me. He'd been distant lately, sick with worry over his friend. I took his hand and wrapped my fingers tightly around his. His hand practically swallowed my own – I hated my tiny fingers they were so skinny and small. He looked at me – a smile in his eyes. Blinking, he seemed to remember that I'd just asked him a question. He stared down at our interlocked fingers.

"What?" Lucas said. "Oh yeah, he's doing great. He's started building model airplanes. It certainly helps distract him from his mental anguish. He's happy for now."

"Well, what's bothering you? You know I'm always here for you. Is there something you need to talk about?" Lucas walked over to a barren tree and leaned his back up against the base. He patted a spot next to him, motioning for me to sit next to him. I felt uneasy, but I walked over and sat with him, leaving a space between us.

"We never get much time to be alone – just the two of us, you know?"

"I suppose," I said apprehensively. I wasn't sure what he was getting at.

"Listen Mina, I think I deserve a shot with you. You haven't given me much of a chance because you've been so obsessed with Mr. Elliot, and I know that I care about you more than he does."

"You don't know that for sure."

"Yes, I do. I see what he doesn't see. Someone daring and

selfless, a beautiful girl who rescued me on her first day, and who wants to be a hero. Mr. Elliot doesn't want to be the hero. I know you see him that way, but he just isn't. He will never be the hero you want him to be. I don't think there's an ounce of good in him."

That was debatable, but I was tired of arguing over Mr. Elliot with him. I would let him think whatever he wanted to keep the peace.

"So you want to be my hero?" I asked curious.

"No, I don't want to be your hero, Mina. I don't want to rush things, but since you say you're done with him, I want you to know that I am here. I feel so strongly about you that there's just no way that the feeling isn't reciprocated, even if it's in a miniscule way, you must feel something for me. I could love you Mina, if you'd let me. I could be your partner, not your hero. I would stand by your side, and I would never manipulate you." He pushed himself on to his knees and leaned down to look at me. "Tell me what you're thinking. Could you care about me? Or will it always be him?"

Lucas was my best friend. I didn't want something like this to muddle our friendship, but I couldn't keep denying how I felt about him. He knew those feelings were there.

"I don't know anything right now, Lucas. I do care about you, but I think it would be unwise to give you hope when I am enamored with him still. We haven't ever been romantic with one another, so it's hard for me to know exactly how I feel. I just need some time."

"Come out with me then – just the two of us," he said so

hopeful that I couldn't deny him. "We'll go see a movie in Chamonix tonight. I'm just asking for a chance to be a bigger part of your life. You won't ever know how you really feel until you've explored all of your options."

"That would be good," I thought for a moment. "I do love spending time with you. You make me happy." I grinned at him and he seemed to swell with sudden confidence.

We agreed to meet up later that night, and walk to the small theater together. I was excited about being alone with him – he was right I hadn't given him a chance. I'd convinced myself that if it couldn't be Drew, then it wouldn't be anyone. Drew was the first person I'd ever been attracted to, but I was attracted to Lucas too, and I had been from the very beginning. If I chose to be with Lucas I wouldn't have to worry so much. Lucas was more comfortable – like the difference between staying home on a Friday night or going out and partying. I had to decide which lifestyle I wanted – the comforting one, or the dangerous one.

I spent the rest of that day studying. There would be a test in Drew's class on Monday, and although I felt that manipulation was the worst of all the things I could do, I realized it would be necessary when dueling other Logosts. If I could master it, then I wouldn't have to fear Cassandra or Ms. Whorton anymore. I skipped dinner that Saturday, deciding it was best for me to practice controlling the elements alone.

There was a small pond near the school. I had mastered the wind, but I would need to take everything else step by step. First, I would master water, then fire, and then the Earth. I would be their master and they would beckon to me for power. I needed to be the one in control – not only of the elements, but of myself. I would have to master my emotions and who I was meant to be.

The pond was frozen so I focused on warming it, on the increase of the temperature, little by little until a layer of water rested above the ice. I didn't need it be completely unfrozen, I just needed enough water to practice. I flew over the lake and manipulated the water, controlling it with the motions of my hands. I shot it into the trees, and towards the sky allowing it to rain down upon me.

I practiced until I made mistakes due to my fatigue. A second to close my eyes and rest my mind was all I really needed, so I decided to nap by the lake for just a little while. I made a small flame and lay down on the cold ground, closed my eyes, and drifted off in to the freedom of my dreams. Only a few moments had passed before Drew was there. He stood in a dark meadow surrounded by hazy, golden clouds. The moon shined on his pale features, his eyes that fearful shade of light green.

"Mina," he sang my name as he spoke. "Come to me Mina, please? I miss you quite terribly, my love," his tone so alluring I wanted to follow the sound.

A black, wrought-iron gate surrounded the meadow and Drew called out to me still. I saw myself paralyzed, terrified to be near him. Something was stopping him from moving closer to me. He circled the gate in a blinding, pale blur. Searching for a way past it, and then I saw someone else there. Lucas stood by my side, holding my hand in his. Drew roared at us. He couldn't get to me because Lucas was blocking him, I was blocking him too. There was fire in his eyes, and the fire spread in the meadow. I saw the gate for what it was – a cage. Flames flew out from Drew's eyes, enraging in time with his anger.

Drew watched on, as he delighted at the sight of Lucas and me burning together. We sank further and further in to the flames until I was jolted awake.

{16}

My throat burned and my face felt like fire. But I was still there near the pond, still lying on the snowy ground. I stood up, splashed the ice cold water on my face, and contemplated how much danger I was putting Lucas in by agreeing to be alone with him. I didn't think Drew knew what my plan was, about Lucas, or the fact that I was practicing without him.

A lonesome feeling gripped me and I raced back to the dorms, realizing I was no longer safe enough to be alone. Had Drew put that dream there, or did I conjure it out of my own free will? Was my subconscious telling me something that I couldn't focus on? Should I be afraid of Drew and his desire for control? Lucas was convinced that I should. When I got back to my room, Lily was lying in bed reading.

"Are you alright?" she said when I stepped through the doorway. "You look like you just witnessed a massacre."

"I'm fine, I was just out practicing. I must have over-exerted myself a bit." I grabbed my bag of toiletries and headed for the showers.

"Where are you going?" Lily asked concerned.

"I'm going to shower. I'm meeting Lucas tonight."

"That sounds nice," she smiled. "He mentioned wanting some time to be alone with you. Mr. Elliot was looking for you earlier." That was strange. He always knew where to find me. Maybe I was getting better at blocking him. "He seemed upset, and a bit erratic."

"Isn't he always?" I asked and Lily laughed without humor.

"Yeah, but you might want to stay away from him for a while," she warned me. "He seemed nervous and obsessive – like his life depended on knowing where you were. He asked about Lucas, he asked if you were with him, and I told him that you weren't, but I hadn't seen you since breakfast. Then he just dashed off. He seemed different, almost frightening."

Lily put her book down and I walked over to her canopy bed.

"Are you afraid of him?" I said.

"No, not really, but I never really pay him enough attention to feel anyway about him. Are *you* afraid of him?"

"I don't know. I don't if I should be, but I'm worried. He's very powerful."

"Yeah, he is, but I don't think he'd ever hurt anyone. He seems harmless – a little creepy, but harmless none the less."

I showered quickly, but I made sure to look nice. I spent extra time on my hair and makeup, and put on a pair of dark blue jeans and a lavender top. I rushed out to meet Lucas in the courtyard, and he stood there waiting for me in the dark.

"You look stunning," he breathed as he took my hand. He looked down at the star filled stone that hung around my neck. The stone was a shimmering pink color, filled with warmth from my happiness of being with Lucas. I forgot to take it off. But he didn't ask any questions about it, I think he knew who had given it to me.

"Do you miss him?" Lucas said.

"How could I miss him? I have to see him almost every day. Do you miss Cassandra? It just seems strange that you would ever desire someone like her."

"I could say the same about you and Mr. Elliot," he sighed. "But I see your point, Cassandra can be intimidating. And maybe that's why I like her."

"Do you find me intimidating?" I said. Lucas took my hand and wrapped his fingers around my own. He moved in closer to me, staring down in to my eyes.

"Not at all," he said, then he laughed and leaned in to kiss my neck. "You're much sweeter than Cassandra, more honest, and trusting. You think you're tough, and I know that you can be tough. But you don't show that side of yourself very often, which makes it easier for me to be around you. Elijah's told me that you're too arrogant, but I don't think that's true. Your confidence falters more than he sees."

"Tell Elijah to suck it," I said and folded my arms across my chest.

Lucas laughed. "Do you even know what that means?" he

asked. I'd heard it said plenty of times before – I guess it meant shut up, I told him. Lucas just laughed again, then he paused to stare down at his feet. "What do you like about me?"

"Honestly, I like everything about you, except for the fact that you can be a know-it-all sometimes." I narrowed my eyes. "You always stand up for me and Lily though, you make me laugh, and I love how awkward you are. But you're still always confident, not arrogant like me. You're brilliant, but you're not a show off, and you manage to only focus on the things that are important to you. It seems like you don't care what anyone else thinks."

"Well, that's not true. I care what other people think. I just try not to let the thoughts and feelings of others affect me. People always have something to say, and you should listen, but that doesn't make what they're saying right. Sometimes, I can't stand to be around other people. But you are someone who I always want to be around." Lucas wrapped his hand around my waist and pulled me to him. He brushed a strand of hair out of my face, and took my hand again.

His eyes were soft, sullen, and we walked in to town and to the theater in silence. We didn't need words. There was an understanding of peace that we didn't need to draw attention to.

Lucas picked the movie, but it was in French without any subtitles, so he had to translate every word for me. He pulled my hair back gently, placing it behind my ear as he translated the film. It was about some teenage girl who obsessed over her mother's boyfriend, it bored me, but there was nowhere else I'd rather be than with Lucas. He was my shy, awkward angel – always so overly confident. He didn't bolster me up or try to control me like Drew. He accepted me for everything I was. I never felt self-conscious near him. There was nothing I would change about him, and I knew he felt the same. He touched me softly, not urgently as Drew always did.

When the film ended, Lucas walked me back to my dorm, and I was sad to see the night end. He confessed that it made him anxious to be far from me, and even though I felt the same, I didn't admit to it. He worried that I would go back to Drew. But his worries were useless. There was no way I could go back to Drew now. He would hate me too much once he found out what I had done.

Lucas looked down at the star once again, and held it in his large hand, examining it.

"You're better at keeping him out now," he said still holding the stone, watching the colors change.

"How do you know that?"

"Because he's given you this," he said looking at me. "It moves in tangent with your thoughts and feelings. He wants you to always be exposed to him."

"It doesn't matter," I breathed. "He'll never have me. There's someone else, now. Someone who respects me and doesn't treat me like a child."

Lucas stared at me, waiting for me to say more. But I just leaned in to him then, and pressed my lips to his feeling the warmth. I folded myself in to his massive stature, and wrapped my arms around him under his coat. I jumped back suddenly, as if the warmth of his flesh had burned me. Something changed. Someone was watching us. I sensed him there, and he was more nervous than angry. But I couldn't let Lucas walk back alone. I knew Drew would kill him.

"Good night," I said and Lucas looked confused.

"Did I do something wrong?"

"No, I just – I can hear Lily, she's worried. I better make sure she knows I'm okay." He turned to walk away. I pretended to close the door, and then I snuck out behind him to make sure he got home safely. I followed him silently until he was inside the boy's dorm. Drew jumped out from behind me the moment I let out a gasp of relief. But he was motionless and unspeaking. He just stared down at me, but I couldn't see his face. It was hidden by the shadows of the night.

"What are you doing, Mina?" his voice a blank monotone as he grabbed my hand.

"Whatever I want," I said. "And I owe you no explanation for my actions," I pulled my hand from his. "You're just my teacher. Stop following me, and stay away from Lucas. You know he fears you."

"Not enough obviously," he said moving his face out of the shadows. "Or he would have followed my advice from the beginning, and kept his distance from things that are not his."

"I'm not a thing," I screamed at him. "And I'm not yours. You have no claim over me and you have no say in the choices I make."

"Oh, but I do, my love," he said his voice so sweet, so enduring. "Do not forget that you owe me everything. I brought you here, and only with my help will you reach your full potential. Practicing on your own? Did you think I wouldn't find out? I am no fool, Mina. What you're doing is wrong. You'll only hurt us both. You may think you love that boy, but you love only me. We are destined for one another. I've seen it. If you go down this path with him, I may never be able to find you again. He eludes me. When you think of him, when you're with him, I can't see you. Your thoughts are cloudy, your feelings about me uncertain."

"My feelings have changed," I told him my voice shaking. "This has to stop. You're acting like a crazy person."

"That is a lie," he said his emotions changing like the flightiness of a teenaged boy's interests. "You love me, I know it, and if I'm acting crazy it's because of you. You force me to behave this way, to stoop so low as to have to follow you around while you *swoon* over him. And to have to watch you through his mind because you keep me out. Don't keep me out, Mina," he begged. "I love you."

I was done with this. It was cold, it was late, and there was no point in having this conversation if he wouldn't listen to reason. I turned to walk away from him, but he was suddenly in front of me.

"You're not leaving until you've heard what I have to say." He said and leaned in close, holding me in place with his eyes. I couldn't move, and there wasn't any time for me to make an attempt to block him. "I saw you kiss him Mina," he whispered to me, stroking my face. "I saw you touch him. Be that way with me again Mina, please. Kiss me," he said, and I fell in to him without thinking.

He pressed his lips to mine, and fell in the snow, pulling me on top of him. "I love you Mina, please love me, not him." He kissed my neck and hair, cradling me in his arms. "Wilma and I are through. You were right. My quest for power is not worth losing you. I'm sorry that I ever believed it was."

"Do you want me to be happy?" I whispered, afraid that his mood might change once more.

"Of course, more than anything," he replied so sure of himself.

"What if I could be happier with Lucas than I could be with you," I said. "Would you let me go? Would you allow me happiness without the threat of your presence?"

Without thinking, Drew answered my question. "That doesn't matter, Mina," he shouted. "You belong with me and that's all that matters. Didn't you just hear me? Wilma knows about us, I told her the truth. She knows I don't love her."

"Will she try to kill me," he shrugged as I spoke. "Isn't this illegal? Won't she turn us over to the Informants now? Our relationship – our ages."

"She may try to kill you," he said calmly. "But I won't let her. Her jealousy will pass. She'll eventually see our relationship for what it was – a matter of convenience. And she won't say anything to the Informants. I know too much about her. If she sold me out to them, I would reveal all of her secrets. She doesn't want them to come here. She's afraid they'll find out she's training students to destroy them."

That was her plan all this time. Was I ever in any danger of being sent to them? She must have just been trying to frighten me. I looked in to Drew's eyes and they were wide with the truth of his words. I'd pushed him far enough, but how could I be positive that he was telling the truth? He certainly wasn't the most trustworthy Logost.

"Why tell her now?" I asked, gently tracing his cleft chin and the base of his neck with my finger.

"I knew you were swaying from me, and that you were considering choosing that boy over me. I do love you, Mina, more than he loves you," he whispered as he kissed my neck. "Come back to me. I promise to be good," he smiled darkly and I could hear a creaking noise — a lonely sound behind his words. But I ignored it. This is what I wanted, to be with him always, and to be his one and only. But there was still a hesitancy faltering that desire.

"Show me," I told him. "I won't take you back until you prove yourself to me. Prove that you love me."

"How?" he asked. "You know that I love you. I've risked everything by bringing you here. What more can I do?"

"Not that," I told him. "Let me inside of your mind. Show me what you said to Whorton, and I'll know that I can trust you." He sighed and his eyes were filled with an antiquated sadness that was indistinguishable. He still wanted me to believe that this was who he was — a gentle neurotic man, who was strange, but kind, and who loved me dearly.

"I must be honest with you, Mina," he spoke so softly I could barely hear the words. "My mind is a dangerous place. I don't want you to get lost there, like I am, and so many others. It's a very frightening place, and I mean only to protect you, never to harm you, my love."

"You don't have a choice. Either show me, or I choose Lucas," I said bluffing. I didn't know if I could choose Lucas over Drew. My feelings for Lucas weren't strong enough, they were still clouded by Drew's control, by my longing for him. He stood up, cradling me with him. He placed me firmly on the ground and put his hands on my shoulders. He stared deep in to my eyes, deep in to my soul, and I watched as his eyes turned dark, almost black the same way mine did when I concentrated on control. But I could still see the gold swirls, they were so much clearer now; they looked like tiny crescent moons.

I felt powerless, then I was no longer standing with Drew outside in the cold. I was swirling in and out of a fiery vortex inside of his mind, falling in to the heat. So many faces passed me as I fell through Drew's mind – hollow faces, haunted with pain and loss. They called out to me, an eerie sound that was not a voice, but a screeching noise, "Mina," the hollow faces said. "Help us, Mina, he's trapped us here. Don't go too far," they warned me. "He'll keep you here too." I could feel myself falling from grace. I reached out searching for something to stop my tumbling. I could feel the bottom growing closer, the cold earth beckoned to me from below. But I caught myself before I crashed in to it, then the image changed to that of Wilma Whorton's office.

Drew walked through the doors of the office – he wore an evil grin hidden behind a solemn expression. He was happy to have the chance to break her heart.

"Good evening, Drew," Ms. Whorton greeted him.

"Wilma, I have no time for formalities. I've come here to confess something."

"You love the girl?" she asked unimpressed by what he'd planned to have shattered her.

"Yes, you know that I do."

"I've seen your feelings for her – the way you watch her frightens even me." Whorton admitted.

"This doesn't have to change anything, Wilma. We can still destroy the Five Leaders together. This world can still be ours."

"Not ours, Drew. It will be mine, and I will kill you both when the time comes. I warned you when I offered you this teaching position, to not let your thirst for power become your undoing, but it seems you have ignored my cautious tale. I will show you no mercy. Leave me now."

"How long can I stay?"

"I'm not banishing you Drew," Whorton said. "You're one of the best teachers I have, and I need you here to prepare the students for battle. Mina will fight on our side and when the battle is won, when the Informants are all dead, I will kill you both. There is nothing you can do, do no try to undo this end. You've seen this coming for some time."

Drew bowed to her, "I understand, and I apologize for the inconvenience. I hope our deaths bring you joy, and no sorrow."

"Goodbye Drew," Whorton said. "I will not mourn your loss. No one will." He shut the door to Whorton's office, and I was brought back to the cold and silent night where our bodies stood.

"She will kill us both then?" I asked him, my legs nearly giving out from under me. "There's no way out."

Drew laughed manically. "Wilma Whorton is an imbecile – she's far too gullible. I've been manipulating her for years – ever since I came to this hopeless place. She knows nothing about me – about who Drew Elliot really is, she believes in the mask. Trust me, my love, I've timed everything in an immaculate way. Wilma Whorton will be dead long before the battle has begun. It will be the end, but it will not be our end. It will take a much greater Logost than Whorton to stop us. We will rule," he whispered and pressed his lips to mine.

{17}

The week that followed was complicated. I was anxious about Paris coming to visit, but I worried Drew would eventually realize that I feared him, more than I loved him. What he showed me that night could not be forgotten, and I knew that I was more afraid than in love with Drew Elliot.

I kept my distance from Lucas. I didn't want Drew to be suspicious. Lucas was terrible at blocking so I couldn't tell him or Lily what I'd seen in Drew's mind.

The souls of those he'd killed haunted him, but he only wanted more power, he only wanted to end more lives. He was convinced that he was doing the right thing for me and for himself, as well as for all the other Logosts he hoped to control.

Lucas knew I was behaving strangely, but I was able to convince him that I was only worried about my brother visiting. He was only staying for two days – Saturday and Sunday in Chamonix and then he would visit a few other cities in France. He arrived in a black taxi that Friday night, and he ate dinner with Lily, Lucas, and me in the dining hall. He was staying at an Inn in Chamonix, and I walked him there after dinner that night.

"So what's the plan for tomorrow?" Paris asked as we reached the door to the Inn.

"We'll go for a walk in the mountains, and then we'll have lunch somewhere in town. Do you like France so far?"

"It's beautiful. The school isn't what I was expecting though. Everyone seems so normal." Paris had yet to see anyone use their powers, and Lily and I had focused on protecting him that evening. I needed to keep him away from the other students. I didn't want anyone trying to hurt him. He seemed to like Lily and Lucas. I wouldn't let Drew see him even though Drew wanted to. Drew wouldn't be a part of my life the way he planned on, and I didn't want him getting close to my family.

"Will Lily and Lucas be there?"

"Yeah, why," I asked.

"I think it should just be the two of us. There's a reason I came out here to see you, and it was more than me just wanting to get away from Mom." I racked my brain for what the reason could be, but nothing lit any flames of thought.

"Is this about Dana? Don't tell me you want to marry her or something."

"No, no! We broke up! It's about Dad, and me sort of. I'll explain tomorrow. It won't be easy."

The next morning, I was anxious to meet Paris in Chamonix. Lily was still sleeping when I woke, and when I walked outside Lucas was standing next to the entryway.

"Going to see your brother?" he asked. I nodded, told him I was late and walked past him. "Mina, what's wrong? Is it me? You've been so reserved lately. I feel like there's something you aren't telling me and it has nothing to do with your brother being here." Lucas loved jumping to conclusions. "If you don't want me, just tell me. I'm not like Mr. Elliot, I know how to bow out politely when I'm not wanted."

"I do want you Lucas. I do care for you. I'm just trying to protect you. You were right about Mr. Elliot. We can't be together Lucas, I'm sorry, but he'll kill you."

"You don't need to spare my feelings. I'll stay away from you, so you can be with him. It was foolish to think you could ever feel something for me. I don't need you to lie to me and lead me on. Just stay away from me and I'll do the same." Lucas walked away from me, and I called out to him in vain. There was no point in trying. He wasn't right, but if hurting him was what it was going to take to keep him safe, then I would just have to deal. It hurt to have him think that I didn't care for him, it hurt to know that he probably wouldn't be my friend anymore.

I met Paris at his hotel, and we walked along the base of the mountains through several courtyards near the school. Paris didn't really like hiking and I didn't either. I showed him how high I'd learn to fly and that I wasn't afraid of my powers anymore. He watched me uproot trees with my mind and fling them in to the mountains. I made the snow stop for him and the sun shine brighter.

"You seem tougher," he said. "But definitely sadder. So sad that it almost makes me wish I could take you home with me. And then you'd be forced to transform back in to my wide-eyed, innocent little sister." There was no going back now. He knew that. He heaved in frustration. "Talk to me, Mina. Tell me what's really going on in your life. I feel like I don't know you anymore. There was a time when I knew all your secrets."

"Nothing's going on," I urged him. "Nothing more than teenage troubles. I mean this is a big change. It's natural to take some time to adjust. I wish I was stronger is all. That no one could defeat me."

"You sound insane. Defeat you how?"

"It's not important. You seem to be hiding something yourself, while you try to pinpoint me. What is it you wanted to tell me about Dad?"

Paris reached inside the pocket of his coat and pulled out a small, silver and oval-shaped trinket that hung from a small chain.

"I stole this from Mom, it was Dad's. It has his name on it." Paris placed it in my hand, and I turned it over, examining it.

It was a silver pocket watch, tarnished with age. There were tiny white sapphires engraved in it, and when I turned it over my father's name was engraved there as well – Ernest Culvert. The hands of the clock face stood still, and I wondered why Paris would give this to me.

"How long have you had it?"

"Since I was twelve, since I found that photo of him, I kept it in my bedside table but I never showed it to you. I wasn't sure if it belonged to Dad, but I always hoped. I tricked Mom in to telling me his name after you left, and then I knew it was his. Our Dad's name is Ernest and this pocket watch belongs to him," he beamed with pride for our father. "I'm giving it to you because you have a better chance of figuring out its significance than I do. I'm sure some of the teachers here must have known who he was – at least the older ones, anyway. Have you asked anyone if they know anything about him? If there's some chance we might find him?"

Paris didn't know that our father probably wasn't a good man. How could he be if he'd been a Logost? A good Logost was an anomaly – I was still in awe that Logosts like Lucas and Lily existed. Our father must have been a horrible man, and that's why my Mom never talked about him. I wondered how many people he had killed.

"I haven't asked anyone about him," I said. "And I don't plan on it, Paris. Don't search for him. This is something that is best left unknown. There's a reason Mom doesn't talk about him. I'm surprised you haven't caught on – you're usually much quicker than I am."

"So you've taken her side then?" he said. "You think there's no point in knowing more about the man that we came from. The man who may want to know us, but can't. What if she's keeping him from us on purpose?"

"Of course she is, Paris! Don't you see? That's why she didn't want me to come here. This is why she didn't want me to be a Logost. They're all evil, controlling spawn – hungry for power. They kill, they torture, there's no way that our father was a good man, and there's no way that we would be good people if Mom had allowed him to be a part of our lives."

"You're lying," he said. "I don't believe you."

"You don't have to. It's the truth. Why do you think I'm so miserable here? I don't belong. But our Dad did. He probably loved it here."

The man who had been a part of my creation had been a murderer, I cried at the thought. I worried about how big of a part of him lived within me. How much of my own mind longed for power and bloodshed the way Drew's did. Maybe I was fooling myself in thinking that I had any control of my own end, of my own destiny. Maybe what Drew was saying was true. We were meant to be together, there was no chance I could escape, and eventually I wouldn't want to. What if one day I wanted nothing more than to have Drew by my side, and the only thing I would ever crave would be power and control?

"Don't cry, Mina. It's not like I think you would lie to me intentionally, you're just going off what you know of Logosts, but you didn't know our Dad. He could have been good. Maybe he was so good that other Logosts wanted to kill him, and that's why Mom had to keep him away from us. Maybe he even kept himself away – to keep us safe. I think he loved us. I'm sorry, but I think you're wrong."

"I know I'm not," I whispered. "I just hope that I don't turn out to be anything like him. I don't want to be a murderer."

"If this place will only make you bad why do you want to stay? If you're so determined to be good then leave with me."

"I can't, Paris. They'll come for me, and they'll kill me. I have to learn how to defeat any and every Logost if I don't want to be a part of this *lifestyle*. I have to be deadly. They must fear me or else I have no chance at survival."

"I can help you, Mina. I can help you fight them."

"Paris, I would never put you at risk like that. You'd be killed instantly. You can't even defend yourself – you're human."

And in that moment, I watched as Paris' feet left the ground. He flew above me and forced the snow from the mountaintops. I watched as the fluffy clouds floated down near us – Paris controlling its movements. He told me that he couldn't control any of the elements, but that he'd always been able to read minds – a rare gift, and he could control whatever he wanted. He'd rejected it from the beginning – always desiring a life of normalcy, rather than greatness like I longed for. He had been ashamed of his difference – I had always valued my own.

{18}

The weekend had come and gone, and I found myself feeling lighter with Paris there. I was less weighed down by the mass of the world as it caressed my shoulders. That Sunday evening, after I wished Paris well, and watched him leave in a taxi, I went for a walk in the city to clear my head, and to avoid Drew. He'd been calling to me in my mind all weekend, and I wasn't ready to face him. I needed to leave him convinced that I still loved him, but I wasn't sure how I could lie to him.

My feelings were changing, my fear growing.

Chamonix was small, like the town that existed only in a child's toy train set. I walked along the cobble stone roads, trying to sense Drew's erratic presence, but I couldn't place him. I worried he might be following me. It was late, and instead of gaining a feeling of peace, I grew more frustrated as the sun set lower and lower. A feeling of hopelessness gripped my insides, making it hard for me to think. It was a feeling of uncertainty, of never really knowing what was to become of me. I wanted to rip my skin off and run as fast, and as far away as I possibly could.

I wanted to stand at the end of the highest mountain edge and jump – allowing myself to feel the wind rush in to me. I needed something to wake me from this nightmare. I'd been numbing myself for so long that I'd forgotten about most things that mattered to me before I came to Winchester. I forgot about my love for fashion. I forgot about my love for playing the piano and for song writing. I'd forgotten how on any holiday my mother would bate me until I gave in, and sat down at the small player piano that had belonged to her mother to play a quiet melody just for my family. Being a Logost had stolen these things from me, but I hoped to find joy in my life – if I were ever to have one.

My calves were sore from walking when I came across a stone, snow-covered bridge. It was icy, and I guessed that it would be unwise to cross it. But as I always went against my better judgment – trusting my own thoughts and opinions had never been easy for me – I trumped across it. It covered a small, man-made brook where water fell upon smoothed stones. An innate happiness flowed from the sound, and before I'd taken three steps to cross the stone bridge, I found myself retreating. I jumped down, and walked along the small ledge where the sound of the brook was heaviest.

The sound grew louder – a pulsating noise like the beat of a faltering heart. The act of blocking was becoming natural for me, and it took me only a moment before I realized that the sound was someone trying to break through my mental defenses. Someone stood behind me, attempting to cause me great suffering. I turned around to see Cassandra there, her friends Amy and Sasha flanked at her sides. Without hesitation, I froze several streams of water and shot the sharpened icicles at them. But Cassandra was clever and quick. She shattered each icicle in to tiny speckles of frost.

"That really is the best you can do." She scoffed at me, and Sasha and Amy giggled. Cassandra's eyes bore in to me, and I felt my access to oxygen cut off. She choked me with the strength of her mind, and I couldn't scream out in pain – there was no air left in my lungs. The timing of my death beat closer and closer, but I refused to be killed by someone as trivial as Cassandra.

"I'll be sure to tell Lucas how much you despise him," she said. "And how peculiar it was that with your last dying breath, you told me that you wanted him to know you hate him," she laughed, that piercing metallic sound. Happiness was unobtainable for Cassandra. She wasn't happy even now that she would get her wish. To watch me die. Her eyes were dead, dark and emotionless. And even though she was killing me, I pitied her still. Poor girl, I thought as I waited for death.

The Earth quivered as it tried to save me from my untimely end. But I wasn't the one controlling it. Cassandra fell to her knees and shrieked in torment. Her limbs flailed, and her body jolted upward towards the sky. Sasha and Amy made no move to help the girl, who they called a friend. They stared at me with horror-struck eyes, and jolted away from the scene. I got up from the brook and stood over Cassandra, watching as her eyes rolled to the back of her head. She would die soon, and I had no inclination to save her. But I also had no desire to watch her die, so I turned to leave.

It was then that I saw him there, out of the corner of my eye. He leaned against the bridge, wringing his hands and watching me. He came over to me and stood behind me to whisper in my ear.

"She's not dead yet," Drew breathed, his voice a low, creaking sound. "She made an attack on your life. It's only fair to end hers. Look at her, Mina. Focus on her heart stopping."

"No, I can't." I thought about leaving, but I couldn't stop watching her die. She looked like she would ask me to save her if she could speak.

"You were meant for greatness, my love," he whispered. "And this is what it takes to be great. She's nearly there. It wouldn't take much," he said, persuading me. But I made no move to end Cassandra's life. "Fine," Drew said as if murdering her were inevitable. And I watched her body stop shaking.

Her eyes didn't shut once she was unmoving. They stayed open, and I kneeled beside her lifeless body. It twitched again, and I felt her tormented spirit escape her chest. I waved my hand over her face and shut her eyes. Drew kneeled behind me, slowly placing his hands on my shoulders.

"Don't mourn her death, Mina. She wanted you dead. It wasn't her first attempt to end your life. She wanted your friend Lily Andrews to kill you." Drew knew that it had been Cassandra that morning when Lily choked me.

"Someone will find her – they'll come for us. Wilma will kill you. She loved Cassandra, or coveted her abilities anyway." I corrected, knowing that Wilma Whorton loved no others but herself.

"She tried to kill you Mina. Ms. Whorton will understand why you did this."

"But you did this. This wasn't me, Drew."

"Mina," he purred. "You won't be punished for defending yourself, but I could be put to death for murdering a student. No one can know that it was me. Prove to me how much I mean to you. You must tell them it was you, my love."

Drew stood up, touching his finger to my chin, pulling me with him as he rose. He kissed me like he never had before. His lips were always urgent, but cautious in more ways than others. But this kiss was like fire. The heat of it burned my lips, leaving them swollen. His mouth tore in to mine, and when I could no longer stand the temptation, he pulled away.

"You're lucky I love you so much," I said breathlessly, penetrating his tortured soul with my eyes, trying to make sure he believed my words. "I will lie for you because it would kill me to see you hurt. But I'm not happy about this. Lying is not something I like to do. I am a good girl, you know."

"Good girls don't sneak around with idiot boys," Drew said. "Are you still entertaining your feelings for the boy who haunts my dreams about you?"

"No, it will always be you. He's hurt, but it will pass. I ended our friendship. Lucas is no longer a part of my life." The words sounded desperately heartbroken. Drew would see right through the lie. But he was silent. He looked at me, and I couldn't turn away from those damning, green eyes. I wanted to fly inside of them and hide there. I wanted to be a part of him. He frightened me, but I loved him still. I couldn't let him go, not yet.

Drew grabbed my hand and glided with me across the frozen bridge.

"Where are we going?" I asked as he led me further from the city and closer to the outskirts of the town.

"To my home. I trust you enough now to show you, to reveal a tiny bit more of myself to you."

We landed near the edge of the Mediterranean Sea and Drew let go of my hand. We were far from France, and I found it odd that Drew would bring me here. He walked up to the black coast of the sea, dark because the moon refused to shine upon it.

He asked me to create strong waves in the despondent water, to lead us to a lighthouse in the distance. I did as I was told. I asked the water to lead us, but this water was unlike the Hudson River. It wanted to resist me, but it didn't, it gave in without a fight and its apprehensive obedience terrified me. The water seemed like it had been abused, or possibly just seen far too much grief. It was the water Drew used to practice controlling the elements.

I sensed danger. The water wanted me to retreat. But Drew was with me, he would protect me from whatever the water was afraid of. Once I gave my faulty confession about killing Cassandra, he would be my only hope. The one thing that I could rely on, Drew would never leave me. He did not have the strength or the conviction to ever do so.

We rode the waves to Drew's home, and we stepped on to a small grassy knoll once we'd reached a small island. The light house seemed to spring from the water and meet us. It looked as though no one had ever lived there.

Drew sensed my reluctance. "There's nothing to fear. This home will be your own soon."

The lighthouse smelled of old, damp wood and stale skin. It was decrepit, clammy, and lit by candles. Hundreds of candles lit the space and they were placed on the floor, the shelves on the walls, and a small wooden table near the entrance. I shivered as Drew led me by the hand. But my shivering was not due to the cold – his home frightened me, and I felt uneasy, even with him there. Drew told me to touch nothing as we walked through the tiny living room, which housed only a small wooden table and one wooden chair. On the floor was a tan fleece blanket. There were books, torn pages, and newspaper clippings scattered all over the floor.

He led me up a winding staircase and into an open space where he slept. A bed sat in the farthest corner to my right, and a stone claw tub filled with settled water lay under the one window. Next to the bed was a tattered packing box, with a small black camera and a gold pocket watch with green emeralds laying on top of it. I reached for it, but Drew grabbed my hand. The shape of the watch was identical to the silver one that hummed inside the pocket of my coat.

There were photographs tacked to every space of the wall, and most of them were of me. Pictures of me when I was as young as eight years old – still smiling, widely in the park that brought me happiness.

"You took these?" I asked not caring if he could hear how appalled I was. Why would he bring me here? Why would he let me see this? The other photos contained suicides, but I knew that these people didn't choose a lonesome death out of their own free will. Drew chose for them, and he had photographed them right before ending their lives. He had used mind control to force them to either hang themselves or slit their own throats.

Now I knew, I didn't want Drew to trust me. I wished that he'd kept this piece of himself from me. I didn't want to know just how psychotic he was. He never answered my question about the photos. He just watched me as I wondered around his bedroom in near tears, over the horrific murders he'd committed. They died by their own hands through his control.

"You don't love me," I said. "It just isn't possible. How could you love anyone?" I said, still not looking at him but feeling his eyes on me.

"Are you afraid of me?"

"Should I be? Why would you bring me here?"

Drew dropped down to his knees, holding my hands, forcing me to stare in to him. He took a slow breath, his eyes never leaving mine.

"I thought you would understand," he said. "Of all people, I prayed for you to see my intentions. Their deaths were necessary, my love. But I promise they were insignificant. They were lonely souls –

desperate for me to end their lives."

I felt the room shake, but it wasn't my doing. My mind wouldn't stop shaking. Nothing in the room could stay still, my legs wobbled and I could no longer stand. I sank to the floor, and couldn't catch my breath as the tears fell down my face. Drew sat down beside me and held me until my breaths were even. He whispered to me, "I'm sorry, Mina."

"I want to go home," I said. "Please, let me go home. Save me, please." I cried out to no one in particular. There was no one who could save me from the demented man who believed he loved me.

Drew continued to console me, through useless attempts. He told me he was sorry, but he thought that I was prepared to know more about him. I wasn't. He flew me back to the school, carrying me in his arms. I screamed in my sleep, convinced that I could feel their pain, the ones he murdered. And I watched through their eyes as Drew forced them to kill themselves. A strange man who they didn't know, but who they were powerless too, just as I was.

{19}

"You look ill, Ms. Culvert," Mr. Maynard, the Levitation teacher, said to me the next day in class. "If you're not feeling well, you should go to your dorm and rest."

"I'm fine," I lied. "I just didn't get much sleep last night," I said to him truthfully.

My feet dragged as I walked through the halls of Winchester that day. It seemed my doom was inevitable. My will was bent, and I could no longer see the good, even in myself. I did love Drew, and I pitied him far more than he deserved. He was unworthy of any forgiveness and his aspirations for control were unchanging. I wanted to convince him that he didn't have to be this way. I wanted to convince myself too. He could have a normal life that didn't involve murder and manipulation. The song of us that I had rewritten so many times was ever-changing. If he knew how I felt about all of this would it change him? I knew that his devotion and obsession with me was wielded by things beyond his control.

The news of Cassandra's death had expectedly traveled with great speed, and little knowledge as to who should be held responsible. My participation in the killing of Cassandra was still a secret as far as I knew. No one had come for me yet. But an aching of guilt rotted away at my insides; I watched him do it. Murder was inconsequential for Drew – a necessary thing. But did he gain any feeling of satisfaction from killing? I needed to know, but I couldn't ask.

I passed by a group of chatty followers and complacent evil-doers on my way out of Mr. Maynard's class. The group of would-be innocents glared at me.

"Hey Culvert," a brave one shouted. "Whorton's looking for you. She says for you to go to her office."

Of course Wilma Whorton would have caught on soon enough. That much was foreseeable, and I walked to her office to confess a lie. I didn't huff this time as I slouched down in the wooden chair across from her desk.

"Mina Culvert," Whorton said. "Did you murder Cassandra?"

I thought for a moment before answering. "Yes, in an act of self-defense I killed her. She choked me with her mind. I had no other choice. This was not her first attempt, either. She manipulated Lily Andrews in her sleep and meant to have her strangle me."

"As odd as it sounds, I believe you. Her closest friends Sasha and Amy told me what they saw. Cassandra confessed her plans to them." She was silent after that, and she just looked at me, her eyes never blinking.

"Can I go now?" I said.

She opened her mouth wide, just as she always did before speaking, "You certainly don't believe that I would allow such an unjust act to go unpunished."

"But you just said…" I tried to get the words out, but she cut me off before I could finish.

"I'm well aware of what I just said. I don't need your annoying little reminders. The act was unjust because Cassandra's life was worth more than your own. You should have let her kill you and spared her," she paused. "But I'm not entirely unforgiving. I understand that Logosts are naturally inclined to be defensive, so you'll serve detention with Ms. Callaway."

I nodded and grabbed my things to leave. "Wait," she said, forcing me to sick back down. "Is there something you want to tell me?" she asked and I shook my head. "Are you sure?" she asked again. "There isn't anything about Mr. Elliot that you feel an adult should know?" I was quiet and I didn't shake my head immediately as I had before. "Tell me Mina. Tell me what he's done."

"I can't. I'm too afraid. I shouldn't upset him."

"Who cares about upsetting him? This is the one time I'm allowing you to be selfish and talk about your feelings. Tell me what's going on with him. Do you love Mr. Elliot?"

"I don't know," I said pondering the question. "I thought I did. I thought I loved him, but he's not who I thought he was. He's done terrible, unspeakable things. I don't think I could describe them even if I wanted."

"Well, I won't ask you to," she said leaning back in her principal's chair.

"Are you afraid of him?" I said under my breath.

Whorton looked at me and laughed. "No, Mina, I am not afraid of him. Drew is a strange man yes, but he's not one to fear. He's weak. If anything he should fear me."

She still believed the mask. Wilma Whorton still didn't see that he had plans to kill her too.

"I am afraid," Whorton said. "But not of Mr. Elliot. I'm afraid about what is going on with the two of you. He watches you in a way that makes me want to protect you from him. As much as I hate you, I feel like I need to keep you from him. He's a greater danger to you than he is to himself. It would be wise for you to end things with Mr. Elliot, Mina," she continued. "And don't think I'm saying this because I want him for myself. I hold no such desire for the man any longer. The fact that he could be with you, a child, the way he was with me, disgusts me."

"How can I make him leave me alone? I've tried, nothing will deter him. He's convinced that we were destined for one another, and I can only pray that it isn't true."

"I will tell him, Mina. I will tell him what you've told me, and ask that he stop this relationship with you or leave my school. I won't do it now. Such harsh words must be said with caution and perfect timing."

She smiled at me, I'd never seen it directed at me before. Then she motioned for me to leave, and I walked out of her office to go sulk in my dorm room.

My guilt about Cassandra's death swallowed me whole, and I couldn't face anyone. They all believed it had been me and me alone. And I was so intent on torturing myself that I hadn't told anyone the truth. I didn't think it was possible to feel so alone when I wasn't. But keeping secrets causes a forsaken feeling that isolated me further.

Lily wouldn't even look at me. She pretended that I wasn't there. She believed the lie and it saddened me that she would think so little of me, but I couldn't blame her. Someone, probably Lucas, had told her that I'd confessed to Whorton, herself. The truth seemed undeniable in her eyes.

And of course Lucas hadn't spoken to me since Paris' departure. I was ashamed to be seen so I tried to stay hidden. When I came across anyone as I walked around campus, I immediately turned in the other direction. The other students hadn't exiled me like Lily and Lucas. They didn't care about Cassandra's death, and they saw killing as a natural occurrence. But Lily and Lucas were good, and they wanted to believe that I was good too. Maybe they felt I was finally allowing my true self to emerge from the shadows.

"Have you seen my hairbrush?" I said to Lily, early one morning before line-up. She wouldn't look at me. Lily walked over to her chest of drawers and handed me the soft wooden brush, without a word. I didn't need this from her, she was supposed to be my best friend. How could she abandon me? Drew was the only one who cared. The only one who really knew me.

After that, Drew became my star again, leading me through

the darkness and emptiness that this school left me lost in. He didn't show that side of himself to me again. He kept it hidden. And after some time, I was able to convince myself that I'd never seen his home, and he hadn't killed Cassandra and asked me to lie for him. I wouldn't turn my back on him. But I wished I'd cared enough to not let Lily turn her back on me.

"Don't do this Lily," I begged, my hand on the door. "I expected more from you, but I guess I need to learn to stop making assumptions. You don't even know what happened."

"You killed her, Mina," she said. "That's all I need to know. We all knew Cassandra was a bitch, but she didn't deserve to die. You have no respect for the lives of others. She was a Logost! What's wrong with you?"

Without looking at her, I opened the door and walked out. After line-up, I went to Blocking, the class I had with Lily and Lucas. The two sat together, but they didn't save a seat for me anymore. Ms. Davies was disappointed with our level of progress that day. Mostly, because no one was trying. It was nearly the end of April and the end of the semester was approaching. The snow near the school and around the base of the Alps was melting, while the snow in the mountains remained.

Ms. Davies forced the class to the nearest courtyard to take turns attacking and blocking. She even asked some of the more advanced students to duel one another. I watched one of the duels. The blonde, curly-haired girl called Frizz was pitied against Elijah, who made lackluster attempts to attack her.

When it was Frizz's turn, she was clearly bent on impressing Ms. Davies, but not with her blocking. I didn't try to read her mind, but I saw Elijah's body rise above the ground as he begged for someone to save him. But everyone looked like they just wanted the next bell to ring. They were bored by Elijah's torment. I even saw Sasha sighing in to her hand. I glanced in Lily and Lucas' direction, and they were staring at me, chatting. I turned my back to them to watch Elijah's torment, and they walked over.

"Tell us what happened," Lily said appraising me.

"Why? You'll believe whatever you want. You two are supposed to be my best friends. Why not ask me before jumping to conclusions?"

They looked at one another, and my old friend jealousy sprung out to meet me once again. I didn't want them to be close without me. I didn't want their friendship to continue. The way Lucas looked at Lily upset me. But he wasn't mine. Drew was mine, and I would just have to get used to that fact.

"We're asking you now, Mina," Lucas said. "You couldn't possibly expect us to ignore the fact that we knew how jealous of Cassandra you were." Lily made an uneasy rocking on her heels when Lucas finished speaking.

"I didn't kill her because I was jealous. She tried to kill me first."

"That's no excuse, Mina," Lily barked. "You could have subdued her; you're strong enough for that. Murder is something I didn't think you were capable of. Well, not intentional murder," she trailed off thinking of the night I'd nearly killed the whole school.

"It was her that day Lily, when you tried to strangle me," I said. "She wanted me dead this whole time. I had to do it." I said lying to the only people I wanted to know the truth. Lily looked like she understood, but she was still angry.

"I didn't know," she said. "But this is bad, Mina. Killing someone out of anger or revenge will only lead to more killings. You don't want to go down the dark path of so many Logosts before you. This scares me."

The bell rang and I left Lily and Lucas standing there. There was nothing more to say. I had to keep the lie for Drew's sake. But when I thought of what it was costing me, I wondered if it was really worth it. Lily hated me. Nothing could be worse than this, and Lucas – he wouldn't even look me in the eyes.

After school, I met with Drew for my private lessons course. But I couldn't focus. It felt like I was sinking and nothing would respond to my control.

"What's troubling you, my love?" Drew asked, standing behind me as I tried to put out a tree with water, which caught fire from me striking it with lightning. "You're better than this."

"This is pointless," I said backing away from him. "I don't want to do this anymore. I can't see past this place. I can't see my future. I see nothing but sadness."

"Then harness that feeling. Don't let your feelings control you. This has to stop if you want to get stronger. You have to learn control – even in sadness."

"But why bother? Why should I live? Why should you live, Drew? No good can come from us existing in this world. Or any other Logost for that matter — we should all be destroyed." I lost my breath as I spoke. A lump rose to my throat and I wanted to slice it away, to free myself from the guilt. And Drew said nothing as I brewed myself in misery. I think he understood, I think he felt that way too sometimes — that the world would be better off without him. Drew told me to forget my friends, and that I didn't need them. Trust no one, he'd said. They will all forsake you in the end.

"The only person you can rely on is me, my love," he told me, and pressed his lips to mine.

{20}

The next day during line-up, I couldn't help but notice how Lily continuously glanced in Lucas' direction, while Ms. Whorton read the morning announcements. They no longer possessed any regard for my feelings, and cared nothing for the girl who they had once called a friend. I looked at Lucas and he looked distressed. Elijah wasn't standing in front of him like usual. I could hear something, but no one was speaking besides Whorton. Someone was thinking loudly.

"*You have to do this*," they thought. "*Just do it. There is no point in staying here.*"

Everyone else sensed that something was wrong, and all eyes turned towards the sky.

Elijah wasn't missing from line-up. He flew above us near the main building of the school, higher than the tallest mountain peak until he wasn't visible. Then I watched as he let go of his mind and the act of flying. Elijah dropped to the ground below, intent on crashing to the bottom, and never having to see another day. But I couldn't let him do it. I couldn't allow him to break Lucas this way. I wrapped my mind around the frame of his body, slowing his fall, but I still felt weak with sadness. And before I was able to focus on holding him up with the strength of my consciousness, his fragile body collided hard with the ground below. Sasha screamed at the sight, and Lucas ran over to Elijah, who was motionless.

"You fucking idiot." Lucas cried over Elijah. His sadness for his friend was unbearable to watch. I walked over to them, but I didn't try to comfort Lucas. I didn't think it would be okay for me to touch him, even now as waves of guilt and frustration passed through him.

"How could you be so fucking stupid?" Lucas muttered through his sobs. Ms. Whorton screamed at Ms. Callaway to call an ambulance. I stared at Lucas, but he only watched Elijah. It felt like this was my fault. I'd tried to save Elijah and had failed, just like I was failing at everything else. I was failing at life, it seemed. I couldn't be the hero even when the timing for it beckoned to me.

I reached out my hand to rest on Lucas' shoulder, but recoiled once Mr. Maynard and Drew arrived. Drew pulled Lucas away from Elijah, who was difficult to move as he kneeled down sobbing beside his friend.

"Don't you fucking touch me," he shouted to Drew, and Drew took his hands off Lucas once he'd pulled him away. The ambulance came and rushed him to the emergency room. Whorton told us all that Elijah was alive, but in terrible condition. He'd broken both his legs, damaged his skull, and cracked a few ribs. They told us that those who cared would be able to visit him in the Chamonix Hospital within a week's time. We were told to go back to class, as if a student hadn't tried to commit suicide that morning.

Later that day I heard Sasha say about Elijah, "Can you imagine failing at killing yourself?" she whispered to Amy when the third bell rang. "You'd *really* feel like a failure then," she laughed. No one pitied Elijah the way that I did. And it was because I understood. I didn't think I could ever kill myself, but I'd thought about it before, if nothing but fleetingly. The act of suicide tempted me in more ways then I wanted to admit. I still felt that no good could come from me living, if killing was what I was really meant for. Why should any Logost live? They were all corrupt and cold.

A week passed, and I went to visit Lucas' easily corruptible friend. I hated hospitals. Most people see them as a healing place, but I only see them as a place for misery. People die in hospitals. People get terrible news in hospitals. But I wanted to talk to Elijah about why he tried to kill himself. I wanted to convince him that there was a point to this life, and I wanted him to convince me too. I hoped that together, we could find happiness by focusing on the good. I also hoped that Lucas might be there.

As I walked down the halls of the Intensive Care unit, I noticed families huddled in corners. I noticed rooms filled with sleepy people, not wanting to leave their loved ones to suffer in solitude. Most rooms were filled with balloons or flowers. But when I walked in to Elijah's room, there was no one there. No get-well-soon balloons bumped against the ceiling, and there were no flowers or cards.

No one at our school cared about poor Elijah. I wondered where Lucas was.

Elijah's expression grew gloomier when I walked through the door. He nodded at me, greeting me without a word. But I didn't care if he didn't want me there. It wasn't like he could get up and leave, so he'd be forced to speak to me.

"All better?" I asked smiling. He just shrugged and turned his head. But I wasn't going to give up that easily. He obviously didn't know me very well at all. "I understand why you did it," I muttered and that seemed to peak his interest.

"You don't understand shit," Elijah said. "You've been here for all of three months, and you walk in here and tell me you understand. Lucas told me about you. He thinks you're God's gift to this school, but I know better Culvert. You're a disease! You broke his heart and you'll destroy this place. I just hope I'm dead so I don't have to see it."

"Wouldn't you want to see it though?" I said bating him. "Doesn't the thought that I wouldn't leave a single one of them alive, thrill you just a little?" I winked at him. I knew that it did. And he knew it too. But he just shrugged at me again.

"Lucas already came by here today," he said staring out the hospital window. "So if you came here looking for him, then just shove off because I don't want to see you."

"I'm not here to see Lucas. I came to see you. I wanted to make sure you were okay. I know Lucas and I aren't friends anymore, but I still don't want to see you hurt."

"You don't give a damn about me, don't act like you do. No one does. You're only here because you think you're crazy. You want to see what a crazy person looks like so you can compare yourself to me. Well, I can tell you right now Culvert that you're not crazy. When you're crazy, you stop worrying about being crazy."

"I'm sorry I hurt your friend. I'm sorry I'm so messed up, and I'm sorry that you tried to kill yourself and failed. But I do understand. Sometimes, I think about that too. I think that things would be easier if I didn't exist anymore. It's hard to deny that feeling. I know it's selfish to feel that way. I try to think about my family – about the people I'd hurt if I took my own life. But then I think about what I'm capable of, and all the people I might hurt if things continue down this road."

"You're lucky," he said. "You only have to think about the people you *might* hurt. Not the ones you already have. When I close my eyes I see their faces – dead faces. They won't ever go away. I use to relic in that fact that I never got caught. That I'd killed so many humans and no one knew it was me. Now I hate myself so much that I only think about ripping out that piece of my brain – that piece that forces you to remember. If I could rip that out then the voices would stop."

"I'm sorry," I said feeling stupid for worrying about something that hadn't happened. "None of us deserve to live. We're all unworthy of this life. Miserable beings who can never really be happy."

"Not one of us should be allowed to live." Elijah said.

"Are you mad at me because of Cassandra?" I asked him. I knew that they had been friends.

"I'm glad actually. It was only a matter of time before I killed her myself. No one will miss her. If she'd lived, she would have been very powerful and she was already so dark, so frightening. I'm certainly not mad at you for killing Cassandra. I'm mad about how miserable you've made Lucas. There will never be another Logost as kind and as brave as Lucas. And you missed out Culvert. Go ride your hurricane of destruction with Mr. Elliot. You'll kill yourself soon enough. You're too good to live with bad things done in the dark."

I didn't have any more to say to Elijah. I told him I hoped his sadness would pass. Elijah seemed happier when I left, as if the failed suicide had shown him that living wasn't so bad.

Drew called out to me that night, and I spent the evening with him practicing in the mountains. We didn't sleep, and I didn't want to go back to my dorm, where Lily would be there judging me with her nonchalant glances and condescending ways. She thought she was better. But she wasn't. She probably thought that she deserved Lucas more than I did, and that part was probably true. The two of them were such good Logosts, they deserved each other. I wouldn't taint them with my misery any longer. I would step back, and out of the picture.

The next day, I realized that I wanted to apologize to them both, they'd earned that much from me at least. I went to go see Elijah that Saturday morning, hoping again that Lucas would be there, but of course he wasn't. And when I walked in to the hospital room where Elijah had been, the bed was empty.

The nurse told me that someone from the school had come by last night and brought Elijah a razor blade. He'd locked himself in the bathroom and she'd found him there that morning with his wrists slit. If Elijah couldn't escape his destiny what made me think that I could escape my own. I slid further in to Drew's arms.

{21}

When most kids are little they dream about their future. They imagine what type of person they'll marry, and what kind of career they'll have. When I was little I didn't dream about my future at all. I never thought about the person I would grow to be. That seemed strange to most people, and it seemed strange to me too. I knew that I was destined for great things, but I never had a plan for my life, always hoping that things would fall neatly in place. But now it was clear to me why I never dreamed about my future, and that's because I wasn't meant to have one. Drew still planned on murdering Whorton and the Five Leaders, and he believed I was the only Logost strong enough.

He wanted me to kill, and I couldn't tell him no. He wouldn't allow it. I didn't want to hurt anyone who hadn't tried to hurt me, and I'd made up my mind. I would destroy the dreadful school, this hopeless place. Not a single Logost would live. I would kill Drew and then myself.

This was the only way to escape my own fate. But I didn't

have a plan. And I only had myself to ask for help. I could be brave though, and selfless like Lily. I wished I was more like Lily. Maybe if I'd been more like her, I never would have let Drew persuade me to come here.

The clock on my bedside table reminded me that it was 3:00 a.m., and I should be asleep, or I would be a complete waste of space at school in the morning. But I couldn't sleep. I couldn't stop picturing my own death. I couldn't stop shuddering at the thought of having to murder the man that I loved. I didn't want to kill Drew, but I would do what I had to. The world needed saving from Drew, and from me. That was the only way I could be the hero. I would have to end it all. I missed him though, he hadn't called to me that night, and I thought that was peculiar. I longed for him, and then a familiar voice sang in my head.

"Mina," he called to me. *"Come to me my love, I'm waiting for you. I miss you angel. Come to me, Mina,"* he thought and placed the words in my consciousness.

I ignored him, rolled over, and thought about what I wanted to do before I died. I'd wanted to learn French and Spanish, I'd wanted to travel to Latin America, but I only had a month before the end of the semester, and I guessed that it would take longer than that to cross those things off my bucket list. And so I thought of other things – more tangible desires and my own thoughts made me uncomfortable. I didn't want to die a virgin, and I never planned on waiting until marriage. My reason for waiting had more to do with the fact that I'd never really been interested in sex. I'd never been a very sexual person. Sexuality wasn't something I ever dwelled on.

But I dwelled on Drew. If any one were to be my first, it would be him. And whenever it seemed like I was ready to take our relationship to the next level and he was giving me those signals, the passionate ones that made me want all of him, he would pull away from me. He always stopped himself. And I was glad, even though sometimes I wanted to be that way with him, other times he scared me. It confused me, and that made me think that I wasn't really ready. I wondered if he thought I was ready would he be intimate with me. Would he make love to me? I didn't know. I didn't even know how many women he'd been with. I'd always been too afraid to ask, worried that the number would intimidate me.

I climbed out of bed and snuck outside to meet him. He dressed in a suit just like he always did. His face absolute perfection – his hair manicured in an effortless way. On the outside, Drew looked like the kind of guy most girls would want to marry, and I hoped that I could make him just as desirable on the inside. Even though he was dangerous, Drew would never hurt me. He loved me. And I loved him more than anything.

I knew that I could fix him.

I knew that he could be good.

When I saw him standing in the darkness, I ran to him and jumped in to his arms. I kissed him violently, and he kissed me back even more violently. I wanted all of him. The sex part too. But I was too innocent. I didn't know what I was doing. He'd probably ask me to stop. When I tried to be more adult, Drew got annoyed. He liked me to be innocent, just as I was, and that didn't make sense.

"Why do you love me?" I said, and he put me down on the ground.

"What a thing to say," Drew laughed and kissed my hair, pulling me close to him. "You silly girl, what is there to not love about you. Your beauty, your power – your innocence." His breath was heavy, uneven, and it frightened me, but I ignored it.

"Would you still love me if I was older? It just seems weird that you wouldn't want someone your own age." I said walking away from him, hoping he would follow, and he did.

Drew frowned at my words and looked away. "Of course I would." He sounded like he was only trying to convince himself. "Women my own age are boring. They're not as honest and as trusting as you. They don't deserve me like you do. And you are the strongest Logost, no others can compare. Besides, you won't be young forever. You'll grow, but you'll always be my Mina. You'll always be my love."

"How long have you known about me? Those pictures you took. I was so little. It doesn't make sense."

"I haven't been completely honest with you, Mina," he said without looking at me. Drew sat down on the ground. I moved in close to him and nestled my way under his arm. But he still didn't look at me.

"And I hope that you will respect the fact that I can't be honest with you now," Drew said. "I'm not sure how long I've known about you. There are parts of my life that I don't remember –

parts of me that are lost in my mind. It's not like I haven't looked. I just can't seem to find them," he laughed to himself. I understood what he meant, and I tried not to remember the time he let me see inside his mind. His mind was one that I would never want to read again, not ever.

"There's something else, Drew," I said and he visibly tensed when I spoke. "There was a watch — a gold one with green jewels in it. How did you come by that watch," I asked in a nervous whisper. The positioning of his body was defensive.

"I made that watch," he said with certain confidence and that same antiquated sadness. "The first Logost I'd ever met had a watch like that. He could control the wind and rain, just like you, but not all the elements. His watch was silver and he used it to travel through time. That man was a great Logost, he was a real genius. But he was a very bad man with a very dark soul," he paused and walked away from me, but not far enough away that I couldn't hear him. "He taught me how to control things with my mind; he taught me how to manipulate people. He believed in me and my power. And I wanted to kill him so I could steal that watch. I tried, but he caught me. He turned me over to the Informants. And they nearly tortured me to death. He told them I killed my parents."

"You killed your parents?" I said trying to hide my fear, trying to detach myself from the meaning behind the words.

"I had too. They were insufferable, no one would miss them, not even me," Drew said, his voice flat, uncaring. "My father was a drunk. He beat her, my mother. Once, he beat her so bad that I knew she was dead, she lay bloody and motionless on the floor of our small, white kitchen. I killed her because I pitied her. I killed him because he deserved to die."

"That man was my father," I said. "The man with a dark soul, the first Logost you ever met. He was my father." I whispered. Since I came to Winchester, and learned what it meant to be a Logost, I had guessed that my father had been a bad man. But that didn't make the confirmation any easier to hear. I cringed, and pictured the photo of him that Paris kept. I wanted to see that picture again. I wanted to look at it with new eyes, and see if I could see that darkness in him. I remembered the wisdom in his eyes.

I wanted to ask if Drew knew where my father was now, but I didn't. I wasn't brave enough. And I worried that if I asked, and found out where he was, I would try to find him. That was a risk I didn't want to take. I had enough psychotic, dark Logosts to deal with already.

"I know he was your father," was all Drew said, and lay his head on my shoulder. He'd never done anything like that before, but I let him. He seemed so sad. I didn't want to make him sadder, so I didn't ask him anymore questions about my father. And I didn't tell him about the watch. If he'd wanted it so bad that he would kill for it, then I couldn't tell him I had it.

I loved Drew, but he was unpredictable. His emotions hit like a hurricane. It was best to keep some things from him because it would upset him if he knew the truth. Like if he knew the truth about my longing for Lucas, who was gone at the moment.

Lucas had been in Colombia for the past week, mourning the loss of Elijah. One of his older sisters sent for him. I hoped he would be back soon. I missed him more than I wanted to admit, even to myself.

We both laid down on our backs, resting side by side, staring up at the sky.

"Drew," I said working up the courage to ask what I knew I shouldn't ask. "How many women have you been with, well not just been with, but *been* with?" He rolled over on his side to look me in the eyes. He wrapped his right arm around me, and stared in to me. But I looked away. I didn't want him to see what I was thinking.

"Why would you ask a question like that," he said, and he took my hand and touched his face with it.

"I don't know," I said feeling embarrassed. "It's just – I wonder when would be the right time for us, if there were such a thing."

"Mina, I don't want to take your innocence. I've told you before that you'll appreciate it more once you're older."

"Please, just tell me. Just tell me how many," I said desperate for him to answer.

"There have been a few. Wilma you already know about. The others were women that I didn't care about, but there were eleven."

"Eleven?" I didn't want him to say that number. That was far too many. I buried my face in my hands. "Were they all older than me?" He nodded. "Then why did you pick me? Do you even desire me at all? I know I'm not sexy."

"I've never been with anyone as young as you are, but I know this isn't a mistake. From the first time I saw you I knew that I wouldn't ever be able to stay away from you. I knew that I would ruin you, just as I'm ruined. I waited for you, though. I watched and I waited. I knew that you were lonely, and that you needed me. And I knew that I would always need you. And I do desire you, my love. I just don't want to hurt you. I'm worried I might hurt you. You're not ready."

"But what if I say I'm ready? Would you be with me then?"

"No, I think I know better than you. I'll know when you're ready."

He was confusing me and pissing me off at the same time. Only I would be able to say when I was ready. He wouldn't be able to control every part of me, but he believed he should. I stood up to leave. I was too upset and embarrassed to continue.

"I don't want to listen to this anymore. You think you know everything about me. You think that you can control everything I do, and the fact that I keep letting you is driving me insane. Why can't you just be normal? Why can't you just be good? You don't have to hurt people."

"You're confused, Mina. I think you're tired. You should go to sleep."

I didn't want to do whatever he told me. But I *was* tired, and it was getting hard for me to think clearly. I was still upset though, and I wasn't done releasing my frustration.

"So you had sex with Whorton," I said sounding tough and

brave. I knew it would piss him off. He liked me timid. He liked to intimidate me. "But you won't be with me, who you claim to love? This is really messing with my head, all of this is, Drew. It's like you're able to convince me that I don't think or feel a certain way, even when I'm certain I do."

"Those aren't my intentions, Mina. It's not my fault you're so impressionable."

"But you picked me because I am so impressionable. You picked me because you want to be able to control me, because of all that I can do. And you lucked up because I'm so young. You're not fooling me, Drew. I know you think you are, but I'm smarter than that. And I let you control me anyways because I love you, and I'm scared of you."

"Don't say that. You know those things aren't true." He stood up from the ground and pulled me close. I was still pissed and I pushed him away. "I'm sorry I frighten you. But I don't want you to be scared of me. I just want you to understand, and to love me."

"You know that I love you. But I won't ever be able to understand you. You won't let me in enough for that. And I won't ever be able to understand why you kill people, mindlessly. I don't think I ever want to understand that part of you. I just want you to change. I want you to stop. Tell me that you will, Drew. Please, just tell me that we'll have a normal life together, with no power and no murder. I want you always Drew, but I don't want you this way."

I envisioned Drew as a mangled wired, twisted and distorted with hate. But I pictured myself straightening out the wire, and comforting him with love. I wanted to make him feel better. I wanted to make him believe that he could be good.

He leaned in and kissed me, his lips aggressive. He was so beautiful. I wanted him to want me. I wanted him to want to be with me, and only me. I pulled him to the ground as we kissed, and pulled him on top of me. I wasn't strong enough to pull him anywhere, but he let me lead him. It felt like this was his way of telling me that he wanted to be good, that he didn't want to hurt people anymore. I reached my hands up to his shoulders to take off his jacket. I wrapped my legs around his waist, grabbed his shirt, untucking it from his pants, and put my hands underneath, touching his bare chest.

Drew pulled back and his body left mine.

"Don't do this to me, Mina. You know that I can't stop killing. I can't be good, even for you. I don't want to be. Don't tempt me this way again." Drew said nothing more.

He walked away from me then, leaving me on the ground panting like an idiot. I screamed in frustration. I wanted to hit something. If Drew couldn't be good, then I had no choice. My attempts to change him were useless. We both had to die.

{22}

At breakfast, I overheard that Lucas had returned. The other students made fun of how sad he'd been about Elijah's death. They thought that it was stupid for him to care about anyone else that much. I didn't understand Lucas' friendship with Elijah, either. Elijah had never been a good person, but he tried to be in the end. I think he knew that death was his only escape, just as it was mine. I had sunk in to a lonely state since Lucas and Lily had exiled me. But I tried not to let it bother me. I wasn't completely alone. I still had Drew, even if he was evil. He was still my partner. But Drew was cold during our private lessons that day. When I tried to kiss him, he recoiled. And it made me feel disgusting.

Lucas still hadn't been in class, or even at line-up. I knew he wouldn't want to see me, and I knew it was selfish to want to see him. I knew I should leave him alone, but he was hurting. I didn't want him to feel the way that I did. So when Drew dismissed me from practice, I walked to the boy's dorm.

The front door was the same as the girls – oak with gold

metal trim, and green colored class. I banged on the door, it opened, and a red-haired boy stared at me.

"What are you doing here, Culvert?" The boy said my name with obvious disdain. I'd seen him in line-up before but I didn't know his name, I just knew that he wasn't very nice, and I didn't like how he called me Culvert.

"I'm looking for Lucas," I said. "Is he here?"

"Oh, that loser's here alright. His flight got in last night. He doesn't want to see anybody though, especially you, Culvert." The way he said my name made me want to crack his skull open on the ground outside.

"Just tell him I'm here."

He made a move to slam the door in my face, but I blew it open with the strength of the wind. Fire burned at the heels of his shoes. He screamed and jumped around trying to put the fire out. I doused it with my mind and gazed at him. He looked terrified, and it made me feel good. I wanted to scare him even more, but I needed to talk to Lucas.

"Go get Lucas," I said.

He walked away, afraid to turn his back on me. When he returned, Lucas was with him. My heart pulsed at the sight of him. I hadn't thought about what I'd say if he agreed to see me. He was wearing a face that wasn't Lucas' though. It looked more like Elijah's – tired, bored, and stricken with grief. He seemed different, more grown up. I wanted to touch him. I wanted to hold him until his eyes didn't look like that anymore.

"Mina, why are you here?" Lucas said, his hand on the edge of the door like he wanted to slam in it my face.

"I wanted to talk to you. I wanted to make sure you were ok. I still care about you, you know, even though you stopped caring about me."

"It doesn't matter. Go find Mr. Elliot and let him manipulate you some more." And then he *did* slam the door in my face. I couldn't stop ruining things. It was then that I started to hate myself.

The next few days passed like the growing of my finger nails. I had to force myself out of bed in the morning. I had to fight back tears as I brushed my hair in the mirror. Crying in the morning was not a good sign. That was something my Mom did. I didn't want to be sad like her, so I controlled the tears, but some fell, some would always fall.

At lunch that day, I didn't go to the dining hall. I went to the closest courtyard to skip. I knew my absence wouldn't go unnoticed, but I didn't care. Why bother when my plan was to destroy the whole school? It seemed too easy. I would need a distraction – like a storm, or a fire, maybe even just an awful buzzing in everyone's mind. And then when they were all inside, I would build a wind tunnel to demolish the school. I would tell Drew about my plans because I didn't want him to die with everyone else. I wanted his death to be more intimate.

In the courtyard, stood a stone fountain with owls shooting water from their eyes. A cement path enclosed the fountain and there were several iron benches in the circle. It was surrounded by green trees, the season was changing. I put my books down on the edge of the bench, rested my head on them, and cried. I wanted to live, but I knew I couldn't. I didn't want to be afraid of death, or of Drew, but I was. Crying was no good, I had to stop being so sad. I'd made my decision, and the plans I had couldn't be undone. I sat up and tried to calm down. I tried not to think of it as the end.

Lucas walked across the courtyard. He glanced my way, and I thought he would turn in the opposite direction. But when he saw me, he walked towards me. He came over to the bench and sat down without saying a word. He faced me, and I just started crying. I honestly don't know what came over me, but I couldn't stop. I think it was the look he gave me. He looked like he wanted all his troubles to disappear, and that included me. The rain began to fall, and I didn't want it to stop. My mind was hazy, and a cloud of fog began to circle the fountains where we sat. The fog helped calm me down. The sun shining through it was an enchanting sight.

"Don't you see what he's doing to you?" Lucas said. He made no attempt to comfort me in my sorrow. "No one who's in love should be this sad about it."

"I'm sorry," I whispered through my tears. "Please, just be my friend again, I'm so alone I can't stand it. You were right all along about what he's doing. Lucas, I didn't kill Cassandra. It was him, I thought I had to lie for him. I'm sorry she's dead, and I'm sorry I lied to you."

"You lie about everything, Mina. You're probably lying now just so I'll forgive you. I can't trust you."

"I know I don't deserve your trust anymore, but you *can* trust me. I'm not lying about this Lucas, please believe me."

"You're too far gone. You'll be his puppet soon enough."

"Don't say that to me. What good can come from you saying that?" I asked and he said nothing more. "Why come over here and make me feel even more miserable then I already do? Go away, and stay away since you hate me so much."

"Stop this," he shouted at me. "Stop this stupid pity party. You know I don't hate you. You know that I wanted to be in Mr. Elliot's place, but not in control of you like he is. I just wanted you to be my Mina, not his." And he reached out his hand to wipe the tears from my eyes. "I love you, Mina, you know that I do. And that's why I have to stay away. It will always be him. I know you well enough to know you'll never love me. I'm not dangerous enough it seems. You know that he'll only hurt you. You know that no good can come from you loving him."

Lucas seemed to know me better than Drew, but not better than I knew myself. I wouldn't let things go that far. I would end it all. But I didn't want to end things for Lucas or Lily. They at least, deserved to live.

"What should I do then, Lucas? You seem to have all the answers, so tell me what I should do. If Drew found out just how much I care for you, he'll kill you and me." I admitted to myself more than him. I'd seen Drew's desire to kill me in his eyes if ever I spent too much time with Lucas. "And what will that solve? He won't ever leave me alone. You know that just as well as I do. There's no way to escape him."

"You've got to leave this place. I know you're strong enough, now. Go where he can't find you."

I knew that Drew would always find me. But he said something to me before, after my date that night with Lucas. He told me that when I was with Lucas, he couldn't see me anymore. Lucas was the only thing that could keep Drew away.

"Come with me. I can't leave you with him. He'll kill you just because he can."

"I can't." Lucas said, staring across the courtyard. "You know I love you, but I can't. I belong here."

"But you hate it here. You're a good Logost. You're not like them Lucas and you certainly don't belong here. You could belong with me though, if you wanted to. I know you think that I couldn't love you, but I know that I could. You already feel like home to me."

"Don't – Mina, don't say that. I can't go with you. I'm sorry, but the way you feel about him would haunt me. I wouldn't ever be able to stop picturing him coming back for you one day, and taking you from me. It would be too much to bear."

"That's not it, you're lying," and then I said something without thinking, but it was what my subconscious wanted me to say. "You love Lily. She's the reason you want to stay. Do you love her?"

"I can't answer that. And it's unfair for you to even ask. You can't spring this on me after telling me you choose him over me, after letting me know you weren't even willing to give us a chance."

"I was willing, Lucas. I was just afraid. I was too afraid of

Drew."

"You're stronger than him, Mina. When will you see that? You don't have to be afraid of him," Lucas said. But I knew that he was wrong. I might be more powerful than Drew, but I certainly wasn't stronger. If I wanted to kill him, I would have to incapacitate him first.

"I made a mistake, Lucas. I should have told him that I didn't want him. I should have told you how I really felt. I'm sorry I messed up. I'm sorry – just don't love Lily anymore, ok? Just stop feeling that way towards her. It hurts more than it would if it were someone else."

I wanted to make sure that it was only me that he dreamed of, and that was so selfish. He was right. It would always be Drew. I would die loving Drew. But I did love Lucas too, it was just a different kind of love, and I couldn't describe it then, but I thought I could get him to stop thinking of Lily. I wanted him to miss me once I was dead. I didn't want him to ever forget about me. I grabbed the collar of his coat and kissed him the way Drew kissed me. I wanted to swallow him whole, so that I wouldn't have to be without him. His reaction was intense, and he kissed me back with equal fierceness. I knew that he still loved me. But then he pushed me away, and stared at me like I was the bad guy in the film, and I felt like the bad guy. I couldn't have them both.

Lucas pulled my hands off his coat collar.

"What do you think you're doing? This won't change anything. I can't help how I feel. I'm sorry for this, but I can't go with you." I wanted him to love me, but I didn't want to endanger his life any more than it already was. He couldn't come with me, even if he wanted to, it just couldn't be. Lily would make him happier than I ever could.

"You're right," I said. "I don't deserve you, but Lily does. I want you to be happy, and I know I'd only bring you sorrow. Drew and I are the perfect matches for death." I smiled with anguish. "But I won't let him have me. I'd rather die. Listen, tomorrow morning before line-up, you and Lily have to go in to the city. If you stay in the school you'll be killed."

"You sound crazy. Is this what he's asked you to do – destroy the whole school?"

"He hasn't asked me to do this. But this is the only way, we all have to die – me, him, Whorton, all of us. No good can come from any of us living, except you and Lily. So promise me you'll run away with her. And promise me that I am something you'll miss. I do love you," I said, "I really wish that it was enough." And I got up and left him sitting there. I hoped he would heed my warning. The last thing I wanted was to kill the kindest Logosts I'd ever met.

***

The next day at school, I was so nervous it felt like I might pass out. When I got to Drew's class that morning, Lucas was sitting there. He hadn't listened to my advice. When class ended. I followed him out. He walked in to the boy's bathroom and I walked in behind him.

"Mina, get out of here," Lucas said. "There's nothing left to say, just get out." I ignored him, and focused my mind on searching for anyone that might be there. I couldn't hear any thoughts or sense anyone's presence.

When I was certain we were alone, I spoke. "Didn't you hear what I said yesterday? I'm going to kill everyone in the school today. I don't want you and Lily to die too. Go find her and leave."

"You can't be serious. This is pointless. Why are you doing this? It won't save you from Mr. Elliot."

"It won't now. But I plan on killing us both. It's the only way to keep the world safe. As long as we aren't in it, everyone will be better off."

"Are you listening to yourself? You sound demented. Just leave, Mina. You don't have to *die*. Please don't do this," he said, with enough sadness in his voice that it almost made me reconsider. But I couldn't go back now. "Think about how badly that would hurt me," Lucas said. "How much it would hurt Lily? Kill Mr. Elliot, don't kill yourself."

"I won't be able to live with myself once he's dead. This life wouldn't make sense anymore."

"Please Mina, don't be this blind. I love you still, even though it only hurts to say that. I don't want you to die like Elijah. I know that you don't want to do this. You need to get out of your own head. You're trapped there, Mina. Don't let sadness turn you in to a monster."

"Lucas, stop. This really is the only way. Just leave with Lily. I don't know what's meant to happen after life, but I won't ever forget you."

"Don't talk like that. You will live," and he paused to look away from me. "I'll come with you if you leave. Just tell me you won't kill yourself."

"I was wrong yesterday, Lucas. You can't come with me. I don't want to put you in that much danger. Drew won't ever stop searching for me, and he would kill you. I couldn't live with that. You should be with Lily, not me. She's safer for you. She'll protect you."

He walked up to me then, slowly. He touched his hand to my face, and pulled me to him, kissing me without hesitancy. It was too much. I couldn't stand him kissing me this way. It only made me want to be with him, when I knew I shouldn't. When I knew I was no good, and I would always hurt him. He deserved better than some selfish, arrogant, self-loathing wench. But I couldn't pull back, no matter how many warnings ran through my mind.

And then several things happened all at one. The door to the boy's bathroom flung open and I saw Drew standing there. He looked different, as if he were detached from everything in that moment. His eyes were light with fury, and there were no golden crescents around them. I heard him shout something I didn't understand. Lucas flew back from me, in to the bathroom wall, sliding to the floor. He wasn't moving. I ran to him, but Drew grabbed my arm. He stared at me without speaking. Lucas' body moved again, and floated towards us. His head cracked to the right like Drew was trying to snap his neck.

"Don't," I screamed. "Please, don't do this Drew." Drew

looked at me, and I couldn't speak anymore.

"I told you to stay away from her," Drew said, practically singing to Lucas. "I warned you, and like the overly-confident scum you are, you didn't take me seriously. Did you really believe that I would let you live when you continue to try and steal from me?"

"She's not yours," Lucas whispered, and Drew's body flew up and slammed hard against the ceiling, but he didn't fall to the ground. He laughed and floated down to the floor. I still couldn't move. Somehow, he managed to keep his control over me. I thought about Drew leaving. I thought about him getting up and walking out, but my powers of manipulation were no match for his.

"I don't want her," Lucas said walking towards me and Drew. He *was* overly confident. He was no match for Drew, and neither was I. "You two monsters can have one another." And he left me there with Drew.

"Just leave," I shouted before Lucas slammed the door. "Find Lily and leave, please."

Drew looked at me, smiling, but it was the most frightening thing I'd ever seen. I flung him in to the line of sinks, and ran for the door. But he threw me in to the wall with his mind. He moved in close, and brushed off the shoulders of his collared shirt. I couldn't move, and I couldn't gage just how lethal he was in that instant. He didn't want to kill Lucas. If he had really wanted to then he would have. I started to shake, and that made his evil smile widen with pleasure. He put both his hands on the wall near my face – one on each side of me, staring down at me.

"Should I have killed him?mYou told me that you don't love him, and I find you kissing him and contemplating leaving me for him." He laughed. "He doesn't want you. His feelings are changing. I'm the only one who loves you, Mina. When will you stop resisting me, and just be happy, my love. That's all I really want, to bring you happiness." He kissed me and I wanted to fight him, but I was too afraid.

"I'm sorry," I said pulling away. "I lied about Lucas. I do still care for him, but you're right. He doesn't want me anymore. He loves someone else. And it doesn't matter, anyway. They'll both be dead soon." I lied, hoping that Lucas would take Lily and run. "I'm going to kill everyone in the school today. I love you more than anything, and I want to gain your trust back. Everyone will die, and then we can be together. But you have to go in to the city," I said, "so that I don't kill you too. Wait for me at the lighthouse."

"You're lying," he said. "You're trying to trick me so that you can leave with that arrogant idiot." But then he looked down at the star filled stone that hung around my neck. It showed the truth of my words. "What's your plan," he asked. I opened my mouth to speak, but he ignored me.

"Never mind," Drew said. "Whatever it was, I'm sure you would have failed. This is what you'll do: create a lightning storm over the school and strike it until it's on fire. Make the fire strong, and freeze everyone so that they die slowly. And they'll have no control over themselves."

"I can't do that, Drew. I don't want them to suffer."

"Yes, you do, my love. Think about how cruel they've all been to you. They deserve a very slow, very painful death. Remember every detail," he said. "Read their minds when they die, and place your thoughts in my head so I can watch too," he chuckled nervously and wrung his hands.

"My powers of manipulation aren't strong enough for something like that. How could I keep everyone still all at once, and focus on building the fire?"

"You must focus on your hatred for them – you must focus on your fear of having them live. When you harness those dark feelings, you'll be able to do it. You are the strongest Logost, my love. Trust me, Mina. This will work, and then we'll go after the Informants. I wanted Whorton's death to be more intimate than this. She really does deserve better," he said to himself. "But no matter, this will work out perfectly. I'm so proud of you, my love. I knew your desire for power would grow with time."

"It's not power I desire. We should die too, once it's done. I don't want to live anymore, and I don't want you to live without me. I want us to move past this world together. I love you." And I leaned in to him, kissing for one of the last times. I wished it could be otherwise, but I knew we had to die. He was too psychotic to live, and I loved him too much to live without him.

"We don't have to die, my love. That seems hardly necessary. The world will be a much happier place once we're in control of it."

"Don't Drew," I said. "Don't lie. I know you well enough to know when you're lying, even without reading your mind."

I didn't look at Drew when I walked out of the boy's bathroom. I knew he would only manipulate me, and I couldn't take any more of his games. The time had come to end it all. I had warned Lucas enough, if he hadn't already escaped with Lily, then they would have to die. If I went looking for them now, I might convince myself that it didn't have to be this way, and I knew that it did.

With my mind, I shut and locked every door to the school. I made sure that everyone was inside, and those that weren't, I pictured them walking to the school, even the ones who stayed in bed sick. Once they were all in, I put a dense fog over the school so they couldn't see the outside. I flew as high as I could. I called to the clouds of lightning, but there were none that day. The sky was clear, a perfect shade of blue atmosphere.

I used my hands and the strength of my mind to strike it with lightning. I forced everyone inside to remain motionless, but I wouldn't read their minds as they burned alive, that was something I had no desire to watch. Drew wouldn't get his wish, and it wouldn't matter once we were both dead. I pictured the sight of our lifeless bodies, and I thought about what my Mom would think. I felt bad that I would die without saying goodbye to her, or Paris, or Carter. I wanted to see them. And as I thought of my family, and the life I had before, I felt myself weakening. I screamed, and it felt like someone was sticking hot needles over every inch of my skin.

My body fell towards the school courtyard. Someone from the ground below was trying to stop me. I assumed it was Whorton, but I could feel her mind still inside of the school. My balance faltered, but

I kept striking the school with the lightning from my hands. Then I could stand the pain no more, and I rushed to my death as I fell from the sky, just as Elijah had. But unlike Elijah, I would die. Surely, whoever it was wanted me dead, and I made no attempt to save my own life. If this was to be my end then so be it, the world would be destroyed if Drew lived and I didn't, and I found myself uncaring.

I floated up, just before I slammed to the ground below. I saw Lily there, standing near the school. She looked so disappointed in me. I didn't want to have to face her now that she'd stopped me from going through with my plan. Lucas stood by her side, and I lashed out at the sight. I lunged at them, but Lily forced me backward, and I fell on to the cement ground. She walked over to me and wrapped her arms around me, restraining me with her love. Lily loved me still, even though I didn't deserve it.

{23}

"I promise not to kill again, my love," Drew said as he held me close. Once Lily and Lucas stopped me from killing the entire school, I'd gone to the lighthouse to meet him. At first, he thought I still wanted to kill him. I told him that I had failed with my intended course of action. He told me that he wouldn't have allowed me to go through with it anyway.

"I love you more than anything, Mina," he said. "I didn't know you felt this way. The world won't need saving from us anymore." He kissed my hair. "We'll have a normal life, I promise to be good from now on. We'll get married when you're old enough. We'll have a family with no murder, and no power. I promise to let you, be you. I won't control you anymore. Do you still love me, Mina?" he asked, and I kissed him. This was what it took to get through to him, finally. He did love me. We would be together forever, and we wouldn't have to kill anyone.

"I love you so much," I said. "I didn't think you would ever change for me. That's why I believed we both had to die. I'm sorry for thinking that way. And I'm sorry for kissing, Lucas." I whispered. "He pushed me away the first time," I admitted. "You don't have to hurt him. He loves Lily Andrews, the girl in your second period class."

He looked down at me and put his finger to my chin, tilting my head upward to look at him. This time there was no gold around his irises. He really wasn't going to manipulate me anymore.

"I know," Drew said. "I know that he loves her. Why do you think I allowed him to live? I'm sorry that he hurt you. But he can't be yours; you know that it was meant to be me. Can you feel it now?" he asked. And I could feel it. It felt like I was meant to stay this way with him, forever. We would grow old together, and he would stay this obsessed about me. He loved me enough to finally stop the murders, to finally deny his thirst for power. My happiness in that moment was indescribable.

"So you promise it's done then?" I asked. "There won't be any more killing? What about Whorton? Doesn't she want us to help her battle the Informants? She expects me to protect the school when they finally come for her."

"We'll have to leave soon," Drew said. "We can't stay here and escape them. Before I brought you here I had to register you with them. I told Narc, who is under Sophia in terms of rank, about your gifts. I regret it, but I had no other choice at the time. He forced me to allow him to read my mind. I don't know how we'll be able to stay hidden. They'll be here very soon — within a week is what my instincts tell me."

A week was all we had to stay at Winchester and then I could go home. And Drew would stay with me. I hoped that I'd be able to finish at a real school, my old school. Even though it was beat-down and ragged I wanted to go back there, and see all those familiar faces. At the time, I wanted nothing more than to leave, but the comparison was easy to make. I had it much better in Inwood than I knew. It sucked here, it sucked being with people of my own kind. Paris had the right idea all along. Being normal is easier than trying to be great.

I looked Drew in the eyes and thought for a moment. "Why would the Informants come now?"

"They're coming to investigate Cassandra's murder. She was a daughter to one of the Five Leaders, called Louis. He is upset by her death, and hasn't received any answers from Whorton at my urging. I've asked her not to give your name, but I'm afraid she may have to. And if she does, we'll have to leave. She'll tell me when they're coming."

"We can't trust Whorton. She might set us up."

"Whorton owes me," Drew said. "I don't trust her, but I'll blackmail her if I have to. It's impossible to trust anything the Informants say anyway. They lie about everything, like most Logosts, and they're experts at Blocking. If they capture us, we won't be able to escape. Their underground castle is surrounded by mental protection that even I haven't been able to break."

"Is there anything we can do to save ourselves?"

"If they see us, we won't be able to leave," he said. "We'll just have to be on our guard. I have a surprise for you though, my love." Drew said and took my hand. He led me down the lighthouse's winding staircase.

"Wait," I said and ran up the stairs to his bedroom. The photos were still there – a constant reminder of the man he'd been. I grabbed each one and began throwing them in to a metal trash can I found near his bed.

"Let's take these awful pictures down," I said. "You don't need these now that you've changed." I removed only the photos of the forced suicides, leaving the ones he'd taken of me.

"Don't touch those," Drew shouted. I couldn't hide the question in my expression. "Sorry, I just need to be alone with them, before I throw them out."

He helped me take them down and put them in the trash, but he said he needed to wait a while before getting rid of them, and I guess I understood. But he was always difficult to pinpoint. I never really knew what he was thinking or how he felt – his erratic and nervous behavior hid everything.

"Give me a moment to straighten up," he said looking at his hair in the only mirror in the house. A crack ran down the mirror and rust coated the edges. "Go wait outside," Drew said turning his back to me.

There wasn't much land around the lighthouse except for a small grassy knoll. I sat down and let the cool breeze from the ocean blow in to me. I wondered if anyone else but I, knew that Drew lived here. It could only be reached by the water or the sky. It probably looked abandoned to all others who were unaware of the existence of Logosts. But Drew had told me that some humans did know about Logosts, but for the most part legends of our kind had died off years ago.

Drew told me that there were Logosts who lived among humans unregistered, and the Informants put a bounty on their capture. He told me that the only reason they hadn't killed me is because Drew had sacrificed something for me. He wouldn't tell me what, but I knew he'd shown Narc the memories and thoughts he had of me.

Drew was silent and stealth-like when he moved. It was difficult to hear him coming out of the lighthouse, but I sensed him there, just as I always did. I fell over when he walked out; pretending that he was choking me with is mind. He was always so serious that it was hard to have any fun with him.

"That is not amusing, Mina," he said sounding irritated.

"Well," I said getting up from the ground. "Where's the surprise?"

"Just watch," Drew told me. And I did watch as the ocean began wailing in a way that I was sure only I could hear. It cried as Drew forced the water in to crashing waves that nearly overtook the lighthouse. The water formed in to the face of a man – I recognized it at once as Drew's face, but it was hollow. Drew beckoned the water back and it slunk away from us, shuddering in fear all the while. This didn't make sense, where was the surprise?

"Was that it?" I asked.

"What do you mean?" Drew said.

"I thought you had a surprise for me?"

"That is the surprise. I can control the water now. I thought you'd be impressed. Pretty soon, I'll be just as powerful as you are, my love."

The Earth quivered as he kissed me.

"You can move the Earth?" My voice tinged with jealousy.

"Only a little. Don't be jealous, Mina. We're partners in this life. We don't need to fight over who's the most powerful."

"You're right," I said but I was still jealous. I would just have to learn to hide it better.

I stayed at the lighthouse until nightfall. And once the moon rose in to the sky, I flew in to the night, chasing the stars, and went back to the school. Lily was fast asleep when I walked in to our room. I wanted to talk to her. I *needed* to talk to her, but I was afraid to wake her. She might still be upset with me. I certainly deserved the wrath of her anger. It seemed like it had been so long since we'd really had a conversation.

"I'm awake, Mina," she said rolling over on her side. "Say what you want to say."

"I'm sorry, Lily. I'm sorry for letting my sadness get the best of me, and for detaching myself from you. I just didn't expect you to desert me the way you did after Cassandra's death. Are you angry with me?"

"No, I'm not. I wasn't ever really all that angry. I was just afraid, I think. You were showing a different side of yourself, and that worried me. Lucas told me that he thought Mr. Elliot was the worst Logost of all. And I disagreed at first, until I started to see the changes in you. I was really just trying to protect myself. I was so hurt when my old roommate Maria got sent away last year. I didn't want to care about you anymore, because I didn't want to miss you once you were gone."

"That makes sense," I said. "I didn't kill Cassandra, though. Drew did. Did you know that she was Louis' daughter, one of the Informants?" She shook her head. "Well, I think they'll be coming here to investigate. Whorton's worried."

"Are you worried?" Lily asked.

"Not really worried, more cautious than anything, I guess. I know Lucas thinks Drew's bad, but he's changed now. He promised me that things would be different. He'll leave with me if I have to go in to hiding. Drew will keep me safe. He told me today that he wants us to get married someday, and have a real life together."

"That's great, Mina. I'm glad things between you two aren't as complicated as they were before. I know you were in a dark place. I just hope you don't go back there again."

"I won't. I'll never let anything like that happen again, but I really do think that it's this place that makes me crazy. I mean I was lonely back home, the same way I am now. But I've never been sad like that before. I've never seen Lucas that sad before either." I cringed knowing that I'd just opened the door of an asylum. But we would have to talk about it sometime. I would try my best to keep my feelings in check, and be happy for her. She deserved happiness, even more than me. Lily was genuine.

"He was pretty shook up after Cassandra's death, and I'll admit that I instigated the whole thing between you two." Lily said. "I told him you were jealous of Cassandra. And he was so sad that he believed me. I initiated everything, though. I think I've always loved him, I was just too afraid to give in. When his feelings for you surfaced, I was jealous. I didn't think you were right for him. You're so in love with Mr. Elliot. I knew you would just hurt him, and after Elijah's death I just couldn't bear to see him hurt by anyone. Not even by you, Mina."

"I know," I said. "I knew that I would only hurt him too. And I am happy for you two, I *really* am, but I'm jealous nonetheless. I just hope that the more I see you two together, the more desensitized I'll become," I laughed out of anxious habit. "You're better for him than I am, anyway. You hid your feelings for him so well. I never suspected a thing."

"Honestly, I thought that you two would end up together. And really, I didn't think Lucas would ever want me. I'm so socially inept, don't deny it," she said as I tried to disagree, but we both knew it was true. "And Lucas is beyond me," Lily said. "He's had girlfriends before and had sex. I just didn't think that he thought of me that way. I don't know if I'll ever be able to be intimate with him. There's a reason why I keep most boys out, and it's not just because they think I'm some kind of psycho genius."

"What is it, Lily?" I asked tense by the strain in her voice. "You can be honest with me. I know it probably seems like you can't, but I really am a good Logost."

"I've never told anyone except for my Dad," she said. "I don't even know how to talk about it really. There aren't words to describe this kind of grief."

I didn't understand what she meant, but I was silent and waited for her to say more. It really wasn't my business, but I wanted to help. Even though she was with Lucas I loved Lily.

"Just tell me, Lily," I said. "I'm always here for you."

"I'm ashamed," she said. "I don't want you to think less of me. And you never asked me why I was able to be a good Logost. I've never met a Logost as good as myself besides Lucas, not even my Mom is a good person. I'd never say that to her though," she laughed. "And I'd never tell her about this, either. I think she would say it was my fault if I told her what her brother, my uncle, did to me when I was little – I was six the first time," she whispered. "He told me that we weren't doing anything bad. I cried, and I didn't understand why he would touch me that way. Why he would force me to be motionless as he did it. I believed it was my fault, and I still believe that sometimes." She finished her sentence and her voice was shaky.

"It wasn't your fault, Lily. He did that to you. He should be the one that's ashamed. Only a sick individual would hurt a child like that. He knew what he was doing. Don't blame yourself."

"Well, it's because of him that I'm so good. He had a troubled soul, and he tortured and killed a lot people. He was the worst kind of Logost, and I thought I had to be bad too. But I knew that I couldn't be. After what he did to me, I knew that I couldn't ever hurt anyone, not even humans. I just didn't want to kill. I got no joy out of pain, because I'd been on the other side of that pain."

"And that's why you don't think you can be intimate with Lucas?" I asked.

"I don't know. Honestly, I'm too afraid to try. I have nightmares about it sometimes, and I wouldn't want Lucas to know about it. He just realized his feelings for me. I don't want to scare him off."

"Lucas is good, Lily. He would understand. He wouldn't pressure you to do something you don't want."

"I know, but he's a guy. All guys want sex, don't they? I mean he was with Cassandra just for sex. If I can't be that way with him why would he want me?"

"Lily, don't be such a pessimist. I think you just need to be honest with Lucas about the limitations of your relationship. If you gain trust in him maybe you'll eventually want to be that way with him. And Lucas isn't like that, he respects you. And not all guys think about sex. Some guys think it's better to wait."

"Does Mr. Elliot think it's better to wait?" Lily said. It made me nervous to imagine being that way with Drew. He was so much older and experienced. I understood the way Lily felt. Lucas wasn't as experienced as Drew, but he was more experienced than her, and I could imagine that would make her just as nervous.

"He wants to wait," I said. "He says it will mean more once I'm older."

"Do you want to wait?"

"I don't know. Drew scares me sometimes, and other times when we're kissing I want to be with him. I've tried before, but he always pulls away. He doesn't like when I'm the one who's in control."

"Of course he doesn't," she said. And I asked her what she meant. "He just seems like the type who wants to have the upper hand with that sort of thing. He'll probably only want you that way when you don't want him."

"That doesn't make any sense."

"If you really think about it Mina, it does. Mr. Elliot wants to control everything, and that includes you. If you're the one initiating, and he wants to be in control, then it makes sense that he would tell you that it's best to wait. He won't let you decide for yourself, and that's the part that worries me."

"There's no need to worry. Drew promised to change, he promised he wouldn't be so controlling anymore."

"People don't change overnight. I would bet that he's still banking on being able to control you. And I'm not saying this to make you sad. I'm only trying to look out for your best interests, and I hope that you start to look out for your own best interests too."

I disagreed with Lily, but I kept quiet about it. I didn't want to start another argument between us, but really I didn't think she knew what she was talking about. She'd never even had a boyfriend before, or been intimate with anyone. I did have my best interests in mind, and I wouldn't let Drew control me anymore. If he ever tried to be that controlling again, then I would leave him for good – it was the *how to leave him* part, which I hadn't figured out yet. But I would only worry about that if his controlling nature resurfaced. And I hoped that it wouldn't. I wanted Drew to be good, and he finally wanted that as well. I didn't want anyone else but him, so I would give him space and time to change.

{24}

Lily and I sat alone at breakfast, while Lucas sat clear across the dining hall with some of the boys in his level. I kept turning my head to look at him, and he kept looking away from me. Things between Lucas and I were over before they even started, but I didn't want our friendship to end with our attraction to one another. Lily watched me out of the corner of her eye as I picked at my bowl of oats, feeling too anxious to eat anything. She pretended that she wasn't watching.

"Why don't you just go talk to him," she said looking up from the book she was reading on serial killers. "You know you want to, and he wants to talk to you too. Things don't have to be this cumbersome, Mina. You two should be more adult about this, and go back to being friends. Or else I'll shun both of you."

"I planned on talking to him this morning. He's the one who's avoiding me. Do you think he's still mad?"

"Possibly," she said. "But I'm not sure. Lucas has a hard time expressing his feelings. And I think he doesn't want to talk about you in front of me. I think he worries I'll be hurt or jealous or something, but I wouldn't be. People change, and I'm not banking on our love for eternity. I'm not even sure I believe in love at all."

"So you don't think you love Lucas?" I asked.

"I care about him, and I want him around for the moment. But nothing lasts forever, and love is just a temporary chemical reaction in the brain. Who knows if it will last, but I hope that it will. Besides, it doesn't make any sense to be jealous of you. We're friends. I know you'd never do anything to hurt me, and I'd never do anything to hurt you."

"You're right. I'll try to talk to him during free period."

"Why wait? Don't you two have Manipulation together?"

"We do, but I want to wait until we're alone. Drew tends to eavesdrop, and he doesn't need to know about everything that goes on in my life."

Lily nodded and went back to reading her book. I loved Lily, but she could only engage in conversations for a minute or two before she got bored and needed something more intellectually stimulating. She made me feel stupid sometimes, but I knew those weren't her intentions. She couldn't help how brilliant she was.

***

In Manipulation, Lucas didn't save a seat for me the way he would have before. I walked by his desk on my way to my seat, and I leaned down to whisper in his ear.

"I'm sorry," I said. I asked him to meet me after my private lessons with Drew so that we could talk and practice flying together.

I told him that Lily had suggested those plans. He was silent as I spoke, but he nodded his head apprehensively. He probably believed I still wanted to be with him, and I did, in some ways. But I loved him and Lily more than I cared about my own impractical and selfish desires.

When I knocked on the door to Drew's class, he took a while to answer. When he opened the door his eyes were red, and had puffy bags under them. He told me he wasn't feeling well and would have to cancel. I could understand why Drew felt so tired. With everything that had gone on in the past few months, I felt mentally exhausted. What I really needed was a day to myself – a mental health day where I wouldn't have to talk or be bothered with anyone, not even Drew.

On my short walk home, I closed my eyes and focused on finding Lucas' thought patterns among the other Logosts at the school. As I searched through each mind I came across, I found Lucas sitting in the common room of the boy's dorm. Luckily, he wasn't very good at blocking, and never bothered to keep other Logosts out with any consistency.

"Can you meet with me now?" I thought and placed the words in to his thought processes. *"Drew canceled my private lessons. I'll be near the pond at the base of the mountains if you want to meet me."*

"Give me a minute," Lucas thought in reply. *"I need to go see Lily first, then I'll meet you there."*

I headed to the tiny, circular pond, where I had practiced controlling the water on my own. I tried a few new things as I waited. I tried to move all the water from the pond and empty out just the bottom level. I thought about Lily's reaction to me doing something like this, and it wouldn't have been pleasant. She would have worried about the fish, but I wasn't even able to budge the water from the pond's enclosure. It took too much of my mind to focus on controlling the water, and levitating it at the same time. Another task I undertook was creating tiny clouds of precipitation, as I asked the water to evaporate in to the atmosphere. I made several small, white puffs, but they dissipated before I was able to do more with them. I sat there levitating the weak clouds, when Lucas joined me at the small pond. He kept his head down when he reached me, and it made me feel like a leech – sucking the life out of him, little by little.

"You don't have to do this, Mina," he said not meeting my eyes. "I already talked to Lily. We can try to be friends again if you want. I just don't think it will ever go back to the way it was. I'm sorry for that. But I think you realize it isn't my fault."

"Yes, I do realize that," I said. "I'm happy for you Lucas, and Lily too. And pretty soon you won't have to worry about me anymore. The Informants will be here soon, and I'll finally get to go home."

"Won't you have to go in to hiding?" he asked. "You won't be able to stay in New York. They'll know where to find you."

"How do you know that?" I asked.

"Because," he said releasing a deep sigh. "Because Sophia is my grandmother, that's how I know. It's not something I tell people. I wish I weren't related to that loathsome dictator, but unfortunately we don't get to choose our family."

"So your mother is her daughter?" He nodded. "Does that mean she'll be the leader when Sophia is too old to rule?"

"Yes, she will be. And if you were to ask my mother, she would say that Sophia is already incapable of keeping a grasp on our world."

"Do you believe that?" I asked.

"I don't know what I believe," he said. "But I hate Jaclyn, I never call her mom, and I really want nothing to do with her or my sisters. Jaclyn's plotted to have my grandmother executed in the past, but Sophia misses nothing. Jaclyn only wants power. She never cared for me or my sisters. Growing up, I never saw much of her. We have money, so I was raised mostly by housekeepers and our nanny."

"Your mother wasn't around at all? That's really sad."

"Neither was my dad. My sisters always were, though. But they're just as corrupt and malicious as my mother. My three sisters go on killing rampages from time to time. They torture humans and other Logosts," he paused sounding as if he pitied his evil older sisters. "They're very powerful, and their mental capacity goes beyond most Logosts. I share a bond with them, and I've tried to save them from themselves. They killed our father when I was thirteen."

"Why?" I asked.

"Because he wouldn't do what they said. Jaclyn didn't even mourn his loss. She's like ice, I swear I think she's frozen sometimes, and my sisters are becoming just like her."

"They all live in Colombia?"

"Yeah, they all live in our villa. They pillage the smaller villages and burned several. My oldest sister is Isabella, then Melissa, and Claudia is the youngest. She's the only one who still has a chance to change. Claudia still has goodness in her, but she wants to deny it. I think Jaclyn is the reason I'm different. I had to watch her torture and kill, and living with her brought me to a level of compassion and resistance."

"Do you have any desire to stop her?"

"My only desire is to stay as far away from her and my sisters as possible. So you'll leave with Mr. Elliot then when the Informants come?" Lucas asked.

"Yes," I said and then something resonated when Lucas wouldn't meet my eyes. "You knew, didn't you? You knew they would come for me. Cassandra told you Louis was her father." He stared down at his feet. "Why didn't you tell me?"

"I don't know, Mina," he said. "Maybe it was because I was still angry with you about her death. And really I don't think Louis would kill you over Cassandra. He never saw his daughter, and Cassandra didn't know anything about him."

"Do you miss her?" I asked.

"Of course I miss her. I know she wasn't a good Logost. She was like Jaclyn in so many different ways, but she gave me the attention I desperately needed at that time. I feel bad about being with her now, though. I never knew then, how much it hurt Lily to see us together."

"Would you marry Lily?"

"It's too soon to tell. But I love her more than she loves me." I laughed, but stopped once I realized how rude I was being. "Why's that funny?" Lucas asked.

"Because Lily thinks she loves you more. She says it took you so long to realize how she felt about you. She's worried your feelings will change."

"I don't know if they will. We're so young. But I do love Lily. I want to protect her, and keep her safe. She's so naïve sometimes, and she needs me. She's not like you Mina, you don't really need anyone. But for some reason you think you need Mr. Elliot."

"He's changed Lucas. He promised me his quest for power is done. And he does love me, I know you think he doesn't, but he does."

"I'm sure he really believes he loves you, Mina. But Mr. Elliot is all fucked up. I think he manipulates himself sometimes. He doesn't know what truth is, and what lies are. He lies to himself, and he lies to you. Leave him behind when the Informants come."

"Can't you just be happy for me, please? Don't you think it hurts me to listen to how you feel about Lily? I'm able to be mature about it though."

"I am being mature," Lucas said. "I'm not saying these things because I'm jealous. I just know that you can do better than him. Almost any other Logost would be better for you than Mr. Elliot."

"How long did it take before you were able to be yourself with Lily?"

"I've always been myself with Lily," he said. "If you can't be who you really are around Mr. Elliot, how do you know you love him?"

"I just do. He's frightening, but he makes me feel special. He comforts me and he'll protect me. Isn't that all that anyone wants?"

"How should I know?" he laughed. He placed his arm around my shoulders and smiled at me.

I wish he wouldn't look at me that way when he knew wanted to be with Lily. He would have to stop looking at me as if I was the only person in the world who mattered, it would only hurt her. And even though I knew that was what should happen, I didn't want him to ever stop looking at me that way.

{25}

My eyes were black as Drew and I drifted through clouds of night, our bodies hovering above the Earth. "Can you feel it," I whispered to him. His eyes were that dangerous shade of light green, which always made me tremble with distrust. The earth turned only a miniscule amount in the opposite direction of its rotation. I wondered if the people on it could feel the difference. I felt the strength of its cosmic pull beckon to me.

"Stop, Mina," Drew said keeping his voice even. "Set it back as it was. This isn't something you should play with."

"Why do you have to be so serious all the time?" I said. "You should try not to be so neurotic," I laughed but his face was still serious. I grabbed his arms and pulled him close to me, kissing him as we floated down to the Earth below. "There's more. But I'll only show you if you promise not to get jealous."

"I'm not jealous," he said sounding more frustrated than he probably intended to. "You just worry me. You're so strong, and so young – a fatal combination. You *should* take things more seriously, especially something as detrimental as moving the Earth. Do you want to mess with the passing of time?"

"I moved it back," I said. "And why would I want to be as serious as you are? So I can be nervous all the time?"

"I'm not always nervous, Mina. And when I am there's usually a reason behind it."

"You're nervous now," I said looking at his hands. He was wringing them together the way he always did when he was contemplating something. I grabbed his hands and pulled them away from each other. "Stop being so twitchy," I shouted. "It makes it hard for me to see what you're thinking. I can't read your mind, so your actions are all that I have to go off."

"Don't criticize me that way. You know I can't help it."

"I know," I said kissing his hand. "Do you want to see more or not?"

He nodded. "Just don't rotate the earth. I am impressed that you've learned this on your own. I'm sorry I've been distant lately, but I am trying to change for you. It's difficult, and it's easier for me to be alone right now – to keep the bad thoughts out. But, if I'm being honest, those urges are still there. I don't know if they'll ever go away."

"Just don't give in to them. When you distance yourself from people it makes it easier for you to kill them without compassion. Think of them as beings. They all have thoughts and feelings, you know? How would you feel if you died as they had?"

"That isn't something I think about. Don't ask me to do that, I won't."

"Fine," I said giving up. "Just watch."

I flew away from Drew and down towards the sea. He followed me, but kept his distance. My body hovered over the black coast of water, and I became stormy as the sea. I created large nimbus clouds, and floated across the ocean, striking it with lightning. The water began to turn and rise, as a wave of the ocean enveloped me. The rushing water circled me and gushed in to the sky.

I couldn't see Drew past the water tornado, but I could sense that he was even more anxious than he'd been before. I knew he was jealous. He'd been practicing for years, and all he could do was create waves in the water. My lips curled as I pictured the troubled look on his face. I let go of my focus, and the sea returned to its calm. Drew flew over to me and his reaction was not what I was expecting.

"That was amazing," he said. "I'm so proud of you, my love." He pulled me close, kissing my hair, and that uneasy feeling returned. He was lying to me, but I wasn't sure why. He seemed like he was forcing himself to be this way with me. As if he was pretending, but I couldn't be sure. I pulled away from him to see the truth in his eyes, and there was nothing there. His eyes were flat, almost dead looking – like he wasn't present. We flew back to Winchester, and stood outside the door to the girl's cottage. I looked at him and his eyes still hadn't changed.

"Something's wrong," I said. "What is it?"

"You fear me, Mina, don't lie to me. And I'm beginning to fear you as well," Drew admitted. "Whorton's told me that you don't really love me. You're only keeping up this charade because you're afraid. I've seen the way you recoil sometimes when I touch you."

"That's not true," I said the words rushing out. "I did say that to her, but things have changed now. You've changed, Drew. Don't let Whortons's words come between us. There's no need to fear me," I said and he ignored me. But his eyes wouldn't leave mine.

"She's asked me to leave Winchester, and to stay away from you. But you know that I can't. I won't ever leave you, no matter how frightened of me you become."

"Stop, don't say those kinds of things, Drew. You're worrying me. Just love me," I said. "You're convincing yourself that you're afraid because you're jealous. You're concerned, but I would never hurt you. I couldn't, you know that, don't you?"

"I don't know, Mina. I'm beginning to think that you're not as trusting as you once were, and perhaps I have only myself to blame for that."

"Look at me," I said, but he wouldn't. "Drew, please just look at me. You're going to lose me if you continue to let fear drive all your thought processes. You *can* trust me," I told him and pressed my lips to his. But his mouth was tight. He wouldn't kiss me back.

"Go inside, Mina," Drew said making no move to hold me. "I'll see you tomorrow."

He didn't call to me again that night, but I wasn't too bothered by it. It was becoming a habit that I was getting used to, and that saddened me. He always called to me, but he hadn't since the day I tried to take the photos down in the lighthouse. It was becoming hard for me to picture his face. It was hard for me to focus on him, and the way I felt. It felt like we were separating, and pulling away from one another. As if our forces were going in opposite directions.

The next morning, it was Ms. Callaway and not Wilma Whorton who sent out the morning alarm through our inner ears. Their minds are different, the sound was different. It made everyone, including me, stressed.

When Lily and I walked to line-up, Whorton was nowhere to be seen. All eyes darted about searching for the dark-haired beauty, but she kept her mind blocked and her body hidden. No one could sense her there. I was the only one who seemed to notice that Drew was missing too. My thoughts took a turn for the worse, and I pictured the two of them running away together. He must have believed every word she said.

Lily turned around to face me and the terror in her eyes spoke worlds of darkness.

"What is it?" I said. "Do you know why Whorton's missing?"

"He's here, Mina," Lily said looking past me.

"Who's here? Is it the Informants?"

Lily nodded her head. "My uncle is here, I can sense him. I can't stay here, Mina. I have to go. I have to leave until they're gone. I can't face him. I'm sorry to desert you, but I have no other choice. You understand, don't you?"

I flung my arms around her. Of course I understood. Lily's uncle was her abuser, but she hadn't told me he was one of the Five

Leaders.

"I have to go now," she said. "Tell Lucas for me. Tell him that I'm sorry." And then Lily was gone. She flew in to the sky, and several other students took flight at the sight of Lily rushing off. I knew I needed to leave too, but I couldn't without Drew. I just couldn't leave him behind. I turned to the back of the line, and saw Drew running towards me. He grabbed my hand and pulled me with him, preparing to take flight.

"Drew Elliot," called a voice I had never heard before. "Surely, you would want to see me before rushing off with this young girl." The man speaking walked up to me and Drew, as we stood amongst the crowd of students.

"Narc," Drew said trying to hide his nervous behavior once again, but a tense smile ran across his lips. "I wasn't expecting to see you here," he said.

"I'm sure you weren't," Narc smiled. "But I am here, nonetheless. And here is Ms. Mina. How lovely she is. She's much prettier in person than she was in your memories." Narc looked me up and down. "But still just as young."

Narc took my hand and pulled me away from Drew. "It looked as if you were planning on leaving before we've reached a decision regarding the death of Louis' daughter. Whorton's given us Mina's name, you're very lucky Louis is not here. He would have killed you the moment he sensed your presence. Chance and Andres stayed with him to guard our home. Sophia and I came alone," Narc said.

Drew told me that the Five Leaders always leave the castle in pairs. They have so many enemies in our world that they're always in fear of leaving their home unprotected.

"I'm afraid we can't allow this to continue Drew," Narc said. "Wilma's told us everything about this *inappropriate* relationship, and we cannot ignore this. Mina will die for the death of Cassandra, and you must be tortured for stealing her innocence."

"Please, Narc, must you be so unforgiving," said Sophia as she walked up to us, Wilma Whorton following close behind. Sophia's voice rang like the bell on an old-fashioned bicycle. Her demeanor was so calm and polite. I couldn't believe what Lucas had said about her being evil. She looked so sweet – like the kind of grandmother who would bake a pie for you whenever you came to visit.

"Let us not prove the stereotype, but rather be the exception to the rule," Sophia said her voice controlled with the strength of her authority. "We should let all know that the Informants are forgiving in some ways. Release the girl," she shouted, but Narc did not let go of my hand. He just stared at me with anxious eyes. "No decision has been made as of yet."

Sophia's top lip tucked in when she finished speaking. Prominent wrinkles formed around her eyes and her hair was no longer blonde, as it had been in the painting in Whorton's office. It was a shimmering silver now, and fell past her shoulders in big curly locks. Her beauty was still present, it was just more aged.

She did look ancient, just as Lily had described her. There

were frown lines around her mouth and deep creases in her forehead. Her eyes were glossy, almost colorless, and the sight was eerie. I couldn't stop staring at her even though I knew I was being rude, even though I knew my fate lay with her perceptions of me. I didn't want to die, not yet. I thought that perhaps Drew would admit that he had killed Cassandra. But I knew that he wouldn't, he was too selfish for that good of a deed. No amount of love would leave him risking his own life to save me. That much I knew about Drew Elliot.

Sophia walked to the front of the crowd of students, facing everyone. She beckoned Narc to stand with her. Wilma kept her distance, but stayed close to the Logost queen. Sophia's eyes turned dark and I felt my mental defenses slipping. It was sudden, but I realized that I wasn't able to move. I glanced in Drew's direction and his eyes weren't blinking. She must have frozen us all – indeed Sophia was the most powerful Logost. The sound of her high-pitched voice rang in my head.

"The Informants have reason to believe that there is foul play taking place here at Winchester. We no longer trust the school's leaders." Her eyes flickered to Whorton. *"Nor do we trust the students here. We are displeased with the way you all are being taught. I have asked Ms. Whorton, to showcase Winchester's most gifted students. You all must prove that this school is worthy of the support of the Five Leaders. If you cannot prove that, you will all die. But we will give each of you a chance, and those who do exceptionally well will be asked to join us, and share in the power of the Informants. Tomorrow there will be a display of power, and tonight Ms. Whorton has planned a banquet in our honor."*

Sophia turned to Whorton. "Where is my grandson?" Sophia

said. "Where is Lucas?"

The look on Wilma's face was invaluable. I wished she always looked that shocked and vulnerable. She regretted the day she'd tortured Lucas in front of everyone. Sophia walked over to Lucas and embraced him. Lucas was motionless, but he allowed his grandmother to hold him. She turned away, facing Whorton.

"Wilma, would you show me to your office? I believe we have several matters to discuss." Whorton nodded and took Sophia's hand, leading her to the main building of the school. Narc followed them. "Not you, Narc," Sophia said. "Your egotism is annoying me more than usual. Stay behind and monitor the classes today. We need to be aware of everything that's going on in this school."

Narc bowed to Sophia. Whorton dismissed the students, who stood there motionless from the tension. They scattered, trying their best to go unnoticed. It was a moment of weakness that I found myself in as the seconds ticked by. Drew looked defeated, and his eyes were focused on Narc. I could feel the anger pulsating under his skin. Narc let go of my hand finally, and took a few steps back to examine us. I ran to Drew's side, fearful that he would attack us.

"Narc," Drew said addressing the strange man. Narc craned over the two of us. His eyes were flat and black as if he were concentrating on levitating some large object. His head was shaved, and he wore a black suit with a black collared shirt. He looked older than Drew, but not as old as Sophia. "You've seen in my memories what Mina is capable of, but there is so much more to this young girl. She is stronger than all of us, even you Narc, and Sophia. The girl is the most gifted Logost that anyone's ever seen. Cassandra was useless, she died with reason. Do not throw away this girl as if Cassandra was more valuable."

"You seem certain of this fact," Narc said. "And you make no case for yourself?" Drew shook his head. "Very well, we will allow Mina to make a case for herself. If she can prove to Sophia and me that she is as great as you say, she will live."

"That sounds splendid," said Sophia staring up at the faint morning clouds. "I do love a good display of Logost strength. It has yet to be determined whether Cassandra was more valuable than Mina. She deserves a chance, and naturally we would want her to display her power tomorrow along with all the other gifted students."

{26}

The rest of that school day passed with a quickness and great tension. Everyone was on edge – especially Whorton. But after that morning Drew seemed more at ease.

Narc sat in on one of every teacher's classes, and it was no surprise when I walked in to Manipulation and saw Narc chatting with Drew at the front of the class. I strolled to the empty seat beside Lucas, but Narc grabbed my arm. I pulled out of his grasp, and he winked at me. Drew saw what had transcended, but said nothing. He laughed awkwardly, and I stood there waiting for one of them to say something.

"Take your seat, Mina," Drew said. "I apologize, Narc. For whatever reason Mina has been unbelievably unobservant today, you'll have to excuse her insolence." Drew motioned again for me to take my seat and I obeyed.

"Where's Lily?" Lucas said as I pulled my books from my bag.

"There was a situation," I whispered. "Lily had to leave. She can't be around Narc. Narc is her uncle."

Drew shouted at both of us to be silent during class time. Narc sat in the back of the classroom, scribbling in to a leather journal. He nodded approvingly at some points of Drew's lecture, but shook his head during others. Every time I faced the back of the class to gage his thinking he locked eyes with me, and I turned around, not wanting him to know I'd been watching.

When the bell rang I rushed out, but Drew asked me to stay behind. He told me to take my seat, and stepped out of the classroom to rush the students out of the hall. Narc lingered around, standing behind me, staring down at me. I wanted to leave. I didn't want to have to sit there and endure the looks he was giving me. It made me feel like I was standing there naked – as if he could see every part of me. He placed his hand on the top of my shoulder, and leaned down near my ear.

"You are beautiful Mina Culvert," he said. "I can see why Drew chose you. But I can also see you don't really love him, you're only with him because of his power."

"Drew's just a teacher. He possesses no power."

"But Drew is no ordinary Logost, his powers of manipulation are godlike. A girl with your beauty should stand beside a man with much greater influences in this world. You would be an exceptional Informant," he said. "Drew is too corrupt to join our ranks, but you are someone we could mold."

Drew shut the door. He walked over to Narc and I, but he didn't look upset by the way that Narc leaned in to me. I would have expected him to attack Narc, just as he had with Lucas.

"Mina," Drew breathed my name the same way he had months ago, when he sat in that black and tan booth at the pizza place. "Narc, wishes for you to escort him to the banquet tonight. You will sit with him and Sophia at their table with Ms. Whorton and the other teachers."

"No," I said looking straight at Drew. "Why would I? That makes no sense."

"You will, because Narc has asked you to. He is one of our leaders, and you must respect his wishes. I'm sorry Mina, but my hands are tied. You have no choice."

I was silent because there was nothing left to say. I would have to accompany this creep, and what he wanted with me I still did not understand. I wanted him dead that much I knew. He'd hurt Lily, scarred her for life, and yet he was able to walk around as if he had done nothing wrong. This wasn't right, but nothing seemed right anymore.

"It's settled then," Narc said and he rocked backed on his heels in anxiousness. "I'm having lunch with Sophia and Wilma. You're welcome to join us Drew." Drew bowed and Narc stepped out of the classroom.

"What's going on?" I said to Drew.

"Listen, Narc has agreed to excuse our relationship if you accompany him to this banquet. He says that I will not be punished if you agree to go, so just go, look pretty, and be charming. Narc has a weakness for beautiful, young girls and unfortunately he's set his radar upon you."

"He's foul and disgusting. I want nothing to do with him."

"I understand Mina, but please don't be selfish about this. I'm asking you to do this for me. I'm afraid that you must. And in all actuality this may work to our advantage. If you can lure Narc to you, then you can kill him once his protections are minimized. But you must keep him distracted in order to go in for the kill. If he tries to kiss you, let him."

"You're not serious? I can't believe you would ask something like this of me. I thought you loved me. Why would you be complacent with me having to kiss that sleaze? You don't own me."

I stood up to leave, but Drew pulled me close to him. He stared down in to my eyes, the gold swirls turning around his dark green irises. My face flamed.

"Do you want to see me hurt?" he asked. "If you don't do this then I will be tortured. This may be our only chance to take out one of the Informants' strongest leaders. Do as I say, my love, please."

"If I kill Narc, the blame will fall to me. I don't love you enough for that. And you don't love me enough to even consider that using me like this is wrong. I will escort Narc to the banquet, and I will *only* kill him if he tries to touch me. I won't do your bidding. I thought you were changing, but you always lie." I pushed him off me and walked out.

That was the end of it. I made a promise to myself that if Drew ever tried to manipulate me again I would leave him. So that's exactly what I would do – leave him. Now was the time to tell Whorton the truth about Cassandra's death. If she knew, then maybe the Informants would leave. If I had to go in to hiding then I would have to hide from Drew as well – I was reaching my breaking point.

When I parted ways with him that day, it was then that I knew he was a passing movement, and not a permanent fixture in my life. He would not be the one I would introduce to others, but rather just a sad story to tell. My love for Drew Elliot was fading fast, and I had finally broken through the rose-colored glass. He would never change, and I didn't care anymore.

I stepped out of my last class, and Lucas was standing across the hall, his eyes smiling at me. I walked over to him, and the pace of my feet told him enough about how I was feeling.

"What is it now?" Lucas asked.

"Everything," I grumbled. "Lily's gone, Drew's an asshole, and now I have to escort Narc to that stupid banquet."

"Well, I've been telling you all this time that Mr. Elliot was no good. But why would you escort Narc to the banquet?"

"I have to because he wants me to. What choice do I have?"

"None, really, the Five Leaders always get what they want. They pretty much own us all."

I asked Lucas to speak to Sophia, she was his grandmother. But Lucas said there was nothing he could do, if this was something Narc wanted then Sophia had no say in the matter.

"She wouldn't get involved with something like this anyway," he said. "I'm sorry that monster has it out for you. It seems like you attract every creep within a 20 mile radius."

"He's Lily's uncle," I told him again. He was upset that Lily hadn't told him herself. I explained how Narc had abused her when she was little. He was horrified and sad that Lily had to endure something like that.

"So what's going on with you two?" I asked.

"Lily doesn't know what she wants," he barked. I'd never heard him say her name like that before. "She says that she does care about me, but she doesn't want to be with me. She told me that it would be best if we just stayed friends."

His words weren't sinking in. Lily told me that she loved him. Why would she give him up so easily?

"What did you do? You must have sullied it somehow."

"I swear, I didn't do anything, a few nights ago we were walking around the city. It seemed like the perfect moment, so I tried to kiss her. She stopped me and said we should just be friends. She said she didn't feel the same way about me anymore. She echoed your words and said she didn't want to lead me on."

I could tell Lucas was hurt, but he didn't seem broken like he had after Elijah's death. It made me suspicious, but I ignored my instincts only because I wanted to. It was selfish of me, but I wanted there to be a chance for us still. He held my hand as we walked back to the dorms, which wasn't anything out of the ordinary. He used to always hold my hand. I didn't want to lose Lily as a friend, but if she didn't love him anymore maybe she would understand.

***

The banquet was starting and everyone else was already there. My hand gripped the entrance door to the girl's dorm. Narc was on the other side. I could sense his presence and read his mind. He allowed me to read his mind because he wanted me to know what he was thinking. The images his mind continued to replay made me that much more nervous. How could any one person be that repulsive? I couldn't get myself to budge, and as hard as tried to convince my hand to just turn the doorknob – I couldn't.

"I know you're there, Mina," Narc said, his voice loud enough that I could hear it as I stood inside the common room. "Just open the door. I'm not going to hurt you, I promise."

Narc banged on the door when I didn't say anything in response. I jumped at the sound, and then opened it and stepped outside. The grin he wore made me want to slap him. He looked so pleased with himself, and he took my arm and wrapped it around his own.

"You look very nice," he said. I wanted to run, but it wasn't worth the risk. He wasn't stronger than me, I decided. If he tried anything he would regret it. I thought about what he'd done to Lily. I wanted to kill him for that.

The banquet was held in the same tent as the dance. And Lily was right, they did use the same decorations, but it was still beautiful. I found myself unable to enjoy any of it though with Narc by my side. We sat at a table with Sophia, Whorton, and the other teachers. Lucas was there, seated between Sophia and Whorton. His chair was pulled back from the table, his arms folded across his chest, and his eyes stared down at the floor.

Narc kept placing his hand on my thigh during dinner, and I shocked his fingertips each time he did. After a while, he caught on and left his hands in his lap. Drew watched Narc and I intently, and even though it was childish I kept sticking my middle finger out at him – I did it discreetly though, and pretended to scratch my head, but I'm sure he saw it.

"Dance with me," Narc said once dinner was finished. He pulled me from the table before I could answer. On the dance floor, Narc kept his body close to mine as we swayed in time with the music. He wouldn't stop pawing at me, and it made me feel like a curtain that a cat was intent on destroying.

I was in a hurry to get out of there, but I was searching for a moment to tell Whorton that Drew had been the one to kill Cassandra. There was not one moment where she was alone. Sophia stayed by her side, chatting away. The seconds were ticking by and still Whorton was occupied. Narc pressed his body in to my own once again, and I could feel his erection. I backed away from him staring down, but I saw nothing. I told him I had to leave, and that I needed sleep to prepare for tomorrow's demonstration. He didn't offer, but told me he would walk me back to my dorm.

When we were outside, he wrapped his arm around my body as if he were a strait jacket, trying to constrain me. I made several attempts to move his arm, but they were useless. His walk was unsteady, and our bodies rocked from side to side. Drew walked several feet behind us. I couldn't hear him, and I was certain Narc hadn't noticed him following us. But I could sense Drew there, just as I always could. He seemed hopeful, he still wanted me to try to seduce Narc so that I could kill him.

After a moment, Narc stopped walking and touched my face. He grabbed the back of my neck pulling me to him, trying to force me to kiss him. He was stronger than me, and he held me in place as he ran his hands across my body.

"I want you," he whispered. I wanted Drew to save me, but he stayed hidden, watching. The wind blew Narc back and away from me. I knew I was only further endangering my own life, but I didn't care.

Stones rested on the path we walked across. I levitated them, and pelted him with each one on the back of the head. He dodged them, and they fell to the ground. He lunged at me in an attempt to tackle me to the ground. I jumped out of the way. I lit his body on fire, and he dropped to his knees, screaming in agony and then I doused the flames. I blew my breath at him, sending waves of pain through his body.

"Are you done?" I asked him as he lay on the cold ground. I stepped over him, looking in to his eyes. He stood up, brushing the dirt from his black suit.

"You stupid little bitch," he said. "Do you realize just how much trouble you've made for yourself?"

He jolted my body away from him. My access to oxygen cut off, and it felt like I had been dropped in to a freezing lake. I stood there shivering and gasping for air, when Drew stepped out of the darkness and in to the light.

"Narc," Drew called. "Let her go." And I was shocked to see Narc obey. My breath came out in gasps as I tried to fill my lungs with air.

"Fine," Narc said. "It's obvious she doesn't want me."

"You should return to the banquet. I'll walk Ms. Culvert back to the girl's cottage," Drew said. "I apologize if she's bruised your ego."

Narc scoffed, and squinted his eyes scrutinizing me. "Culvert is your last name, isn't it?" he asked. "Didn't you kill that loon Ernest Culvert, Drew?"

Drew didn't move an inch. He was as motionless as an old oak tree that couldn't be swayed by the wind. He moved his lips to speak, but said nothing. I stared up at him, boring my eyes in to his soul, but he didn't turn to look at me. He kept his focus blank, and I knew once again that he'd been hiding this from me. Narc took in my expression.

"He didn't tell you," Narc said. "That's love for you. Well, she may have wanted you before," Narc laughed. "But the little bitch won't want you now." Narc walked back to the tent, leaving Drew and I to stand there in the cold, angry with one another.

{27}

"Why didn't you tell me?" I said. "You want me to trust you, but you've given me no reason to. What is this Drew? What is this that you're doing with me? Please be honest, for once."

"I didn't tell you because there was no reason for you to know. I won't discuss this any further, so don't bother pestering me with your juvenile games. Stop questioning me, and just do as I say," Drew shouted, grabbing my arm. His grip was so tight I was sure it would leave bruises. "We've reached the point where you must follow my directions without reason."

"You killed my father. Tell me now why you did that. When did he die?"

"I had to kill him, Mina. If he were still alive there would be no chance of us ever being together, and I knew from the start that we were meant to be. The first time he mentioned you to me, I knew then. Ernest Culvert would never have let me anywhere near you if he were still breathing. You wouldn't be here with me now. Doesn't that mean more to you? It's not like you ever knew him. You have no reason to be upset."

"Stay away from me," I said my voice so low I could barely hear myself. "Don't ever come near me again. My father had good reason for keeping you from me, Drew. I must respect his wishes." Hatred dripped from my every word. But I could hear Drew laughing. That same dark laughter I'd heard in the park – it seemed like ions ago now.

"You're so oblivious." Drew laughed without smiling. I started to walk away but he stood before me, blocking my path. "You don't have a choice Mina. When are you going to realize that you can't leave me, even if you want to? I am yours my love, and you my dear sweet girl, belong to me. There is no doubt in my mind that this much will ever change." He reached out his hand and stroked my cheek. "I love you Mina, you know that I do. In fact, I love you so much that I believe you know exactly what will happen if you try to leave me."

"You'll kill me," I said, and Drew nodded his head ever so slowly.

"I'm afraid I can't let you live without me, my love. And I am sorry for this. I'm sorry that you're the one that my barely beating heart chose. But you'll adjust, that much I can promise. And if you decide that you want to kill yourself again, please do let me know ahead of time. The death I've chosen for you will be long-lasting and much more tragic – the death that a truly great Logost deserves. You deserve better than that pitiful Elijah. He wanted death so badly, but when I was willing to answer his wishes, he prayed for me to spare him."

"You killed Elijah too," I said flatly, no longer surprised by how heartless he was. "I suppose I don't need to know the reason for that either."

"No, I killed him to torture the boy you love."

"I have to go, Drew. Tomorrow morning my fate will be decided, and I need rest if I am to make a convincing case for myself. I'll see you in the morning."

He ignored my words and grabbed me by the waist, pulling me in to him. He pressed his lips to mine, but I kept my mouth tight, hoping he would give up.

"Invite me to your room," he said.

"No, you're not allowed, you know that."

"It wasn't a question. The rules do not apply to me. I do as I please. Your roommate's gone now, isn't she? Yes, of course she is," he answered his own question. "Narc's very presence scared her off. She's so weak – so unworthy of your friendship, why you bother with her I may never know."

"You don't know anything," I said. "He sexually abused her when she was a little girl. He hurt her more than you know."

"Please," he said. "I'm sure she knew what he was doing. She probably liked it. If she'd wanted him to stop he would have." I opened my mouth to speak but he put his hand over it. "No more talking, Mina. Just do as I say. I don't want to hurt you," Drew said.

I led the way to my dorm room, too frightened to argue with

him. I walked in to the cottage and it was completely empty – everyone was still at the banquet. We went in to my room, and Drew sat down on my bed. I grabbed my things and went to the bathroom to change.

"Where are you going?" he asked.

"To the bathroom to change in to my pajamas," I said. "I told you I need to sleep. You can stay here if you want, but you'll have to sleep in Lily's bed."

"Change in front of me," he said. "I want to see you." Drew had never seen me naked before, and he had never asked to see me naked. I guessed that Lily had been right – I didn't want him anymore, so naturally that was when he would decide that he wanted me. He wanted to control every part of me. He didn't want me to be happy, what he wanted was for me to be broken and obedient to him in every way.

"No, I don't want to," I said. "Please just let me change in the bathroom. This isn't what I want."

"I didn't ask you what you want. How fitting that your desires for me should change the moment Lily Andrews is out of the picture. Are you thinking of him now," he asked. "Do you wish that it was him sitting on your bed, and not me?"

I couldn't think of anything to say. I just stood there as his eyes fell upon me in a way they never had before.

"Take your clothes off," he said, and then the tears fell. I didn't even have this much control over myself. He owned every part of me. What I said or wanted no longer mattered. I undressed for him, but I cried all the while. He seemed to enjoy that – the sound of me breaking brought him so much joy.

Drew pulled the covers of my canopy bed over him. He motioned for me to lay next to him. Again, I did as I was told. He held me for a while. He asked me about Lucas, and about Narc. He wanted to know how it made me feel when another man touched me. He wanted me to give details about the times I had kissed Lucas, and I did, but it was hard. He touched me as I spoke. He shushed me as I cried, and I wanted him to leave so badly. I begged him to go. I told him that this wasn't what I wanted, and he ignored me. He kissed my hair, and whispered to me that he was sorry. I knew that he wasn't.

He placed his hand on my thigh and moved it towards the space between my legs. I jumped up and grabbed the sheets from the bed, wrapping them tightly around me. My quick thinking might just save me from him for the moment.

"What are you doing, Mina. You wouldn't want to upset me now, my love. Come back to bed."

"Wait," I said. "There's something I have to show you. I just thought of it now, but my brother gave it to me when he was here visiting." I dropped down to my knees in front of my dresser and rummaged through the drawers, searching for the silver pocket watch that had once belonged to my father, Ernest Culvert. My heart was racing, as if finding the stupid trinket depended on whether or not it would continue to beat.

My body relaxed as my hand gripped the engraved silver and embedded white sapphires.

"Did you know that this was my father's?" I walked towards the bed, holding the watch out towards him.

"Where did that come from?" he asked. "That watch was destroyed, I destroyed it myself so he had no way of ever reaching out to you." He held the watch in his hand. "It's fake," Drew said sounding so convinced of this fact. "He must have made a duplicate. That man thought he was so clever, but no one is as clever as Drew Elliot."

"I don't think it's fake," I said taking the watch from him and running my fingers along the jewels. "See, these are definitely real, but it doesn't matter, it's broken."

"I should leave," Drew said. "Keep that thing away from me." He jumped up from the bed and felt his own pockets, they looked empty. I imagined that he'd left the gold watch with green jewels in the lighthouse. He stormed out of the room, and didn't return that night.

I put on my pajamas, but I kept the watch with me as I lay in my bed. I sighed in relief and I held it in my hands. I wished that it did work, but it had saved me from a fate worse than death. I opened the watch and flicked its face with my index finger, trying to make the hands turn, but they wouldn't. I pressed my lips to its face as a gesture of thanks. And then a faded image of my father appeared beside me. He looked just as he had in the photo that Paris had, and those same gray eyes stared out at me.

"Mina, are you there?" The faded memory of my father was speaking to me.

"I'm here," I whispered. "Can't you see me?"

"No, my dear, I'm afraid I cannot. But I can hear the sound of your voice. I'm here now, and that must mean that Drew has found you, as I knew he would. I'm sorry that you must suffer the consequences of my mistakes."

"How did you know?" I said.

"That watch was given a memory that I created for it. It was told to present itself to you when you began to fear that Drew would end your life. I know what he's told you, Mina. And everything he's ever said has been a lie. I want to show you what really passed between Drew Elliot and me, and how he murdered me and so many others. You must protect yourself against him, in any way that you can."

The flickering image of the man my father had once been walked towards me. He took my hand and led me across the room. Before, we were standing in my dorm room and now we stood in the scene from the photo that Paris had.

My father and I stood in a meadow filled with dandelions. A stone cottage was visible in the distance, covered with vines. He led me to the window of the hidden home, and we both watched as the *real* him, my actual father stood inside in front of a group of young students who sat at a small wooden desks. Ernest Culvert stood near the doorway, teaching the little ones.

"You don't have to be bad, to be a Logost," my real father said to the children. "We all choose our own paths, and by learning to control your anger and fear you won't ever kill anyone. Harness your feelings of right and wrong. Power is not then end all, be all in this life."

"You were a teacher?" I asked the fading image.

"I was. And despite Drew's conviction that I was a dark man, with a dark soul, I was a good Logost, one of a kind, and very powerful. He fakes his nervousness – it's an act to keep his true intentions hidden. And I don't fault you for buying in to his charming and erratic ways – I believed them as well. I took him under my wing as an apprentice teacher. He convinced me that he wanted to be a good Logost, and to help me in my journey of building a community where good Logosts could live together in peace. But it was all a lie. Drew wanted me dead, he wanted to steal the watch, and he wanted you all along. You were just a baby at the time, and he was only thirteen years old. I didn't know it then, but he had already killed his own parents and stolen many more innocent lives."

My eyes turned to the dark-haired, green-eyed, innocent looking boy who sat at the front of my father's small class. There he sat, contemplating and plotting the murder of my father.

The image blurred and changed again. The scene was the same, but it was as if many years had passed. An older version of my father stood at the front of the class, facing a new group of children, and a nineteen-year-old Drew stood outside the door of the stone cottage, grinning in dark satisfaction. He flung open the door frightening the children. He threw up his hand and blasted a hole in to my father's chest, flinging him across the stone floor.

"Where is she?" the younger version of Drew said.

"I can't tell you that, Drew," my father said, straining through the pain. "I love her too much to allow you to be with her. Why are you here? The Informants wouldn't let you go."

Drew laughed. "I escaped, you imbecile, not everyone is as thoroughly as incompetent as you are. I know it was you who turned me over to them – you told them I killed my parents."

""I couldn't allow such a grave injustice to go unpunished. I did what I knew was right."

"There is no such thing as right and wrong, there is only power, and those who deny it must be disposed of." Drew said and his evil smile widened. I covered my eyes as he manipulated my father to hang himself, and slaughtered every child in the room. He went after the women and men in the small village, leaving not a single good Logost alive. The scene left me breathless, but when I was able to breathe again I turned to the fading image of my father.

"Why did you stay away from us if you were good? Didn't you realize how desperate we were for you?"

"There was no other way, Mina. There were many good Logosts during that time, and we all had to stay hidden because the Informants wanted us dead. Sophia had a price on my head, and the only way to keep your mother and your brothers safe, was to stay away. I did what I had to protect you all, and it was unbearable for me at times. And as Drew grew and his interest in you persisted, I sensed that I should keep you hidden from him, even though I didn't fear him yet." I watched as the picture widened, and I saw that the expansive meadow was filled with more stone cottages hidden among the trees.

"We have to go back now," the image said. We were jolted back to Winchester and my depressing empty room. "Drew will return," the memory of my father said. "And he will destroy the watch, because he's convinced it is the only thing that can save you from him. You must save the hands and the stones. If you save them, you'll be able to rebuild it. You're a more gifted Logost than I ever was, and I love you Mina. Tell your mother, Paris, and Carter how much I love you all."

And then he was gone.

{28}

I couldn't sleep after that, and I replayed the events of the night over, and over again in my head. My body quivered because I was afraid Drew would come back. I couldn't sleep so I got out of bed, and threw on a raggedy t-shirt and jeans. I knew I wasn't allowed, but I snuck outside of the dorm and tiptoed to the boy's cottage. It was stupid, I know, but I didn't want to be alone and Lucas was the only person who could bring me solace.

I walked as carefully and as quietly as I could manage around the outside of the boy's cottage, searching for the room with Lucas' mind inside it. And it was by some miracle that his room was one with a window.

It was locked, but I used my mind to open the lock from the inside. I opened the window and climbed inside. Lucas was fast asleep in a bed across from the one that had belonged to Elijah. I tried not to wake him. I climbed in to his bed and pulled the covers over myself. I nuzzled myself deep in to the crevice of his body. His hair smelled like gel. I played with it as he slept, and I wished that he was mine, and that I wouldn't ever have to leave this bed. His lips were so full and pink, and I wanted to kiss them. I held my breath as I leaned in to him and pressed my lips, gently to his.

He opened his eyes, blinking to register my face. "Mina," Lucas said his eyes filled with sleep. "What are you doing here?"

"Quiet," I told him, "We don't want anyone to know I'm here. I'm afraid and I couldn't sleep," I said. "I'm sorry to disturb you, but you're the only person who makes me feel safe. I'm sorry," I whispered, and recited the events of that evening. I told him things I hadn't before – about my father and Paris, and how I had once tried to be intimate with Drew, but after tonight I regretted it.

"You haven't done anything wrong Mina," he said. "You loved him, and you trusted him. I'm sorry you did, but you can't blame yourself, this was his plan all along."

"If I were more like you I would have been able to see through him. I just wish I wouldn't have been so trusting of him in the beginning. I really thought I loved him."

"Being more like me wouldn't have changed anything. There's no time for regrets, we just have to figure out a way to move forward. I'm glad you came here," he said moving closer to me. He wrapped his arm around my waist, and I let him touch me. I wanted to touch him too, but I was afraid of his reaction.

"You're too good to me," I said. "You're so beautiful." And I reached out my hand to touch his face. "I love you," I blurted out without thinking of the meaning behind my words, but it was true I did love him. I just knew that I shouldn't, and couldn't love him for various reasons. "I'm the worst friend in the world. You should just kill me now so I can't hurt myself or anyone else ever again."

He laughed and pulled me close. He stared in to my eyes and kissed me like he couldn't stand ever being without me. I felt dizzy from the passion between us.

"I wish you were mine," I said.

"I love you too," he exhaled. "We'll figure this out, I promise. And we'll figure out a way to deal with Mr. Elliot so that he can't hurt you again. I won't let him, Mina. I'll keep you safe from him."

Lucas held me and kissed my face until I feel asleep. I didn't think anything could ever feel so perfect and so unreal all at once. But I felt guilty, and I knew what we were doing would only hurt Lily. I would have to tell her the truth once she returned, which I hoped would be soon. I missed her terribly.

***

The next day, I was so tired it was hard for me to breathe as I stood in the line of gifted students, preparing to showcase our talents to Sophia, Narc, and the other teachers. Frizz stood in front of me smelling of presumption. She felt that this would be too easy. I smirked a little, knowing she was vastly underestimating the situation, but I respected her confidence.

The demonstration was housed in the school's auditorium. I didn't know how I would be able to control the elements in this space. But I prayed for strength and I called out to my father, but there was no response. He had moved on, and I would have to do this alone.

I watched as Frizz took her first step on to the stage. At the front of the stage stood several glass objects that increased with size as my eyes traveled down the line. The first item was a small glass pitcher, which Frizz shattered without blinking. The next item was a large vase and though Frizz was visibly strained, it too shattered with quickness. Next, she broke a 3 feet tall glass container, then moved on to a small class table.

At the very end of the line of objects was a large mirror pane. Frizz closed her eyes, and all I could think about was how the shards of glass would cut everyone in the audience. The glass cracked at the base of the pane, and the fissures traveled along the center. After several moments, Frizz looked defeated, but the glass shattered and fell in to sand as it blew in to the audience. Everyone clapped, and she exited the stage. After seeing how well she'd planned her demonstration, I felt like an idiot. Why hadn't I thought this through more? I stood there cursing at myself for my lack of preparation.

When it was my turn, I sucked in a deep breath and pictured a successful outcome in my mind. If I wanted it badly enough I would have my wish. I grabbed a paper cup from the fountain backstage, and filled it with water that I didn't plan on drinking. I got back in line, and when Whorton called my name it took a lot of convincing to get my feet to move.

I walked on to the stage, and I couldn't see anything because of the blinding lights. It took me a while to focus my eyes, and the silence of everyone watching and waiting increased my body temperature by at least four degrees. I threw the water from the cup in to the air and froze each droplet before it fell to the ground. I focused on levitating the icicles, then I melted and evaporated all of the water. I created small puffs of clouds, and moved them slowly above the students and teachers sitting in the auditorium.

I blew a wave of fire to scare everyone, and I let the rain from the small clouds extinguish it. My eyes went black and I could no longer see, but I flew a few feet above the stage and created a strong wind tunnel that circled me and pulled in the broken glass, sand, and all the other debris from the stage. The wind and dirt blew all around me and I produced clouds of lighting on stage. I asked the Earth to quiver – just enough so that everyone could feel it. I heard several gasps and that was when I knew I had done enough. My feet fell to the ground and I ran off stage. I heard everyone clapping, and when I walked towards the stairwell Narc bumped in to me.

"How fascinating." Narc pushed himself against me.

"I better go sit down." I tried to walk away, but he held me in place.

"The decision has been made. You will not be killed for the death of Cassandra, but you will be punished, and you will come with Sophia and I back to the Netherlands. This school is no place for a Logost of your caliber, and Sophia agrees."

"Don't I get a choice?"

Narc plainly stated that I didn't. Sophia walked up to us as we stood in the stage stairwell. Her hair was braided on both sides and done up in a large bun in the back. She wore a black pencil skirt and black collared shirt.

She grabbed me by the hand without looking at me. "Mina, we must leave while everyone is distracted," Sophia said. "Narc, kill everyone here – they are no use to us. Mina and I will meet you at home." She pulled me along with her.

"Wait!" I shouted getting her to stop for a moment. "What about Lucas? You wouldn't want him to die, would you?"

She thought for a moment. "It will be fine," she said. "His mother can't stand him anyway."

She pulled me along her side. I called to Lucas – I told him to get out of the school before Narc killed everyone. Sophia and I ran down the hall, past several dark classrooms when she let go of my hand. I turned to see her being jolted backward. Her body slammed in to the floor and slid down the hallway.

Drew stood before me, smiling. He grabbed me and pulled me under his arm. He flung Sophia's body back and forth, like a ball in a pinball machine. I could hear a humming noise burning my ears, and I watched as the waves of sound Sophia created inched closer and closer. There was a blasting noise, and it felt like my head was going to explode. Drew stood there, unaffected by the sound.

The hall floor split and cracked down the middle, leading to where Sophia stood, and she flew in to the air. She flung darts of fire toward Drew, and he dodged each one. Drew's eyes turned light and Sophia wrapped her tiny wrinkled hands around her throat and dropped to her knees, gasping for air.

When Narc appeared, Drew was no longer standing beside me. His body crashed in to the ceiling above, then slammed to the floor below. He was motionless as he lay there, and a tornado of fire shot towards us. I blew the flames away from us, and ran for the closest exit. If they were all going to kill one another I saw no reason for me to stay behind. I spotted Whorton running from the auditorium. She shut and locked the auditorium door with her mind, finally proving to me that she did care whether her students lived or died.

Whorton disabled Narc and crashed his skull on the ground. He jumped back, dodging her mental blows. Drew stood up, winked at me, and went after Sophia. He was distracted enough that he wouldn't notice my escape. I could sense Lucas standing outside the building's entrance. We could leave this place together. I ran for the door, but my pace became slower and slower as it became harder for me to breathe.

I stared down at the star filled stone hanging around my neck, which Drew had given me. Wearing the stone had become a bad habit, and I'd put it on that morning without thinking. The string it was tied to burned my neck as I moved closer to the door. I reached out my hand grasping for the handle, and the stone became heavy as it weighed me down to the floor and choked me. The image of Drew and Whorton battling Sophia and Narc slipped away, and my vision tunneled out until I saw nothing.

{29}

Heaven floated through my mind. And I was sure I was dead when I woke and saw a bright light shining above me. My eyes darted back and forth, trying to make sense of my surroundings. For a moment, I thought I was in hell, but when I saw Lily standing over me, I knew I wasn't. She was far too good for hell.

"Thank God," she said to me. "I was worried you might not wake up. Ms. Whorton told me that you were fine, and to just make sure you didn't try to leave when you woke."

"What happened to me?" I started to get out of bed.

"Don't," she shouted. I tried to stand up, but my legs gave out and I fell back in to my sheets. My head felt like it had been split, it was throbbing so hard.

"Mr. Elliot happened to you," Lily said. I reached for the stone that usually hung around my neck. "Whorton destroyed it. She stopped it from choking you, and she sent Mr. Elliot away from the school."

"She saved me?" What on this earth could possess Whorton to save my life? Maybe the near death experience had changed the woman frozen in stone. "What about Narc and Sophia?"

"They were no match for Mr. Elliot and Ms. Whorton. Sophia set the school on fire, but Wilma stopped her. They left in a hurry, but they'll be back, and they won't be alone. They'll return with their followers and anyone stupid enough to stay here will die."

"Did Whorton give a time frame?"

"She said five days at the least. They won't come if they think there's a chance they'll lose. They'll wait until they've regained their strength. I came back once I sensed Narc was near death – Mr. Elliot almost killed him. But by the time I got here, they were all already gone. All I saw was Whorton shouting at Mr. Elliot for trying to kill you. I'm sorry Mina," she said. "Lucas told me what he did. What are you going to do?"

"I'm leaving." I said. "What else did Lucas tell you?"

"He told me you climbed in to his bed last night, and I must say that was very out of character for you. I thought you loved me, Mina?"

"I do, Lily. I was scared, and I love Lucas still. I'm sorry, but it's true. I don't think that will ever change. What can we do?" I asked her, staring at the ceiling. I was too afraid to meet her gaze. "I don't want to fight over him. If you want me to stay away from him, I will."

"You don't have to stay away from him," Lily said. "I hate to admit to this, but I'm not sure I ever really loved Lucas. I'm selfish, Mina, I know you think I'm so amazing, but I'm not. I told Lucas we were best as friends because I realized I didn't love him. I have a tendency to trick my mind in to believing something's true. When he was preoccupied with thoughts about you, I thought I loved him. But when Lucas finally wanted me, I didn't want him anymore." Lily backed away from me and sat on the edge of her bed, facing away from me.

"Are you sure that's what this is about? Or is this about your intimacy issues?"

"It isn't that," she said. "It was just, when I finally kissed Lucas, I knew. I knew I'd been fooling myself. I don't think I ever really loved him. I just didn't like all the attention he was giving you." She stood up from her bed, moving closer towards me. "Do you hate me?"

"Yes," I said, turning away from her. "No," I laughed, turning back towards her. "As long as you don't care about the two of us I suppose it doesn't really matter."

Lily told me I needed to rest, but there wasn't time for sleep and I didn't feel capable. My mind wouldn't let me sleep. Every time I closed my eyes, I pictured Drew standing at the foot of my bed – his eyes a light green with golden crescent moons swirling around his irises. Nothing could keep him from me, not even Whorton. I couldn't stay here another day. At nightfall, I would have to leave, there was no other choice, and I hoped that Lucas would come with me.

"When are you leaving?" I asked Lily.

"As soon as you're gone, I'm out of here. I have no reason to stay, and I don't want to be here when Narc returns."

"I can't sleep Lily," I groaned. "I have to go see Lucas. I'm worried Drew's going to kill him, or come here and kill me before I get a chance to tell him how much he means to me."

"Just wait. Whorton promised you'd be safe."

"Wilma Whorton has underestimated Drew Elliot since the day she met him, and so have I. But I won't any longer. He's a psycho. I can't stay here."

I showered, dressed, and searched through all of my things for the smallest bag I owned. I threw the essentials inside, which included my father's watch and the shattered star filled stone. I don't why, but I couldn't part with it. I needed to keep it, although I never planned to wear it again. It served as a reminder of how underestimating someone's true intentions can go horribly awry.

When the sun set, I snuck out of the girl's dorm, and I could feel the Earth breathing, warning me of a sudden storm's imminence. The feeling wasn't difficult to place, but it made the inevitable that much graver in my mind. I tiptoed to the window that opened to Lucas' room. I slid up the seal, climbed inside, and saw him standing there waiting for me.

"You're leaving, aren't you?" he asked.

"Yes. When are you leaving?"

"Tomorrow night, my sisters will be here to take me home. I don't want to go, but I know I'll be safest with them."

"You could leave with me if you wanted. But I don't want you to feel obligated to say yes. I want you with me, but this will be difficult. We don't have anywhere to go, and we don't have a plan. And you know that Drew will always search for me, he won't ever stop."

"What about Lily?"

"Lily wants to go home. She wants to enroll in a college near her parents and be a veterinarian."

"I can't let you leave without me," he said. "If you go now, I'll be sick worrying over where you are and if you're alive. None of that other stuff matters," he said pulling me towards him. "I love you, and I won't forsake you. You've become everything to me. I just pray that you won't ever go back to him, and that the hold he has over you has finally been lifted."

"It has been, he killed my father, and he tried to kill me. I won't ever want him again. And I'm ashamed of myself for ever believing that I did. I'm sorry for choosing him over you; it was a mistake all along. I was just afraid. I still am."

"You don't have to be afraid. We'll get out of here, and we'll protect one another. Just promise me that it will always be me. I can't stand the thought of losing you again, Mina. Tell me that you'll stay with me. I want to be your home."

"You are my home," I told him and pressed my lips to his. He cupped my face in his hands and peered in to my soul. It was as if he was searching for something. I hoped that whatever it was he could see it there. I wanted to keep him, forever. He was so beautiful, so sad, so awkward and lovable. Yes, Lucas Ramos was easy to love, and

I wished for it to always be this way, but just a lot simpler as the years passed. I wouldn't ever find another like him.

"You really want all of me – the bad stuff too and the parts of me that might make you sad?"

"All of it. I wouldn't have it any other way. You wouldn't be Mina without the sad and the bad, your sadness and your arrogance makes you beautiful to me. You are perfect in my eyes. Even when you were going off the deep end, I still obsessed about you. About your thoughts, your wishes, and wants."

He smiled ruthlessly and fell in to me, softly pushing me on to his bed. He kissed me for what felt like days and we lay there for centuries as the world faded and disappeared in to the distance. Being with him felt like I was finally home. I wanted him to want all of me the way that I wanted him. I grasped his neck and pulled him further in to me.

I told him he was the most beautiful and genuine person I had ever met, and that I didn't ever want that to change. I asked him to love me forever, and he promised that he would.

There was a thickness in the air and I could see true happiness on the horizon. I wanted it so bad that I could taste it, and if being a Logost had led me to Lucas than I didn't regret who I was, or who I was meant to me anymore. I didn't want to be the hero any longer – I had done enough daring deeds to last a century.

I reached my hands under his plain, white t-shirt and ran my finger softly along the panes of his chest. He looked down at me in anxiousness. I wrapped my legs around him and placed both hands on the top of his waist. He leaned down, kissed me and rolled over on to his side, propping himself up on to his forearm to look at me.

"What are you doing, Mina?" Lucas stroked my face.

"Trying to seduce you," I whispered feeling shy and uncomfortable. "Is it working?"

"Yes," he said and leaned in to kiss me. He rolled over on top of me and kissed the side of my neck. I pulled his shirt off, and he touched the top of my thighs with both hands, and it felt like the room was shaking, and it was. Everything in the room swayed and there was a cracking, a creaking, and a shattering all at once as the Earth quaked. All fell silent – the noiselessness was eerie, out of place and the sound was lonely, filled with grief.

The cold, night air cut in to my skin as the roof of Lucas' dorm room was blown away. My eyes turned towards the sky. It was then that I saw him there, hovering above the cottage, wringing his hands.

"*Mina,*" Drew thought. "*Why have you forsaken me? This isn't what you want, you want only me. You're confused, my love. I promise to be good. Please come back to me.*"

I could hear the damning jealousy and hatred hidden in his words. I looked up and I stared in to Drew's eyes, and then it felt like I wasn't there anymore. A feeling of vulnerability gripped my throat and filled my lungs with iciness. I couldn't move, but I could still see.

And I watched as Lucas flew in to the sky, aiming for Drew. But Drew flung Lucas' body in to the cottage. He pulled him up again to face him, and Lucas hung there like a despondent puppet. Drew shot rounded flames of fire at him, and even though Lucas was barely conscious he deflected each one. Then Lucas' body jolted up and crashed through the school. I screamed, but no words came out.

My voice was gone.

The silver pocket watch inside my bag levitated towards me, but Drew sensed what I was doing. The watch rose from my bag and shattered in to tiny pieces. They looked like tiny specks of silver sparkles as they floated in to the air, but I heard a thud as the stones fell to the hardwood floor.

Drew floated towards me, boring his eyes through my bones. It felt like my skeleton would rip out from my flesh, separating me forever. A shimmering golden crescent flowed out from his eyes, and hooked on to the inside of my chest. My body floated towards Drew. He pulled me close, and said that I had betrayed him. He said that I'd hurt him more than anyone ever had. He wouldn't reason with me as he took me to his lighthouse and across the dark water of the Mediterranean Sea.

"I can't believe you let him touch you. This isn't right, Mina. You know that you belong with me, you belong to me."

"Don't do this, Drew. I don't love you. I don't want you. You tried to kill me! Please just take me back. I just want to go home. You're scaring me," I said, knowing that I would never see any of my friends or family ever again. He wouldn't ever let me escape him.

"You love me, I know it! You're confused, my love. You love me still, I know that you do. He's muddled your thinking, but I know you want me. I know what's best for you. No one's going to hurt you! Stop crying!" he screamed, but there was no way that I could stop crying.

I tried closing my eyes so that I wouldn't have to see him, but he wouldn't allow it. He made me look him in the eyes, and forced me to tell him that I loved him. He wanted to hurt me, I could hear it in the tone of his voice, see it in his eyes. He wanted to make me feel worthless, and he did. He cradled me in his arms whispering dark things in my ear – telling lies that only he believed. He said that I would understand why he had to do this, and why the plan simply didn't work with me being alive and not being with him. He told me that he loved me, and I knew that it wasn't true. Drew Elliot didn't love me. He didn't even love himself.

Drew took me to the lighthouse and he raped me that night. When it happened, I didn't know that it was rape. I thought that rape was a stranger in the night with a knife, and the possibility of death. I felt that possibility of death. All the while, I worried that he might kill me. But I had trusted Drew, had loved him, and had once believed that he wouldn't ever hurt me. He knew everything about me, so my brain couldn't comprehend that this was how a man raped a girl. But he put all of his weight on top of me and pinned my hands down so that I couldn't move.

He ignored my screams, ignored the tears, and he wouldn't let me escape.

He seemed to like the sound of my pleading, the sound of me breaking and shattering in his arms comforted him, as he comforted me from the pain he was causing. I couldn't stop the tears from falling, the screams from escaping my lips, and he shushed me and consoled me as he stole everything from me. I numbed myself, and pretended that I wasn't there.

I'd never felt so powerless in that moment, and I knew that I wouldn't ever feel safe again. He told me how beautiful I was, insulting me further as he apologized for making me cry, but not for raping me. I tried to fight him but I couldn't, and there was no one to save me. I couldn't even save myself. I was so afraid of him – afraid that he would hurt me more, no matter what I said or did. There was no one who knew where to find me and I screamed out in vain, he wouldn't stop hurting me.

He wouldn't stop hurting himself.

{30}

I was still alive, but it felt like I died during the night. It all seemed hopeless after that. And I wished I'd never met Drew. I wished that I'd never been curious about the beautiful man who believed he loved me, but who would always hurt me. I blamed myself for trusting him, for loving him, and letting him in. I wanted to escape this fate, I didn't want to be his doll, but that was how I felt – like a doll that he manipulated and played with, whenever he wanted.

He left me broken. He destroyed my will and those had been his intentions all along. He didn't want me to ever have a choice, and I didn't. He owned every part of me. I said no, and the words meant nothing. I didn't even have control over my own body. I believed that Lucas was dead. I tried calling out to him, but that only infuriated Drew further. He hurt me so much, and I believed that was what he wanted, for me to be powerless to him.

It was an act of power, and he wanted me to be afraid of him, and I was. I blamed myself for all of it. I was so ashamed, so embarrassed. And I believed it was my fault, and not his. But it was his fault, and he had planned all of this. He knew that raping me was what it would take to keep me there, and that I couldn't leave, because I was scared he would do it again.

When he finished, he wouldn't look at me. He stood up from the molding mattress he'd raped me on, and dressed himself, keeping his back turned to me. And I was glad. I couldn't stand to look at him. I shut my eyes and rolled over trying to convince myself that nothing had happened. I wanted to melt away so that no one ever had to look at me again.

"I know that I've hurt you," Drew said. "But I promise not to do it again. Know that I am not the one to blame for this. You only have yourself to blame for trying to leave me, and for making me so jealous. I have to go," he said, and he leaned down to kiss me. "You cannot leave here, Mina. Do not try or you will be killed. Do not try to save him. I know you're upset with me, but I promise that this is what's best for us, my love. You owe me all of you, each and every part – do not forget that. This is only the beginning," he whispered and kissed my forehead.

Drew left and I lay there afraid of his return. I had to go back to Winchester, but my body shook with fear and torment. Drew had tortured me, and my mind quaked with fear. He had finally broken me, just as he wanted. Everything made sense now, and I replayed all that had happened since the first day I saw him. It had all been a trap, and I'd fallen right in and given him all of me, told him everything about me that he needed to know to keep me pacified. I knew that I couldn't kill him, but I needed the watch to figure out what to do. If I could get the stones and the hands, I could rebuild it, and maybe then I would figure out how to put an end to the evil, unfeeling, and dark man that was Drew Elliot.

Risking my own life didn't matter anymore. I shot up through the top of the lighthouse, breaking through the rotted wood. I lit the house on fire, and I watched for a moment, as it burned. The sight brought me some solace, but not nearly enough. I flew above the sea heading for Mount Blanc, but I could hear the water calling me, begging me to retreat.

The sea turned angry and vicious and the waves climbed higher, and higher, the further I flew, trying to escape its storm. I darted right, and the waves mirrored my movements shooting up in front of me, blocking my passage. The water sensed my every move, and outsmarted me each time.

Lighting broke across the water and the waves rolled deeper, as they sought to drown me so I could never leave the lighthouse. The waves formed in to the hollow face of the man I despised, and they attacked and enveloped me. I fought, but I sunk deep below the water's surface. My limbs grew heavy as I flailed them about, trying to reach the surface, but the water pinned me down and filled my lungs. It was sad about it, but it had to do what Drew had manipulated it to do. The sea was powerless to him, just as I was. But then I remembered who I was, and all that I could do. Drew had tried stealing all of it from me, but some parts were still there. I remembered the day I separated the Hudson River to see the boulders at the river's bed. I pushed, and pulled the water away from me until a narrow space existed, where the water couldn't flow. Not a drop touched me, and I flew above the ocean floor. I flew out and headed for the school. I wanted to save Lucas, but I knew that if I failed I had no chance to ever recover the pieces of the broken pocket watch.

My eyes were dark, casks of emptiness from numbing myself throughout the night. I kept a wind tunnel around me, and clouds of lighting above me for protection. I dropped to the cottage floor through the opening in the roof, and gathered the stones from the watch. Then I went searching for Lucas and Drew. I sensed that I wasn't too late, but I couldn't place Lucas anywhere near the school. There was a swarm of chaos, a hazy white fog, above the main building of the school. I landed and flung open the doors, keeping the wind tunnel and lightning clouds close. My feet hovered above the hall floor as I used my mind to search the school.

Everyone was gone, Winchester was deserted. I sensed Whorton and Drew in her office, and when I walked in my defenses evaporated. My eyes fell upon Lily's lifeless body. Her head was twisted. She lay on the ground standing between Whorton and Drew. I was in so much shock I couldn't cry, I couldn't even remember what sadness felt like anymore. It was like I was watching everything from above, and my spirit no longer dwelled within my body. I kneeled beside her in disbelief, cradling her head in my lap. She was cold, and her skin was no longer vibrant. I touched her cheek.

Out of the corner of my eye, I saw Drew move towards me

and I shot him in to Whorton's bookcase.

"You did this." I said my voice a robotic, monotone. "Where's Lucas?" I asked. Whorton was the one to answer.

"He's gone," she said. "His sisters came for him. Drew tried to kill him, and when he couldn't, he went after Lily. She ran here to escape him, but he killed her Mina."

"She's lying," Drew said. "I promised I wouldn't hurt you again, my love. Why would I murder someone you love?" He kneeled beside me, grabbing my face and forcing me to look in to his eyes. "Whorton did this, Mina. She's always hated you. She wanted you dead, she can't be trusted." I stared at him, and all that I could see were the golden swirls inside those dark, green irises he used to force my will.

"Please, Mina," Whorton said. "What has he done to you?" She cried as she took in my emotionless expression. "Believe me, Mina. Drew cannot be trusted."

I paused, forcing myself to think clearly. But everything was cloudy, and I only saw the golden orbs that obstructed my vision.

"You're lying," I said, staring down at what had once been Lily. And I threw Whorton's body across her office. I walked over to her and choked her with my mind. I watched her reach for her throat. Her death was slow and painful, and when her life was over, Drew walked towards me. He took me by the hand and he kissed me. I felt cold, but nothing mattered anymore.

I couldn't see past his powers of manipulation.

"You can't ever leave me," he said. "You know that it has to be this way. If you do as I say I won't hurt you again and you won't ever have to fear me. You still love that boy, I know, but he won't want you now. You're ruined, Mina," he whispered. "And Lucas will never want you again."

I stepped back, trying to break free of his control, but he wouldn't let my eyes go as he bared the weight of his power upon me. I wasn't Mina anymore.

"Don't fight this," Drew said. "You'll only make it worse. I am sorry that I can't give you up. But its better this way, my love, trust me."

I left Winchester for good that day as I stood behind Drew. His domination over me was unquestionable, and he would torture me when I tried to resist him. He led the way in to the city, and he and I destroyed the town of Chamonix. I sent unbearable surges of wind and rain through the city. Drew uprooted the roads, flinging cars in to the tiny shops. With every step we took, the tiny chateaus and shops exploded in to the atmosphere.

And we crumbled the bridges and asked the river to rise up, and leave the town flooded. Drew had known all along that it would be this way. He had wanted this for so long, to become a whirlwind of destruction with me by his side. Without me, Drew Elliot wouldn't have been able to flatten a city in a little over an hour. I was worse than a natural disaster, and I killed and destroyed everything at Drew's command. I was his now, his wish had finally come true.

He pulled me close to him as we walked through Chamonix to whisper in my ear. "This is only the beginning, my love," he said again. "This is the beginning of so many great things to come." But for me it felt like the end of my world. I watched it crumble and shatter before me until I could no longer see, until I could no longer care about not seeing. We left France to embark on a killing spree that spanned across Europe. I couldn't leave, and the killing made it hard for me to remember that I had ever wanted to.

{31}

D rew and I sat in silence in a metro station in the London East End, in the middle of the afternoon. The sky was cloudy and fog rose from the ground like steam from boiling water. People buzzed about, making their way to their trains, completely unaware of the power that sat on the red wooden bench. I still had on my tattered and stained school uniform, and Drew wore a gray suit just as he always did. The days all blended together and I was unconscious, an inanimate object that Drew controlled at will.

I stared across the station without any train of thought. Drew noticed my lifeless gaze, and the fact that I rarely spoke, but he ignored it. He acted as if nothing had ever changed – that he hadn't tried to kill me, raped me, and had me kill Whorton. Drew's presence haunted me. I shuddered at his touch and jumped whenever he called my name. I listened to the sound of my heart beat, wanting the sound to comfort me. It didn't. Nothing could wake me from this tormenting dream.

Drew pretended to read the paper, and I focused on keeping

a shield of protection around us. Days before, Narc had tried to stop Drew's heart from beating. Drew dropped to the sidewalk, gripping his chest, and called out to me, begging me to save him, but I only watched and waited for his death to release me. But Drew was stronger than Narc – he shut him out, but he kept me with him always after that.

The Informants had been searching for us since we left Winchester, and through all the destruction, and mass murders we hadn't been difficult to place. But Drew kept us on the move and they hadn't managed to catch up with us. He swelled with pleasure and excitement, and held me close – restraining me with what he believed was true love. He'd taken my soul away, believing that I could somehow function without it. And I was functioning, but only through his control.

We stole whatever we needed, and only traveled in the dark of night. Today was different though. I didn't know what the plan was, and I didn't want to know. Drew was vague about the path we followed, he didn't trust me anymore.

Across the platform, stood a tiny girl with her mother and father. She pestered them with numerous questions about the train and their intended destination. I stared at her, and she looked back at me. I saw my reflection in her eyes and I looked like a ghastly, porcelain doll. I was the thinnest I had ever been, dark circles surrounded my eyes, and purple bruises colored my neck and collarbone. My skin was pale, fragile looking, and my eyes were sallow, my cheeks sunken in.

My appearance probably frightened her. The little girl's mother pulled her away so that she wouldn't stare at me anymore. I watched the tracks as their train pulled up. Drew didn't lift his head from the paper to speak to me. "Now," he said. And I lifted the moving train off the rails, and flung it in to the crowd of people, waiting on the platforms. The little girl and her parents would never arrive at their destination, and my heart shrunk with power.

Drew blasted a hole through the top of the station, and we soared into the sky, hovering above the city. He pulled me close, and took my hand, kissing it as he stared in to my eyes.

"I love you," he whispered. "You're so beautiful," he lied. I'd begged him to take us to the States, but he worried that I would be able to escape him there.

We had been through Italy, killing at least 10 dozen citizens. Then, we flew to Germany, blowing up several schools and shopping centers. Drew didn't care who we killed as long as many lost their lives. He wanted the bloodshed. He wanted other Logosts to hear of the destruction, and to whisper in terror of a nameless fear. Most didn't know who was killing, but their instincts would tell them that it was a Logost. They would suspect each other, and once they were too scared to trust one another we would emerge from hiding and gain their trust.

We took off once more, flying across the Atlantic and headed towards Ireland. I didn't know why we were leaving England, but I knew better than to ask. I always stayed quiet, and Drew began to occupy the space inside my mind. My own thoughts were lost inside, and I only ever heard Drew's inner voice and the directions he gave me.

The thoughts I had about killing him were subsided, Drew forced them out of my subconscious. I never thought of Lucas, Drew wouldn't allow it. One night as he slept, I tried to escape, but he tortured me and forced me back. I didn't try again, and if the thought crossed my mind, Drew sent waves of pain through every cell in my body.

The sun had set hours before, and the sky was dark. I couldn't see the moon. Drew dropped to a street inside a tiny Irish village, and I followed. Fear permeated the muggy air. There were few streetlights, and it seemed darker because of the overcast of clouds. The starless sky hung in the background. In the distance, there were rolling hills and plains of green. There were white picket fences around some of the homes, and a lake behind them. I stared across the water, and used my mind to peer inside of several small houses. Drew told me to stay quiet, and we walked until I sensed the presence of another Logost. Drew moved us closer to that presence.

We waited outside a two-story house in the dark of night in an ordinary neighborhood. The houses were small and nestled closely together. They were all the same color – white with brown trim, except this one, it had been painted a bright red. Drew told me to get down, and he watched the family who lived inside the home through the back window. I had no inclination to know why we were there, but inside I knew. I knew that we were there to kill, or capture and torture. I just hoped we wouldn't kill any children.

"Make it storm," Drew told me, and I did.

Lightning struck the car that was parked outside the red house we were watching, and the security alarm sounded.

"You're absolutely useless. Can't you see I want our presence to go unnoticed?" I said nothing, and turned my head away from him. "Follow my lead," he said.

We crashed down the door to the house, sending a blast of energy that shattered the windows. A boy and a girl sat on a blue couch in front of a wide television screen, playing videogames. They jumped up, staring at us. They looked at me, and Drew told me to kill them, but I couldn't. I just stood there motionless. He started to choke the boy. Their mother and father ran out of the kitchen. Our sudden entrance startled them, and the father rushed towards us.

He took one look at me and Drew, "Who the hell are you?" the man said. "Get out of my house," he shouted and I could feel his powers of manipulation overtake me, but Drew was unaffected. Drew laughed in his throat, lifted the man's feet off the floor and broke his neck. I heard it snap and the children screamed. The woman in the kitchen shot out at us. She knocked Drew back and out of the front door.

"*Kill her*," Drew commanded. And I focused on the woman's heart stopping. She lifted up every object in her home and pelted them at me. She blocked my attack and flung my body in to the wide television screen. She screamed at her children to run, but Drew killed them instantly. He strangled the woman, and she couldn't fight back.

They had all been Logosts, each of them, the entire family. Killing them sent waves of tension through my limbs as my heartache manifested itself physically. We walked back down the road. Drew lit a few of the houses on fire, and hurled cars on to the other homes and unsuspecting families.

"Why did they die?" I asked.

"Don't look so stressed, my love." Drew wrapped his arm around my waist. "They died with reason, they were very powerful Logosts. We're killing off the stragglers so they can't help the Five Leaders," Drew said. "That man was once an Informant, and he and his family had to die. No more questions," he urged. "With time, all secrets will be revealed."

"Can we sleep, please?" I begged him. I had not slept or ate in three days. My body felt like it weighed a thousand pounds. It had been difficult for me to kill that woman, which hadn't happened before.

"You don't need sleep, be patient and we'll rest soon."

"Please, I can't keep killing with this little energy. I need to rest or I'll be no use to you."

"Alright," he crooned. "You always get your way don't you?" he kissed my hair.

"If I always got my way you would be dead," I whispered. I gripped my chest and fell to my knees, my heart raced and sharp pains pulsed inside. Drew stood over me and a nervous smile ran across lips.

"Don't say things like that, my love. I don't like hurting

you," he lied. "Tell me that you love me, and you want to be with me forever, me and only me. Say it," he said and I did as I was told.

He pulled me from the ground and grabbed me to take flight. We flew to a bed and breakfast that was further down the coast. He used false identification cards that said I was his niece and he was my legal guardian. He called me Lauren, and he told me to call him Richard while we stayed there.

The room in the bed and breakfast was cramped, and filled with cheap knick-knacks. A dusty ceiling fan hung above a queen-sized bed, with a floral comforter. I plopped down on the bed, pulling off my shoes. Drew walked to the opposite side and got under the covers. He fell asleep the moment his head touched the pillow, but his eyes stayed wide open.

Drew never shut his eyes when he slept. He would never tell me, but I speculated that if he ever closed them, I would be able to escape. He was always in my head though, searching through my thoughts for ideas of escape or deception, but there were none. I could see no way to save myself from him.

My family probably believed I was dead. A few weeks before, I'd seen a newspaper that read that Winchester Academy, a boarding school in the French Alps, had been burned to the ground and police were baffled by the cause. They believed that it was ill weather that had left the city of Chamonix in pieces. I wanted to call out to Paris, but I didn't dare try. Drew would probably kill him if he found out he was a Logost. I had managed to erase that bit of knowledge and Drew remained clueless. I prayed for it to stay that way.

When I woke the next morning, Drew wasn't sleeping beside me. The bed was empty, but I could still feel him there – his powers kept me subdued.

I walked down the stairs of the bed and breakfast, following the smell of sweet buns, sausage, and eggs. I entered the kitchen and saw Drew sitting at a table with an elderly, American couple. The man was short, fat, and balding with gray hair and brown eyes. His wife was of a similar stature, her short gray hair framed her face, which was filled with age spots.

The couple laughed as Drew made jokes about Ireland, and the local politics. He charmed them, and they believed he was a nice man who had taken in his only sister's daughter. He told them we were traveling through Europe on vacation. I wanted to kill him, and then a sharp pain ached in my chest. My heart fluttered and Drew turned to me, a faint twinkle in his eyes.

"We're leaving," Drew said to me. "Grab your things."

"I'm hungry," I said. "Can't I eat first?"

"No, go now," he said keeping his voice even, keeping up the charade.

"Oh, come on," said the rotund, elderly man. "Let the girl eat something first."

Drew laughed. "Of course," he smiled at me with an utter phoniness, and patted the man on his back.

He let me sit down, and our hostess served me eggs and sausage. When I finished, I walked upstairs to grab my things. I brushed my teeth, combed my hair, and washed my face quickly.

"I'm ready," I said to Drew as I reappeared at the kitchen's entrance.

"It was nice meeting you," he said to the couple. And as we walked out I heard the elderly man's heart stop. His head fell over and landed on his plate. His wife screamed, and we left the bed and breakfast behind. Drew's eyes turned light again, and he became more lethal with each murder.

{32}

My sense of direction wasn't the best, but I knew we were flying south, back towards Europe. Drew wanted us to stop in Greece, he said we had more business to attend to. We landed outside the city, and the town we walked through looked deserted. Mountains of green sprung up in the distance. Dirt trails treaded through hills and along plains. The terrain was rocky and filled with weeds and grass. Clouds rolled through the blue sky like the sails of ships.

There was no one on the roads – the houses and farmland looked empty in the small village. It seemed foolish to travel so close to the Netherlands, and the Informants' underground castle. I wondered if we were here to be captured, but said nothing. We walked along a small dirt road. In the distance, I saw a large building that looked like it housed tiny apartments. We walked towards the building, and a young man emerged. He stared at Drew, then his eyes fell to me. The boy was tall, blonde, and slender. His eyes were a dark brown, almost black.

"No trespassers," the young man said in an American accent.

"We're not trespassers," Drew said. "We've come here seeking your protection. We're on the run, and the Informants are searching for us."

"You're Logosts?" the young man asked, staring only at me. "Both of you? What's wrong with the girl? She looks sick."

"She's tired," Drew said. "We've been traveling for weeks and we need shelter. Where are the others?"

"Inside, the Informants won't find you here. We've built this place in refuge from them. But it isn't safe. Many have been killed from rivalries amongst the other Logosts. You may not wish to stay."

"I'm afraid we don't have a choice," Drew said.

The young man motioned for us to come inside, but I was afraid. The building frightened me. I could feel its pain in the atmosphere. The windows were boarded and it smelled of mold and rotting flesh. The basement must have been housed with their dead. Drew grabbed my arm, but my feet were rooted to the ground.

"Stop this, Mina," he said. "They will all be dead soon, my love. None of them can hurt us. You're stronger than this, what's happened to you?"

Drew knew the answer to his question, so I said nothing. He pulled me along, and the Earth quaked from my fear.

"Look at me," he said. "If you give us away they will kill us. Stop it, now!" he muttered under his breath. I controlled my fear, and took Drew's hand.

Grown men and young children slept in the stairs and

walkways of the overcrowded building. We walked up a congested stairwell, and I stepped on the arm of a bald, toothless man who lay on a top step, snoring. The man looked at me, and the whites of his eyes were yellow. He grabbed my foot and pulled me down the stairs. I screamed and Drew laughed. I lost control, and shocked the man with lightning.

"Stop," the young boy who led us through the house said. "You'll kill him," he shouted. But I couldn't stop and Drew continued to laugh. A group of young men ran up the stairs, one of them knocked me off my feet, and slammed me in to the wall. They ran past us, towards the sound of a woman screaming. The young boy followed, and Drew and I did too.

We walked in to a large, open space on the top floor, and two women were battling. They flung each other's bodies back and forth, trying to kill one another over a few scraps of potato. The men broke up the fight, and the young man led us back up the stairs.

Dust and mold coated the rotting walls, making it hard to breathe. The smell of urine was ever-present, and I had to hold my nose to keep from vomiting. There were cracks in the buildings structure, and the Logosts who dwelled there were frail from hunger. I wanted to leave – I didn't know how long Drew would want us to stay here.

The young man led us to a room at the top of the building. We couldn't walk in, or we would have stepped on the Logosts sleeping on the cement floors. The boy handed us two dingy and worn sleeping bags, and told us to sleep in the far, right corner. My eyes glazed over the space and it was barely big enough to fit me, let alone Drew and me. We stepped over all the women, men, and children, making our way to the small corner we were allowed to claim. I laid out the foul-smelling sleeping bag and sat on the floor.

"I can't sleep here," I said. "I'd rather seek shelter in the woods. The stench is unbearable."

"Mina, please be patient." Drew said. "Once everyone is sleeping, we'll leave. You mustn't be so obvious about everything, my love." He leaned in and kissed my forehead. An older woman sitting with her young daughter shook her head disapprovingly. The young girl had the bluest eyes I'd ever seen. She levitated a rag doll in front of her, animating it for her own entertainment. Drew shouted at the woman to keep her opinions to herself, and I lay my head down, pretending to sleep.

"Search their minds," Drew thought as we lay there. *"See if any of them are worth saving."*

My eyes darted to the young girl who had been animating the doll. She wasn't asleep, and she created small flames in her tiny hand, blowing on them to strengthen the fire.

"Not her," Drew thought. *"We both can control fire. We'll have to kill them all."*

We waited until their bodies were still, and the pace of everyone's breath was slow and steady. It seemed impossible for us to leave without disturbing the Logosts, who encircled our makeshift pallet. But we hovered above them, making our way slowly out of the disease-ridden building.

When we reached the fresh air, Drew told me to place a shield around the building, and set fire to it so no one could escape. The sound of the screams fueled Drew, and it fueled me too. We watched them burn to the ground, and we convinced ourselves that we were better; more powerful, more deserving of life. They had wasted theirs, I reasoned with myself.

Drew turned to leave, but I stood there, staring for a moment longer. Thick, clouds of smoke from the burning flesh entranced me. Drew grabbed my arm, pulling me along, and we walked back up the road. As we walked, we passed six or seven men from a village that was visible in the distance. They left their horses on the road and ran towards the fire, shouting in Greek. We took flight when they could no longer see us.

***

Throughout the night, we flew towards South America, and it was dawn when we landed in Bogota, Colombia, in the heart of the city. Small buildings fell on top of one another in the overcrowded city, everything was packed together. But it was a beautiful city. The antique structures looked filled with history. Lucas loved this country, and growing up here is what had made him so cultured. I tried not to think of him, but it was difficult when I knew that he was so close. I focused on the city, and not on my longing for Lucas, not on my longing for salvation.

If Drew heard me thinking of Lucas, he would hurt me, and I trembled whenever he decided he wanted to touch me. I hadn't dreamed of anything in ages, and the loss of control over my own mind, body, and future wore away every bit of me. I was certain that I was crazy. I'd thought I was going crazy before, but I knew now that if I were ever to be sane again, I would have to work at it.

"Search for him," Drew said. We walked through the crowded streets filled with food carts, shops, and café's. I stared at him in astonishment. "He's keeping me out," he said looking straight ahead. "But he won't keep you out."

"I'm here with you," I said. "What does it matter if he lives? We don't have to kill him. I won't leave you, you know that."

"This isn't about him!" he shouted. "Just do as I say."

I closed my eyes and searched through every mind in the country. I didn't recognize any of them, and I couldn't feel Lucas there. My thoughts were too cloudy – my mind was overcrowded as Drew stood in a corner, taking up more, and more space. I stopped walking and turned to look at him, but I was too afraid to meet his eyes.

"Let me go," I whispered. "If you love me, let me go, please?"

"You know I can't do that, Mina. I need you with me. Your innocence helps keep me sane."

"My innocence is gone," I said looking away from him. "And you'll never be sane." He pulled me close, squeezing the life from my lungs.

"I'm sorry you feel that way," he said. "But I know that you enjoyed it. You wanted me too," he reasoned. "You wanted me to be your first, didn't you?"

"I told you no, you know that wasn't what I wanted. I don't believe that it was even what you wanted. You did it just to hurt me, just to prove that I'm yours and not his. And to prove to me that you control me."

"I don't control you," he said. "But you are mine. Why would I need to prove that? It doesn't matter anyway, what's done is done. I didn't rape you if that's what you're implying. You love me Mina, and you chose me from the beginning. What we did was meant to happen."

"No, I'm not saying that you raped me." I muttered feeling uncertain, still not knowing how to describe what he'd done. "You forced me. I fought you. I cried… I… All I'm saying is that you knew that I didn't want to, and you did it anyway. Nothing that I say matters to you."

"You're just confused, my love. I know more of what you want than you do, I know what's best for you, and that was best for us in that moment. I made the right decision, and there's no need to discuss this any further. Just do as I say and search for him."

"Leave my mind. If you want me to find him, you have to leave for a moment. I can't think with you inside. I don't want you to read my mind anymore."

"I can't," he said, sounding desperate. "If I leave you'll be able to escape me. I can't bare it Mina, not here, this isn't the right place."

"Well, I can't sense him anywhere. When I close my eyes, all I see is you frightening me. You'll have to find him yourself. I can't see him with you inside."

"Don't say that. That's a lie – you know that I don't frighten you. I love you."

But I could see the truth in his eyes. He knew he had raped me, he just didn't want to admit it. He knew that I didn't love him, and he knew that I was terrified of him. He stared at me for some time, then touched his hand to my face.

"You love me too," he said. "I know you do. You've always loved me. Tell me you do," he said and I repeated the lie, but I felt empty and alone.

Drew pulled me along and we got on a bus that was leaving the city. The yellow bus had been spray-painted with words and drawings of sunsets and birds. We walked to the back row to sit. There was only one empty seat, so I slid in with a group of chatty Americans while Drew stood in the aisle. They looked older than me, but still young. I eavesdropped on their conversation and learned that they were college students, traveling through South America on a study abroad trip.

It was hot, and there was no air-conditioning on the bus. The man standing beside Drew smelled like onions rotting in the sun. I turned towards the window, moving my nose away from the awful smell. One of the girls with the chatty Americans turned to look at me. She asked me a question in Spanish, and I just stared out of the window. I didn't speak any Spanish.

"Are you alright?" She asked and I nodded. Her eyes dissected Drew. "You're traveling with that man. Is he your Dad?"

she said and I didn't say anything.

"How old are you?"

"Sixteen."

"Shouldn't you be in school? Summer hasn't started yet. It seems irresponsible to bring a young girl here, when she should be in school. Where are you two headed?"

"I don't know," I said. "He doesn't tell me anything."

She turned to look at Drew and he was watching us with careful eyes, but said nothing. Drew held the girl's eyes, and she turned back to me in bewilderment.

"Are you in some kind of trouble?" she asked. "I can help you, if you need it."

"Mina," Drew shouted. "Come stand with me, you shouldn't talk to strangers."

"I'm not a child," I said.

"She's fine here." The girl slanted her eyes in Drew's direction. "Mina is such a pretty name. My name's Lisa." She leaned in closer so that Drew couldn't hear, not realizing that he could read everything in her mind. "If that man's hurt you in anyway, you need to get away from him. I can help you."

"He has hurt me. But there's no one who can help me. He'll kill you if you try," I breathed.

She looked at me like I was crazy, and I believed that I was crazy. I continued to stare out the window. Drew was getting angry, and I didn't want to make things worse.

"I have to help you," she said. "Your face is haunted. I won't ever forget it. There must be something we can do. If we all helped…" she trailed off and I could hear her heart faltering.

I couldn't let him kill her – she was only trying to save me. I blocked Drew's attack and flung him towards the front of the bus. He sent waves of pain through my body and I screamed in frustration – he was too strong. He walked towards my seat, laughing at my torment. The girl who wanted to help me looked up at him, screamed and punched him in the face, knocking him out.

The bus stopped. She told me to run, but I grabbed her arm so she wasn't left there to die. We pushed past everyone on the bus and got off.

She dropped my arm and turned to look at me. "What are you?" she said.

"You need to go somewhere he can't find you. Do you want me to take you to a hotel?"

"I'm staying with friends. We can't walk back there. I'll have to find a taxi or catch another bus."

"I can take you," I said. "Just tell me where it is."

"It's outside Bogota," she said. "But I'm telling you, we can't walk there."

I ignored her words, and wrapped her arms around my neck. "Don't get scared," I said. "I promise I won't let you fall." I flew us in to the clouds and towards the city. The house she directed me to was close to the city. And it wasn't a house. This was what Lucas described as a villa – it was enormous and made of stucco with black, wrought-iron gates surrounding it. We dropped to the street.

"Have you heard of a woman named Jaclyn Ramos?" I asked, and she told me she'd only been here for a week, and didn't know anyone by that name. I figured as much, but it was worth a shot. I told her to stay inside, and to try her best not to think of me.

"He'll find you if you think of me," I said.

"Wait," she said. "This mailbox," she pointed to one next to the house where she was staying. "It says Jaclyn Ramos. Is she who you're looking for? I don't know her, but I know she has three daughters."

My eyes fell upon the mansion next to the mailbox and I couldn't believe its size – it was wasteful to have a home this size when the city was so overcrowded. The house was a beige stucco color with columns and tan statues all around it. There was a speaker-button on the black gate and pushed it.

"Hola," a man's voice on the other side greeted me.

"Hi. I'm looking for Lucas. I'm a friend from school. Is he home?"

"No visitors," the voice said.

"I have to see him. Tell him Mina's here!"

But there was nothing.

The voice was gone. I wasn't going to give up that easily, and I was distraught. I banged on the gate and screamed in to the microphone, trying to make someone, anyone listen, before Drew found me. I pulled on the gate handles, but still nothing. Lisa tried to get me stop, but I couldn't. No one cared. It felt like I was losing at everything.

{33}

I sat on the ground, my back to the gate, and started to cry. I hadn't cried since the first night Drew raped me, and my sadness finally manifested itself. My anger was uncontrollable. I couldn't catch my breath. I couldn't stop.

My body shook, convulsed and I vomited in the middle of the road. I tried to calm down, and called to Lucas, but he kept me blocked. And then I sensed Drew's erratic presence. I stared up at sky and there he was, getting closer to Lisa and me. The moment I called to Lucas, I knew he would find me.

"Run!" I shouted to Lisa. "Run now!" I said again when she just stood there, staring at me. I saw her head rise towards the sky. "Don't look at him!" I screamed, but she already had. His eyes held her in place and she fell over to die. There was nothing I could do to save her, there was nothing I could do to save myself. I wanted to run, but he held me there. Just because I escaped, didn't mean he'd left my mind. He was still there, taking up even more space. I couldn't think straight, and I forgot why I was there in the first place.

But I could hear something faint. I could hear Lucas calling out to me.

Drew landed in front of Lucas' home and grabbed the collar of my shirt, pulling me from the ground. I knew he would be the death of me. Some way, somehow Drew would eventually kill me, and I wondered how long it would take before I begged him to kill me. He blasted away the surrounding gate, and tried to walk in, but were thrown in to the street. The mansion was surrounded by invisible barriers to keep enemies out. Drew told me to walk through without him while he figured out another way inside. He was certain they wouldn't think to keep me out, but I was sure they would. Lucas knew I was either dead or with Drew. He would have told his sisters.

"They're not so clever," he said. "I'm sure they've left holes. If you can get inside and distract them, they'll lose focus and I'll be able to get in too."

I walked towards the house, without Drew, but the moment I past the destroyed gate I was thrown back in to the street.

"It's you," I told him, getting up from the ground. "His sisters have put up these barriers to keep you out. I can only pass if you leave my mind."

He looked troubled, nervous. I knew he wanted to kill Lucas' mother and his sisters so that no one would be alive to take Sophia's place once she was dead. But he wouldn't be able to end the Informants' reign if he let me go. He was worried that I would forsake Lucas and run. I could see all of it in his eyes as he racked his brain, searching for a way inside.

"You'll leave," he said. "I'm not letting you go, stop trying to convince me. I'm sorry, but you know it has to be this way. Just call to him."

"I've already tried. He thinks I'm you!"

"No, he doesn't think it's me." Drew said, staring up at the enormous home. "It's not him keeping us out. He's given up, it's only his sisters blocking," he said and pulled me to him. "I'll leave your mind, but if you try to flee I will find you, and it will be much worse. Do you understand? Promise to do as I say," he said. "You love me, don't you?" I nodded. "Go. Now."

I walked towards the house again, and this time I passed through. It felt like I was dangling in time once Drew left my mind. It was difficult to process my own thoughts. I was finally able to think of Lucas. The Earth quaked, signaling to Lucas that I was there. Drew screamed in dismay as he felt it. Lucas rushed out the front doors of the house and I ran to him. He looked at me like he didn't recognize me, but he pulled me close. I nuzzled myself in to his shoulder. I wanted everything to fade away. I wanted to forget everything that had ever happened. I looked out across the drive of Lucas' home, and Drew was levitating a ball of fire the size of the mansion.

I heard a cackling laughter from above.

"Don't let her inside our home," said a voice from above. My eyes turned to the sky above the villa. Three dark-haired girls circled the mansion in flight, taking aim at Drew. He strengthened the fire barrier he intended to have destroy their home. "Kill her," said one of Lucas' sisters. "She's no use to us, Mother wants her dead."

"She loves him, not you," said the oldest sister. "She'll kill you, Lucas that's why she's here. Let her die and be done with this heartache."

"Don't look at them," Lucas whispered to me. "I'm not going to kill her Claudia," he shouted to his youngest sister. "Help us please. Let us inside where he can't reach her. Remember what I told you."

"Don't Claudia," screamed his other two sisters in unison. The door to the villa opened and Lucas and I ran inside. We stood in a grassy courtyard encased by the villa's structure. All of the halls had large archways that opened in to the outdoor space. The home had at least ten floors.

"What do we do?" I asked. But Lucas was silent. He cupped my face and stared in to my eyes.

"What's happen to you," Lucas said. "You don't even look like you're breathing."

I flung my arms around him and kissed him. I didn't know if I would ever see him again, and he was all that mattered in that moment.

"I thought you were dead," he said. "In my heart it felt like you weren't here anymore. I didn't think I would ever see you."

"But you thought that he would come for you? Why didn't you try to save me?"

"I tried," he said. "My sisters saved me from him, but they've kept me here. They wouldn't let me leave. The barrier is for me just as much as it is for him. Claudia is the only one who understands how I feel about you. She knows you are my only hope."

"We've got to get out of here. He'll break through the barrier and take me back." I started to cry. "Please, keep me from him. I can't go back to him now – he'll kill me or worse."

"I don't think we can. I've been trying for weeks and there's no way out."

"There is, he'll break down the barrier, then we have to get out of here."

"I love you," Lucas said. "No matter what's happened, I love you more than anything and that won't ever change."

"You don't know what's happened. Everything's changed. I'm not the same Mina. I've killed too many people to ever be Mina again. You think you love me, but you don't." The memories came back like water rushing through a fall. I couldn't forget, no matter how hard I tried.

"Look at me, none of it matters. He's been controlling you. You are the same Mina. I'll always love you, not even he can change that, and he can't change you, don't forget that."

I felt naked, vulnerable and I knew why. Drew's erratic presence was on the edge of my mind. "He's broken through the barriers, I can sense him," I said. "He's coming for me. He's going to kill us," I cried. "This is my fault, all of it. I never should have trusted him, and now we're both going to die. All of this is my fault," I said again. "I should just let him kill me."

And all I could see was Drew as he stood in a dark corner in my mind, lurking and lunging at me. "He won't stop," I screamed. "Kill him, please! He won't stop hurting me," I cried and felt him ripping me in half. It was all mental, but he made it feel so real. I was sure he would kill me, and I couldn't see anything but him. I lay on the ground of the courtyard, horror-stricken, and I reached out my hand trying to find Lucas.

"Mina, please get up, I can hear him in the house. We have to get out, please get up, please," Lucas begged, but I couldn't move. "Focus on me, Mina. Tell me you love me, remember Mina, remember and he'll leave. I love you," he said. "None of this was your fault. He planned this Mina – this was all him, please don't blame yourself it only makes it worse. It wasn't your fault."

"I love you too," I said. "None of it matters," I repeated Lucas' words and I wanted to believe them. "It wasn't my fault," I breathed and tried to convince myself that it wasn't. But it was so hard with him there in my mind, mocking me all the while. I just wanted him dead, even if I had to die too. All I wanted was solace from him. I don't know how or why but I felt stronger, somehow.

Drew was still there in my mind, but I could hear the wind. I could hear it whispering to me. I called to it and asked it beat down the home – I asked it to save me, and I could hear it blowing at the door. The windows shattered and I opened my eyes. Drew taunted us in anger.

"Don't do this, my love, it's me that you want. Come back to me, I promise to be good. I won't hurt you if you kill him. *Kill him now*," Drew said.

I created a wind tunnel outside the villa, and it grew stronger as my fury and resistance boiled over. The wind blew the roof off Lucas' home and opened up to the heavens. His sisters hovered above. They dove for Drew, and he shot in to the sky, frightening them. Drew lit the house on fire, and Lucas' sisters screamed at the sight of their home burning. I called to the rain and lightning, and shot up to meet Drew and my end. Either I would die or he would die. I wouldn't go back to him.

"What are you doing? You wouldn't want to upset me, my love. Come here," Drew said. "Stand beside me, not against me." I could feel his eyes haunting me, but I refused to look at him. "Don't try to keep me out, you'll only make things worse for yourself."

I closed my eyes so that I couldn't see him, and so he couldn't control me anymore. I was able to focus, and I struck him with lightning. I wanted him to suffer like he made me suffer. I wanted him to admit that his plan had been to manipulate me, hurt me, and use me at will. He never loved me, but he believed he did.

He was psychotic and he really believed that he loved me. And I had believed that I loved him. That was the hardest thing to admit. I had been so obsessed, so enamored with this evil man who killed so many, and who had raped me, and taken advantage of me every chance he ever had. I channeled my anger and the lightning grew stronger, but Drew just laughed. I blew a force of mental strength at him in frustration, but he was unaffected.

"It will take more than that, my love," he crooned. "You don't want to do this. You don't want to kill me. You love me. Look at me Mina, please? I'm so sorry. I promise this time, I won't hurt you again. Just help me now, help me destroy them. I can't do it without you, and you mustn't be so selfish. Everything isn't always about you."

I screamed, and the wind carried my voice in a piercing screech that echoed across the Earth. The strength of my hatred for him blew him away. His expression changed from a taunting one, to a terrified one. But he wasn't afraid of me. Danger loomed, close and ominous.

Drew looked to the outside of Lucas' home, and there was Narc, Andres, Chance, and who I assumed was Lucas' mother Jaclyn.

Drew looked at me and flew away, escaping the Informants, leaving me to be captured and tortured. Narc called my name and my vision was lost. I fell to the ground and he caught me. The pain I felt took me to another place. The Informants had captured me and not Drew. My fate was certain.

{34}

My skin was icy, and I felt a draft of cool air blowing on my shoulders. I opened my eyes and everything was dark. I could hardly see, but I knew exactly where I was. The Informants had trapped me inside the dungeon of their underground castle. Its mental strength and barriers surrounded me.

When Narc caught me, he kept me silent and still with mind control. The Informants and I traveled by car to the airport and then to the Netherlands. We drove to the city of Sneek, but the castle was in the countryside near a black lake. Narc crumbled away the earth to reveal the castle's entrance. Then he and Andres dragged me through the castle, which wasn't visible from the earth's surface.

We walked through underground tunnels and it made the castle look like a train station. The floors were carved of marble, the statues made of stone and granite, but the paintings and statues depicted torture, murder, and suffering. You could hear the screams of others, echoing through the marble tunnels. The home of the Five Leaders was beautifully demented, just as Lily had described.

Narc tossed me down a dark staircase leading to the dungeon, after he and Louis tortured me. Louis was older than Sophia – who I believed to be the most ancient of all Logosts. She was the queen, but Louis was visibly older and angrier than all of the Five Leaders. He antagonized me as he and Narc tortured me. Louis said it was revenge for killing Cassandra. It was the most painful thing I'd ever experienced and their laughter infuriated me, but at least I didn't have to see Drew. He couldn't get to me here. But I could still see his eyes when I closed my own. I could feel him watching me. It felt that way, but I knew that was impossible. No one could break through these mental barriers – not even Drew Elliot, the coward that he was.

Last night, Sophia decided that I would die the next evening. She'd told Andres, Chance, Louis, and Narc that I was too strong to live, too much of a threat to their power. I hadn't tried to defend myself, or describe anything that had happened with Drew. The Informants were not ones who listened to reason, and I knew that it was better to stay quiet than to endure more suffering at their hands.

I stood up, looking around the dungeon, but all that stood out in its darkness was the door to my prison. The steel door was at least ten feet tall, with no windows. There was no way to escape. I couldn't even use my powers, and their mental strength was so forceful I could barely think. I sat back down, pulled my knees to my chest, and waited for death. I didn't cry because there was no escape, and tears weren't going to break me free of this place. I called to Lucas, but my thoughts faded away. I called to Paris, but neither could hear me. My mind was lost here – confined inside the barriers of their castle.

"Mina," someone said my name in such a mesmerizing way, I wanted to follow the sound. But I was cautious – Lucas told me the castle was filled with tricks and traps, designed to lure in the weak-minded. My mind felt weak, but I wasn't weak-minded.

"I'm not upset, my love," the alluring voice said inside my head. And I knew who it was. It was then that I started to cry – he would never let me go. He wouldn't even leave me alone to die in peace. Drew would never be done with me. *"I know that you love me, and I promise I won't hurt you."*

"How are you doing this?" I asked. *"You told me no one could break through, not even you. Haven't you lied enough?"*

"I didn't lie to you! I didn't think that I could break through, but my longing for you, my need for you is so strong – stronger than any power they have. I'm sorry that I left you. Narc would have killed me instantly had I stayed. But I'm here with you now, there's no need to be afraid. I love you Mina, and I'm trying to save you. My thoughts can travel through, but my powers cannot. You're going to have to destroy them on your own, but I know that you're strong enough. You just have to believe it."

"Just let me die," I pleaded. *"I just want them to kill me. I just want to be free from you!"*

"I'm not the one holding you prisoner! You can save yourself if you listen to me, my love. I mean only to protect you, never to harm you. Call to Narc," Drew thought. *"Offer yourself to him and he will let you out. His desire to have you is still very strong. Call to Narc and he will let you out."*

"I refuse!" I screamed out loud. "If I get out of here you'll come for me again, and you'll hurt me. I know you're lying. I just want to die. Please, just go away!"

"They know about Paris," Drew thought. *"They plan to hunt him down and kill him once you're dead. The only way to save him is to kill them, Mina. And I promise once they're dead you'll want me again. You won't be afraid of me anymore. It will go back to how it was before, please just listen – I really mean it when I say I won't hurt you."*

"How did you know about Paris?" I asked, staring up at the dark ceiling as if Drew were speaking from above. He lied about everything – how did I know he wasn't lying now? "And how did the Informants find out?"

"I've known all along, my love. After everything that's happened you really believe that you can keep secrets from me? And I am the one who told them. I had no other choice – it was the sacrifice I made to keep you alive. When I registered you with Narc, he wanted to kill you immediately, but I told him about Paris. As Ernest Culvert's only Logost son, Narc agreed it was an even trade and that is why you're still alive."

I slammed my fists to the ground, scraping my hands. He was lying, I knew he would hurt me the first chance he got. But I couldn't let Paris die because I had been lured in by Drew. I would have to destroy the Informants and risk my life to save Paris. I sucked in a deep breath, and called to Narc.

"Narc," I thought. *"I want to see you. I need to speak to you."*

"The decision has been made," Narc thought. *"You will die tomorrow at sunset."*

"But I want you. I want to be with you before I die. I've always wanted you.

I was just afraid of Drew. I'll be with you now if you come to me."

"You're only trying to escape. Why would I let you lure me in?"

"I just want you to touch me and kiss me — you don't have to let me out of here. All I can think of is how badly I want you." Narc was unwise, his yearning to hurt little girls outweighed all of his other desires. He wasn't as powerful as he believed.

"I'll come to your cell," Narc thought. *"But I don't just want to touch you and kiss you. I want more than that if I'm going to risk death. I want to hear you scream. I want to hurt you."*

Narc wanted me to cry and scream while he touched me, to cause me pain that would arouse him. I didn't know if I was powerful enough to stop him, and I knew that I couldn't stand to have another man rape me. I thought about shrinking in to something so small that no man would ever want to hurt me. But what I wanted was to be strong enough that men like Narc and Drew wouldn't think about hurting me — ever. I wanted them to fear my power and what I was capable of, and now I knew I was capable of murder. I wanted to kill Narc. I wanted to trick him and have him suffer for what he'd done to Lily. He deserved a painful death. All I wanted was to end his life. And I knew I was strong enough to do it.

"You can hurt me," I thought. *"I'll let you do whatever you like, and I promise not to fight back. But you have to let me out of here."*

"You promise not to fight back?"

"Yes, just open the door."

I stared at the steel, gray door. It hissed at me and opened. I ran out the cell and down the hall of prisons. The ceiling of the castle moved like a galaxy of stars and unknown planets. I watched the planets orbit. I could see stars and I began to forget as they entranced me. Footsteps trailed behind me as I followed the planets trapped in the ceiling. I dashed down another marble tunnel. My eyes transfixed on the galaxy up above, staring at the moving stars. I reached my hand up to see if it was real, and someone touched my shoulder. Narc spun me around to face him.

"Come with me," he said, pinning my hands behind my back. Narc walked me further down the tunnel. "I hope you realize there's no way to save yourself. Sophia has made the decision and I cannot overrule her – so luring me in this way will do you no good."

I nodded without looking up at him. I didn't want him to see what I was plotting. But I was sure that he was plotting too, and mapping out in his mind all the things he wanted to do to me. He kept tightening his grip on my hands, and rolling his other hand over my body. He touched my neck and squeezed my breasts. It took strength to not burn away his fingertips. His hands felt like sandpaper and his fingernails were chipped, dirty and yellow.

"I know there's nothing you can do. I just don't want to go back to that dungeon. Where are you taking me?"

"To my wing of the castle," he said. "I have a room you can stay in until your number is called. You won't have to go back to that prison."

"Do the others know you let me out?"

Narc laughed. "I may have a weakness for young girls, but I'm not a fool. I'd be killed for treason if you escaped," he said. Then he stopped and pulled me closer, staring in to my eyes. "Let me read your mind. I feel like you're plotting something. There's too much energy radiating from you."

"There's nothing to plot. I know I can't escape you. I'm just scared. You frighten me."

"And you have every reason to be frightened. I don't think you realize how much danger you're putting yourself in. You may not live to see the morning," he smiled. "I tend to get carried away sometimes. It's in your best interest to not entice me with your screams, I may lose control."

Narc wrapped his hand around my throat. Because of my age and my gender, he saw me as disposable. He could hurt me, even kill me, and would suffer no consequences. In his eyes, it didn't matter what happened to me. He tugged me along, and I needed to keep him talking. I wanted to ask him about Lily, and have him admit to me what he'd done.

"Lily Andrews is dead," I said. "Drew killed her." My voice stumbled over his name. Even though he couldn't get to me, I was still afraid of him.

"Are you talking about Jane's daughter?"

"If Jane is your sister, then yes I am talking about her."

"I know she's dead. I'm not planning on revenging her death if that's what you're asking. I want Drew dead, but for my own reasons – it has nothing to do with my sister's daughter. I don't even remember what the girl looks like. Her father used to try and keep her from me."

"Why? Did you abuse her?"

"I never hurt her. I didn't even try to have sex with her. I only touched her. She was very little when I did it though."

"Do you feel guilty about it?"

"No, why would I? Someone else would have done it eventually. I was just speeding up the process. I wanted to be the first to touch her that way."

"She was your niece," I said no longer hiding my disgust from him.

"You're in no place to judge!" he spat. "Young girls like you and her lure men in. You try to act so innocent, but if you were I wouldn't have wanted you in the first place. I know a bad girl when I see one. And you have no one to blame but yourselves."

"You're sick. It isn't natural to want to hurt little girls."

"I may be sick, but you're a hypocrite. What makes you think I'm any worse than Drew? He's just as much a pedophile as I am."

"Don't say his name. I don't want to hear it."

"So you finally see him for the monster he is?" I couldn't answer him. "Don't worry you'll be dead soon, and you won't hear his name or anything else again."

The tunnel opened in to a large room decorated in white, with gold trim. Torches lit the dim room. The walls were a neutral color with open archways. There were several doors inside the room and he opened one to his left. A king size bed stood in the center, a chair, and a couch along the adjoining walls. There was a large stone fireplace with a poker next to it. He locked the door, and put up barriers to keep me hidden, to keep the others from hearing me scream. I wasn't worried. I knew that once he was dead the barriers would go with him. He was certain this would be my end, but I knew that it was his.

He pinned me down on the bed and pulled at my skirt. I tried to push his hands away but they felt like hot irons. Narc burned my hands and I looked up at him.

"You promised not to fight."

Narc used his mind to convince me that someone was sawing away at my limbs. I felt the pain of it and arched my back in torment, but I didn't scream. I didn't want to give him the satisfaction. He choked me with his right hand, while he used the other to fumble with the belt buckle on his pants. I didn't want to have to see it. I knew that the sight of it would haunt me. He pulled himself out, and I clenched my jaw, but he tightened the grip around my throat forcing all of him inside my mouth. I stared at the floor and bit my teeth in to his flesh until I tasted his blood. Narc screamed in agony and I levitated the poker from the fire to me. I stabbed him through the stomach, and again through the chest. I felt his life slipping away, and the barriers around the room became weaken. I lit him on fire and watched as he burned, screaming all the while. I had expected more of a fight, but he'd let his guard down completely. His lack of respect for women was his end.

{35}

Narc's lifeless body lay on the ivory floor. The barriers lifted, and the Informants sensed he was no longer living. They'd heard him screaming, but I was so entranced by the sound, I'd forgotten where I was. His ashes caught fire to the curtains and I let the room burn. He hadn't raped me in it, but I was sure he'd raped others there, and I wanted it destroyed. I wanted the whole castle to be nothing but dust. I walked out of the room, sensing the danger. I heard someone sprinting towards Narc's wing of the castle.

Andres and Chance's thought patterns weren't difficult to place. They had common minds, with common abilities. Their ominous presence was getting closer to me. But I felt stronger than ever before. Narc's death had brought me more power.

No one was in Narc's wing of the castle when I reached it. I knew I couldn't destroy the castle with just my mind, its protection was too great. But there was a lake directly above it. The castle was so deep in the ground that the water couldn't reach it. I focused my mind on blasting away the matter that supported the lake. No one was focused on protecting it. I wanted to empty the lake, sink the castle, and drown everyone. The castle caught fire and I blasted away the tunnels and walls with my anger.

"Mina's escaped and Narc is dead. Kill her." Sophia's thoughts echoed throughout the castle. She wanted me to hear.

"You won't get out alive," Louis thought. *"You'll suffer for his death, and for the death of my Cassandra."*

Andres and Chance's footsteps chased me. I stumbled, as they took aim at my mind with feelings of pain and images of darkness. It was crippling, but somehow I kept running. Outside of Narc's wing of the castle, the galaxy in the ceiling started to swirl and suck me in. I ran faster, but Sophia sent her endless flames after me. The strength of my own wind kept them at bay. If I flew to escape the fire, the galaxy would suck me in. It pulled me, and I tried to keep my feet on the polished floor. The fire was quick. It moved with speed and grace. The heavy footsteps grew closer, but when I turned the corner I saw Andres and Chance standing before me.

They aimed at me with mental blows. Chance threw out his hand and I was blown down the tunnel, in to the fire. I flew in to the darkness of the galaxy, dodging the fire. It pulled me deeper and deeper in to the abyss. The stars weren't stars at all, but souls of the tormented. Even in death they weren't allowed to leave.

The souls reached for me, pulling me in to the darkness. I was frightened, and Chance and Andres tortured me with more pain. I remembered the ground I was blasting away to release the lake from above the castle. I asked the Earth to quake and shatter the castle, and release the water. The Earth lent me its strength and the castle crumbled, cracked and quivered. The sound of the water rushing echoed through the stone tunnels.

Chance and Andres stood below me, directing the full force of their mental strength at me while the stars pulled me further in. I blasted out of the ceiling, and struck them with lighting. The water rushed in, and I electrocuted them until they were unmoving. Their bodies smoking on the castle floor.

The water flooded the castle, and I had to fly close to the ceiling. At the heart of the castle was Sophia's wing, I headed there to kill her. They'd brought me there when she'd made the decision that I would die. Everything was made of glass in her wing of the castle: the floor, the ceilings and the walls. All you saw was the night sky rather than the surrounding layer of earth.

Sophia's mind was so strong, she could make you see whatever she wanted in the glass, but all I'd seen was the star-filled night sky. The height of it was endless as if you could fly forever and never reach the top. The castle was falling, and the earth that supported it was faltering. I held my breath for good measure, but I knew I only had moments left. When the castle flooded completely, I might not be able to control the water and save myself. And maybe that was best. If I escaped, Drew would kill me.

When I reached the heart of the castle, I approached the entrance, a ghostly, transparent gate, with caution. I didn't think I would be able to pass through, but when I paced in everything was silent, as if the rushing water, and the sound of the foundation crumbling couldn't be heard. I looked for the stairs that led to Sophia's glass throne. The throne looked empty at first, but I could see her pale face, and her silver hair flowing in anger. She didn't attack me, and when I looked in her eyes they were sullen – as if she were vacant. I wondered who was dwelling inside her body. I walked towards her. I wanted to touch her. I wanted to comfort her, for some inexplicable reason I pitied the evil Queen.

"She's dying," breathed a voice from the sky. "The castle has fallen, the others are dead, and she's given up all because of you. She dreamed of your power and told me you would be the end of our reign. Narc and I disagreed, we ignored her. But as you grew stronger, we saw the truth in her eyes. When Drew took you, we searched and we stressed that it was too late. She's convinced there's nothing she can do to defeat you." Louis emerged from the shadows. He blasted me in to the glass wall. My body stuck and slithered down to the floor, like a drop of rain on a window shield.

"Louis, don't." Sophia's voice creaked and echoed in the glass room. "Let her live," she said. "If she doesn't, it will be the end of our world. Drew Elliot will not stop until every Logost is dead. Then he will rule the humans."

"Why should she live?" Louis asked without turning to Sophia. He kept his eyes on me and it felt like I was being swept away in to the sky, in to the piercing cold. "She's killed the others – she killed my only daughter."

"It wasn't me," I murmured through my resistance. My body

floated upward at Louis' command and he choked me with the strength of his mind.

"You're a liar," he said. "I don't care what Sophia says. You will die with us. You've destroyed everything we hold dear you selfish little bitch! I hope you see your father in hell!"

Sophia was no longer protecting this wing of the castle. My eyes looked up at the glass ceiling, and it cracked and broke away. The water from the lake rushed in, capturing Louis' attention. I flew towards him and held him in place with my eyes. I envisioned his body splitting in half, separating him forever, but I was weak now. I could feel my energy draining, and it seemed like too many moments had passed before he screamed, and his body was severed in half.

Sophia rose from her chair, screaming – a high-pitched howl, at the sight of Louis being ripped in half so slowly. She floated down from her throne, her eyes fixed upon me.

"You killed him." Sophia gasped for air. "He's really gone." A faint smile ran across her pale, wrinkled lips. She walked towards me and embraced me. I pushed her back, frightened she would kill me. "I won't hurt you," she said. "All I've ever wanted was to be free of Louis. He's been manipulating me since I met him. He fooled me, filled my head with lies, and used me as a puppet. But with time my mind began to match his, and I couldn't think for myself anymore."

She looked broken, haunted with pain.

"Thank you, for saving me. You should leave. Get out while there is still time."

"You don't have to stay here and die. I know you're weak, but I can carry you. We can be free together."

"No," she said looking away. "I don't want to live anymore. I want peace." She walked back towards her throne and sat down. "I will let death find me. I will not resist this end. But you Mina – you are destined for great things. I've seen it, and I know that you think you're ruined now. But you've grown so strong, and you will only grow stronger. Drew will not defeat you. Don't let him break you as Louis did with me. Don't let his actions control you."

I wouldn't leave her there to die. I just couldn't, so I told a lie when I knew I shouldn't. But I wanted to believe the lie for Sophia's sake.

"Leave with me," I said. "You can have a normal life. Lucas will miss you. He's always loved you – he's always known that deep down you were good. He'd be distraught if you died."

"He would? Oh, but his mother would not. She would probably wet herself in excitement over my death," she mused. "I don't want to give her the satisfaction though," she breathed and I didn't wait for her to finish. I grabbed her and blasted a hole in the castle for us to soar through.

I flew us to the ground's surface and Sophia was silent and unmoving. Her frail spine rested under my arm as I released her. The lake was empty and the water had destroyed the castle. A high cliff in the distance opened up to a rocky valley. I walked towards it, knowing I had to jump or Drew would find me. He'd keep me and he'd kill me in time. I stared at the cliff, but Sophia grabbed my arm.

"Thank you for saving me. I'm still not sure that I want to live.

I'm ashamed of all that's happened. I'm ashamed that I got enjoyment out of it."

She kept speaking. I watched her lips move, but I couldn't hear anything. All I could see was Drew raping me. All I could see was his face and how much he hated me. How much he feared me, and wanted to control me. He would be here soon. I walked towards the cliff again. I reached the edge and I felt free. The wind blew in to me, and the open air called my name. "Mina," I heard it say and I reached out my arms. I pushed off the balls of my feet and it felt like I was flying. But I wouldn't fly now. I smiled, and waited for death to release me of the pain, and all the shame I felt. I was in a blissful state, knowing he wouldn't get the chance to hurt me again, knowing that I wouldn't ever have to feel worthless because I wasn't. I was worth something.

Drew would be upset that he didn't get to kill me, and that brought me joy. I chose my own end, and I couldn't worry about the world. I hoped they would see things for how they really were. That it had all been him, and not me. He'd meant for me to trust him, and love him. It was what he wanted – and he'd planned to rape me all along. He was waiting for the opportune time, and he had not anticipated that I would fall in love Lucas, which had changed everything. It swayed the original blueprints. It made him angry, it made him jealous and he didn't want me to have that power over him. I didn't believe that I would ever heal – I believed I had to die to escape him.

I could hear someone screaming, and I assumed it was me. It

was a woman's voice, and she sounded like she was suffering, someone was hurting her. I opened my eyes and saw the bottom of the cliff. It was so close to me, then I saw him there too. It was really him, though, it wasn't just my mind. I flew back in to the sky, but he shot out at me, his body colliding with mine.

Drew grabbed me, pulling me down. I reached for something to protect me. He slammed our bodies in to the rocks below. I cried and he climbed on top of me. He pinned me down and choked me.

"I love you," Drew said. "Thank you, for everything you've done. I wouldn't have been able to kill them without you." He released one hand from around my throat, and pulled up my skirt. My arms flailed at my sides, as he pinned them down. My hands touched the ground and I searched for something to knock him out with. He was so distracted by his own enjoyment that he didn't see me pick up a long, jagged piece of rock.

I could see the gold swirls around his irises, but I fought their power. I stabbed him in the arm, and then in the stomach. He grabbed my hand, trying to take the miracle weapon from me. I heard the bones in my fingers breaking, but I couldn't feel the pain. I wouldn't give in. I wouldn't let him convince me that I couldn't fight back. He wasn't stronger than me. I blew his body off me, and he collided with the side of the cliff. He laughed, but I lunged at him and tackled him to the ground. I froze him so that he couldn't use his powers of manipulation. And then I saw panic in his eyes. They were dark green and there weren't any swirls inside them. I held him down and I used the jagged rock to cut his eyes out. I cut them out, and he couldn't scream. I cut them out, and he wouldn't be able to control me with them again. They were gone, and I was finally free of him. But he began to stir once they were missing. The rock I held in my hand flew away from me. He was regaining control. I felt him ripping me in half.

I flew in to the sky and called to the wind. I held out my arms, and created a wind tunnel that swept him away as he shot in to air and took aim at me. The strength from my tunnel would sweep him away forever, and he'd never hurt another person again.

{36}

I couldn't feel him there anymore. Drew was really gone. I flew back up to the cliff's edge and saw Sophia, dead on the ground with leaves around her. She deserved better than this. I threw her arm around my shoulder and carried her from the cliff's edge. I needed to find somewhere she could pass on in peace. This dwelling of pain couldn't be her final resting place.

The sun fell lower, and darkness was approaching. My only plan was to bury her, but I wanted to see my family now that I was finally safe from the threat of death. Drew was dead. The Informants were gone. And I no longer had any reason to be afraid.

It was an unfortunate thing, but when I closed my eyes I still saw Drew. I saw him leaning against a corner in my mind, whispering to me with hatred in his eyes. I couldn't hear his words. I kept him silent, but he was always there. And I wondered if he would ever leave, or if I would always see him, and that the threat of his presence would keep me subdued. And there were things I thought of that made me ashamed. I was ashamed for loving him, for thinking that being with someone that much older was appropriate. I still blamed myself, and I knew I couldn't tell anyone what he'd done – ever. I worried they would blame me, and I couldn't handle having to hear their accusations.

I carried Sophia's body through the surrounding forest and in to the evening. She was too limp and heavy for me to fly with her body. And there was a part of me that didn't want to use my powers. I hoped I wouldn't ever have to use them again. I wanted to be safe. I wanted to be happy and free. It seemed like that goal was finally obtainable with Drew gone.

The light from the moon shined through the tall trees. I hadn't eaten or slept in days. The heaviness of everything began to weigh me down. I hadn't traveled far from the Informant's destroyed castle, when I heard something stirring in the distance. I assumed it was a human, but I worried that it might be another Logost. I was still and didn't breathe. I prepared myself to attack whoever was there. Then someone's hand caressed my back. I didn't recognize him at first, but I saw that mischievous smile in his eyes when he looked at me. I saw a longing for me. Who he was didn't register in my mind. I was scared, and I shocked the hand and blasted the figure in to an oak tree. Lucas fell to the ground and pushed himself up, looking at me in shock.

I walked towards him, staring in to his eyes. I didn't have to be afraid to look Lucas in the eyes. He wouldn't try to control me. Lucas valued my thoughts and opinions. He didn't want me to be his puppet, he wanted a partner. I knew I would always feel safe with him. He respected me and he didn't think that I was worthless. I kissed him for the first time without resignation or guilt. I kissed him, knowing that I didn't have to worry about Drew taking me from who I really loved.

Drew believed that I was too young to know what I really wanted. But he was too psychotic to know what he ever wanted. He believed he loved me, but he only loved my power. He only loved me when I was afraid and obedient to him. And I wished that I hadn't stayed obedient for so long.

I still felt ruined. And I knew I couldn't tell Lucas the truth. I was ashamed. But I kept kissing Lucas. I didn't want to let him go, even if he decided he didn't want to touch me again. I knew I should tell him the truth, but what if he didn't believe me?

Lucas pulled me tighter in to his arms.

"How did you know where I was?" I asked.

"I've been to the castle before to visit Sophia. And I decided to search the forest on a whim once I saw it was destroyed. We should rest for a moment," he breathed. "It took me two days to escape my sisters. I thought you would be dead before I got here."

"We can't rest. We have to find a place for Sophia."

Lucas gazed down at his lifeless grandmother.

"What happened?"

"I told you I'm not the same Mina anymore," I started to say.

"You killed her! Don't you realize this is what Jaclyn's been dreaming of?" But then he looked sympathetic. "I'm sorry. I know he was controlling you, and I know you were afraid he might kill you. I

338

was afraid he might kill you too, and me as well. I'm surprised I'm still alive."

"I didn't kill her, Drew did. I killed the others though, one by one. They're all dead."

"You're amazing," he said. "I love you more than anything, Mina. I've never known anyone as strong or as brave as you. Maybe if we're together forever some of it will rub off on me." He kissed my lips and smiled. "How did you kill Narc? He's so strong. I thought he couldn't be beat."

"I don't want to talk about it." And I pictured what had happened. I felt dirty, unclean and disgusting. I'd let two men do bad things to me. I hated myself. I couldn't tell him the truth. I didn't want my nightmares to be his. I thought about Lily, and the fact that I wouldn't ever see her again. I'd tried to avenge her, but that didn't change anything.

"You know about Lily?" I asked but I already knew that he did.

"Yeah," he said trying to hide his sadness from me. I knew he missed her. And I couldn't blame him for missing her, when I missed her too.

"It hurts to know I won't ever hear her voice again. It's not fair that she's dead. How are you feeling?" I asked. He needed to open up to someone, even if it that someone was me.

"I probably shouldn't admit this to you, but I really miss her."

"Drew killed her."

"Where is he? He must be close if he just killed Sophia. We

should keep moving."

"He's dead. I killed him. He won't ever come for us again." I sounded different when I said that, and Lucas looked frightened, but said nothing. "Help me carry her." We lifted Sophia's body from the forest floor. "We should take her to the Wadden Sea." I'd seen it along the coast when we traveled to the castle. "It's not far, if we fly we should make it before dawn."

I prepared for flight, but Lucas pulled me down to the ground.

"We can't fly, Mina. My sisters are searching the skies for me. They probably know I'm here. I think they know that I'm close."

"How can you know for sure? I thought you couldn't read minds."

"I can't, but whenever I can't see them in my mind, I know they're close by. We have to stay hidden until they leave. But the sea isn't too far. It should only take a few hours if we travel by foot."

"Well, I can't levitate her," I said. "I'm too weak. You should do it."

We walked through the forest while Lucas levitated Sophia. When we reached the lake, we rested her body in the water. We used or minds to lift heavy stones on top of her so she would sink to the bottom. I could have easily burned her with my own fire, but I didn't think that was what she would want. Her ability to control fire had made it so she couldn't ever be normal. She'd never been free, but I believed she was now.

"Despite all that's happened, I can't believe I finally have you to myself," Lucas said as we watched Sophia sink to the bottom of the dark sea. "You're going to think I'm crazy, but I want to stay with you, forever. I don't want to go back to Colombia. I just want to be wherever you'll be, if you want me."

Lucas embraced me from behind and kissed my neck. I pushed him off me, knowing that he didn't really want to touch me that way. He didn't really love me. He just thought he did because he didn't know what had happened. Once he found out the truth, he wouldn't ever look at me.

"What's wrong?" he asked sounding filled with desperation. "What's changed? I've risked everything for you. Don't tell me you've changed your mind. I might die if I have to hear you say that."

"No, it's not that. I love you. I really do. I just – touching is going to be hard for me for a while. Whenever Drew touched me, it was because he wanted to hurt me. I know you would never hurt me, but sometimes my mind thinks it's him touching me."

"What an awful thing to say," he said quietly. "I'm not him. And I won't ever be like him."

"I'll always want you. I'm just worried you won't want me." I wanted to cry, but I didn't. I didn't want him to ask me why I was crying, and I didn't want him to see me cry over another man. It wasn't fair to him, and I'd already been vastly unfair to him. He kept trying to meet me gaze, but I felt like I didn't deserve him. I felt worthless.

"Mina, I've loved you since the first day I met you. How could you say something like that? Tell me what you're thinking, please?"

Lucas moved up to me slowly, and put his arms around me. And I didn't push him away this time. I knew he wouldn't hurt me, but it still felt uncomfortable to have him touch me in a loving way, and not an aggressive way like Drew did. I'd gotten too use to having to fear for my life.

"I want to take all the pain away from you," Lucas said. "It's making me insane to have to see you this sad, and to feel like there isn't anything I can do to make it better. I feel so helpless, Mina. Tell me what to do. Tell me what to say to make everything go away. I just want you. I want you forever."

"Everything's changed. I don't think there's anything you can do to help. I wish I was anyone else but myself right now. I just feel like it was so easy for him to trick me. I should have been more cautious. I shouldn't have been so trusting."

"You're young. He wanted you to believe that he was the one, and you did. You shouldn't blame yourself for that. You can only control yourself. You cannot control others. Accept that Mina, and let go of the mistakes you feel you made."

I leaned in to him and pressed my lips to his. Maybe I was free now. Maybe I could love and be whoever I wanted. I could make my own choices and decisions without having to worry about Drew watching, and waiting for me to be alone. I touched his shoulders and his skin felt like velvet. I wanted him to be mine, but I couldn't stop my feelings of uncertainty. I felt unworthy of love.

"I want to come with you to New York. I want to see Paris

again, and meet Carter and your Mom. I want to be a part of your life. I want to show up at your home, and ask your mother if I can take you out to the movies."

"She'd tell you that you could. They'd like you a lot. I know they would." I pictured Lucas being my home one day. And just the thought alone, made me forget everything that had happened. I wanted him to be right. I wanted to pretend that none of this had ever happened. Maybe if I pretended then all of it would go away.

"I need something to rely on, and you're that something. I need your support and I need your love."

"I need you too," I said. "I don't think I could move past this without you. You're the only one who understands. No one else knows me like you. I just want you to love me forever, no matter what's happened."

"Will you tell me what's happened?" Lucas breathed as if he was afraid to ask. "I know it's something bad, I can see it in your eyes. I can see in your face, there's been a change in you. I don't know what though, and it's making me think of terrible things. Don't tell me if you don't want to. I'll try not to be selfish about this."

"I can't tell you, Lucas. I don't think you'll ever forgive me if I confess this. I just can't – I don't know if I'll ever be able to tell anyone. I'm sorry, and I know I'm hurting you by keeping secrets, but I just can't. I'm not ready or well enough to even think about what happened." I started to cry, and I couldn't stop myself. I wanted to, but I couldn't.

Lucas pulled me close to him and let me cry in to his

shoulder. "I understand," he said. "And he's gone now. He won't ever hurt you again."

"But I do long to hurt you, my love. I hope that I'll get the chance to feel you shake underneath me," I heard Drew's voice inside my head. *"I want to hear you scream. I want to watch you cry, but after what you've done I will never see anything. You've done a bad thing, my love. But I forgive you. Come back to me. I promise to be good."*

There was an ache in my chest and a lump rose to my throat. I wanted to slash it away. He was still alive. How could I ever be free from him? He would never die. He would never stop, and he wouldn't ever go away. I screamed in frustration, and Lucas looked like he thought I was losing my mind.

"Calm down, what's wrong?" Lucas said.

"He's here." My voice trembled. "I thought he was dead, but he isn't."

"He is dead Mina. He can't hurt you. I don't sense anyone near us."

And then I couldn't hear Lucas' voice anymore. I was certain it was Drew speaking to me inside my head, but maybe I was crazy now. Maybe Drew's soul was lost in my head, like so many souls had been lost inside his.

"He really hurt you, didn't he?" Lucas asked. "I'm sorry for what he's done. But you are safe now. You don't have to be afraid."

"Oh, but you should be afraid," I heard Drew's voice again. Lucas reached for his chest, and his eyes rolled back. He fell over on to the ground. I screamed again, then I knew Drew was really there. I could

sense him. I cried over Lucas. He just couldn't be dead. *"I won't kill him,"* Drew thought. *"He deserves to watch you die. He deserves to watch you suffer."*

{37}

The morning air was thick with fog. But I saw Drew beckoning me in the lightening sky. The sun was rising. His face held dark circles where his eyes had been.

"You want me, Mina," Drew said. "I know that you do. You love me. I'm sorry for trying to kill you. It was an accident. I don't know what came over me."

"Just like you promised not to hurt me!" I'd never been angrier with anyone in my life. I wanted to watch him burn in Hell for everything he'd put me through.

"Oh, but you wanted that," he said. "You asked for it, remember?"

"I wanted to before, but I didn't then. I changed my mind, and I had every right to. I regret having ever wanted you in the first place! I never thought you would force me!"

"No one forced you!" Drew screamed. "You wanted it that way. I know you did. Don't deny it. And you deserved to be treated that way for upsetting me – for forgetting how much you love me."

Lucas began to stir. I could hear him moving. He looked up at me.

"What's he saying Mina?" he asked.

"You know what's happened," Drew said to Lucas. "I was the first to touch her, the first to have her. It wasn't you, and it won't ever be."

"He's lying," I said to Lucas. "He's making all of this up. He's just trying to hurt you."

But a part of me felt like I was the one lying, there was a part of me that wanted to believe that I deserved that, and it made me shameful. It made me hate myself. It made me so ashamed I couldn't think. I wanted to disappear, but I knew that I couldn't. I was even angrier than I'd been before. But I was also confused, and it was hard for me to remember what had happened.

Maybe Drew was right, maybe I did something to make him think that was what I wanted. It was my fault. I couldn't stop blaming myself. If I'd never been curious about him, none of this would have happened. If I'd decided right away that he was too much older, and that his ever-changing mood was hard for me to keep up with, he wouldn't have raped me. But I knew him, so how could he rape me? I'd been trying to forget, trying to pretend, but that wouldn't make it go away. And when I closed my eyes he was always there laughing at me, delighting in my torment. What he had done in just a few short moments could not be undone. What he had done would haunt me for the rest of my life.

He held me down, he knew he was forcing me. But I knew

him. I knew him and he raped me. He held me down. He put all of his weight on me, so that I couldn't move. It wasn't about him wanting me. It was about him wanting to hurt me. He wanted to show me that he was in control. He didn't touch me or kiss me. He felt that I was unworthy of any of that. The fact that I knew him didn't matter. It was rape because I said no. It was rape because he didn't give me a choice.

The fact that I'd wanted him before did not matter. I should have been able to decide for myself, but I never got the chance. It hadn't been something I wanted or desired, despite him trying to convince me otherwise. He held me down and he raped me. He did that to me. He was the bad one, not me.

I put the strongest barrier my mind had ever conjured around Lucas.

"Come to me, Mina," Drew called. "Please my love. I cannot wait any longer to feel your life escape you."

I shot at him determined to watch him die. I floated across from him. He couldn't see me, but he still believed I would be easily killed.

"I'm sorry," I said sweetly, going along with his charade. "I've missed you, Drew. I want only you. Hold me, please. I need to feel your arms around me."

"You lying, bitch! You want him. But I can make you want me again. I can convince you if you'll let me. Let me entice you once again. I'm ashamed of the holes in my face. My beautiful eyes are gone," he cried. And I was glad that his appreciation for his physical appearance had faded.

"You're still beautiful to me" I said. "I want you. Come closer to me. I need to feel you here."

Drew moved towards me, and I flew away from him. He reached out his hands, grasping for my throat. The water from the sea shot up, placing a barrier between us. The waves pulled him down, but he didn't fall. He just laughed nervously, and smiled.

"Make this easier on me. You know that I will kill you, eventually. The Informants are dead. The only threat to my power now is you, my love."

"Admit that you never loved me and you planned all of this!"

"I do love you. I love you more than anything. And so what if I hurt you. What difference does any of that make to me? You'll be dead soon, my love and I will hurt you again. It will happen. And it won't be so gentle this time."

Drew shot fire at me. The water rose up before me and doused the fire, before it reached me. I shot up further in to the sky, above Drew. But he began to move the mountains in the distance. The rock crumbled, and he attacked me with the broken boulders. I dodged them in the sky, but he could still sense where I was. I used my mind to gain control and stopped the mountains from falling. I sunk the boulders in to the lake, and I aimed one at Drew but he managed to dodge it, even without his eyes. I could feel him choking me with his mind. I could feel him trying to sever my body in half. He was strong, but I was stronger. I called to the clouds, and lightning shattered across the lake.

The rain came down in heavy drops, and I set fire to the rain. Flames ran across the lake, I struck Drew with lightening from the sky, and he screamed in pain. The waves from the lake enveloped me and shielded me from the falling fire. I flew behind Drew and burned him with the fire from my hands. I stuck my fingers in the holes where his eye had been. He screamed again and grabbed me. I tried lighting him on fire, but he drenched the flames. I used the strength of the wind to blow him away, and tortured him with my mind. I wanted him to know what it felt like to be ripped in half.

Drew sank to the ground, and I followed. His torture was slow, but I felt him blocking me. I could feel him trying to stop me. I laughed at his pain, and that infuriated him. He lunged at me. But Lucas immobilized him. He started to break his neck.

"Kill him," I shouted to Lucas, but Drew blurred my words. It felt like there was glass inside me, cutting away at my insides. He blasted Lucas and me away from him. Then he took off in to the sky. He was too weak and wounded to kill either of us. I shot up after him, but I couldn't see him. I could hear him laughing. I could feel his presence. But I couldn't place him.

"You won't find me," he said in his alluring voice. I shot feelings of pain at him, and he screamed, but laughed again. "You won't kill me. I won't allow it. And I won't ever stop searching for you, my love. I can't stop until you're dead."

Then Drew emerged from the shadows of the morning sky. I blasted a hole through his chest. He flew away and I went after him, but he was too fast. I couldn't sense him anywhere. He was gone. He flew so much faster than me. I searched the skies for him. My mind was tired, my body ached. I couldn't find him, and I felt too weak to keep searching.

***

"Wake up. We have to get up now." Lucas stroked my cheek. His hand felt warm against my cold skin. I slowly opened my eyes, and we were still in the forest near the Wadden Sea. My neck stiffened from having slept on the ground. I couldn't count the cuts, scrapes and bruises that covered my arms and legs. I felt frail, raw, as if the slightest touch could break me.

"What happened?" I asked Lucas. He appeared equally disheveled. Leaves tousled his hair, his clothes tattered and torn, but he was still that same beautiful boy.

"You passed out. I couldn't wake you, and I must have fallen asleep as well. I'm worried, Mina. I have a feeling Mr. Elliot will be back." He leaned in to me and kissed my cheek as I lay on the ground in a lush forest. The kiss was meant to comfort, and yet I felt nothing, despite my efforts. "You were so brave. You stood up to him. He may still be alive, but I think what you did was the most beautiful thing I've ever seen. Watching you was like a dream, it was like magic how you moved the water and set fire to the rain. And I don't care what he said, or what's... or what's happened." He paused to look at me, but I couldn't look at him. "I just want us to be safe. I need to keep you safe. I don't want him anywhere near you. He can't ever hurt you again."

My thoughts eluded me. This silver lining, the possibility of safety, it cut me like glass. I couldn't fathom ever feeling safe again. I couldn't see a life past this one. I'd made so many mistakes, but I knew I could rewrite them.

"I have to kill him," I said. "Even if I die too Lucas. He can't live. This is much bigger than you or I. If Drew lives he will destroy the Earth. So many will suffer. He's tortured me, but I can't let Drew Elliot hurt another person. I'm not sure what to do, but I can't hide from him."

But I knew where he was. I could see him there in my mind. I pictured him sitting on the grassy knoll where the light house had been, wishing he could see the ocean. Drew was plotting my death, as I plotted his.

My body felt weak, but my mind was strong. I didn't know how to kill Drew. He was implausibly elusive. He had escaped death so many times. And I was so unbelievably young, but I believed my wisdom could destroy him. All that had happened, it made me wise. I reached inside the pockets of my tweed skirt, remembering that I had saved the stones from my Dad's watch. I thought about where we'd gone in my dream. The stone cottage must hold a key to Drew's undoing. I wasn't sure if it actually existed, but it was all I could think of. I knew where to find Drew, but I wasn't ready to fight him yet.

"I'm here for you, Mina. No matter what you decide, I'm staying. You can't do this on your own. I want to be there with you, and protect you, in any way I can. Tell me what to do, and I'll do it. He seems invincible. How can we destroy him now?"

"He's not," I breathed. "I think... I think I have to go back to him. I'll have to return, and pretend that I love him again if this is going to work. But first, we have to go to New Zealand."

"What's in New Zealand?"

"My Dad's school used to be there. He showed it to me once in a dream. I'm not entirely sure of the location, but I believe it's somewhere outside of Doubtful Sound." Doubtful Sound was a strip of deep lakes and lush green hills that had kept the Logost safe haven hidden.

"But if you only saw the cottage, how do you know it's in New Zealand?" he asked.

I didn't have an answer to give him, because my reasoning was senseless. I'd been dreaming of New Zealand since I was a child. Ever since I saw that photo. I don't know why or how, but I knew. Chalk it up to intuition or what have you, but somehow deep down I knew what was to come. Just as I'd had the premonitions of what was to pass between Drew and I. I knew what would happen, knew what I was supposed to do, but I couldn't act in accordance to stop it. The path was before me, twisted and dark, cloudy and ominous, and I trudged on. Somehow, I kept my spirits high.

I needed to go back to Inwood. We would need Paris to find the cottage, and I owed my Mom an explanation. I thought about who I'd been. I was never happy before Drew. I was always searching, always waiting, rather than enjoying my precious moments. My thoughts of endless time were naïve and ignorant. I knew now, what was to happen. I hoped that Drew would let me live, but my hopes seemed useless.

***

Lucas and I flew to New York. My Mom was so happy to see me that she questioned nothing. She only held me and comforted me. I told her that Lucas and I were the only ones who survived the school's destruction, and that Drew was dead. Lucas needed a place to sleep, and she let him stay on our couch. That night she went all out with cooking. It wasn't tasty, but she tried her best, and her efforts made me feel the love that I so desperately needed.

"I love you, Mina, my dear sweet Mina," she crooned as she braided my hair before bed just as she'd done when I was a child. The tenderness of it all was too much to bare.

Three days later, we ran away. I left a note confessing my undying love to my Mom and Carter. Paris came with us, he was in on our plan. He didn't know the depths of Drew's evil, but he wanted to help. He wanted to keep me safe. He and Lucas believed I would live, but I couldn't dream, it was over. I knew, but that didn't stop the frantic beating of my heart.

Paris' connection to our father was greater than my own. When we arrived in New Zealand, he knew the path we should take. He led us to the cottage, and I felt an unsounding peace within myself.

The remnants of the defiant Logost village still lingered – holding its history and memories weakly intact. It felt like home, more than Lucas or Drew ever had. I couldn't explain it, but wandering through the tiny cottage that once belonged to my father, brought about an inexplicable feeling of harmony. It was all so worn, so broken, yet comforting.

We searched through his things that had remained untouched. Trinkets and common household items like spices and a dust pan all seemed to belong there. He'd carved tiny owls in to the stone, just like at Winchester. I didn't understand, but I wanted to. His books intrigued me the most, they spanned the eras of time. The cottage was much the same as it had been in the photo. It was dark inside. Spiders dwelled, claiming it as their own. I couldn't imagine any other place to feel as this did. I felt power, beauty, sadness and strength all at once. This was my Dad's sanctuary.

We needed something, any clue to how to rebuild the watch. I thought about secrets kept. Places for hidden things that weren't obvious, but Lucas, Paris, and I searched throughout my father's home and felt even more lost than when we first arrived. We brought life back to the cottage, although the village was still deserted. I felt my father's spirit, and Paris felt it as well. When we entered, he couldn't breathe – gasping and choking, clutching at his chest and moving with such caution. I felt his tameness as well. We didn't want to disturb this tomb.

"This is hopeless," Lucas said. "There's nothing here to lead us to Drew's undoing. We've wasted so much time by coming here," he egged in frustration. I walked towards him, as he stared out the large window of what had been my father's bedroom. When I stepped across the mahogany floors, I heard a creaking, an empty sound. The ground was hollow beneath the window. I dropped down at once, and Paris suggested we lift up the floor boards. We found a hammer in a small tool shed in the yard, and pried up the floorboards. And what we found was not what we expected – a diary, a journal of sorts filled with heartache and longing for our Mom and us.

My father had always yearned for us, for a family, and had felt inadequate as a provider because he was a Logost. He'd loved our Mom since they were teens, falling hopelessly for a woman he couldn't ever have. And there in the last page of the book, was diagram of the watch that could tell time, but not telling time the way that you or I would think of it to being told. The watch told what was to come, how to achieve an end. It revealed secrets of the past, and my father had inscribed the words of the very first Logost:

This is it – all it ever will be. Emptiness and longing, no place to call my own. My desires to kill – to hurt and torture are ever changing. The power is too much to bare alone. I will create another to confide in.

But the other could not be trusted, revealed the journal. And I felt that same loneliness as the first ever Logost, the same hopelessness that came with my powers and mental strength. We were not to be understood, and I knew why. We were unnatural – a result of too much questioning, too much self-reflection and doubt, that is how a Logost was born.

We took turns examining the stones and the diagram, but it was useless. Neither of us were skilled enough to rebuild it. I remembered that Drew had an identical watch. The night he raped me and left me in the lighthouse, I'd noticed that he'd taken it with him. I couldn't tell Paris and Lucas. They would want to come with me, if they knew my plan. They wouldn't want me to face Drew alone, but I knew what had to be done. I was the one who had saved this man's life.

If Drew hadn't met me, he would have killed himself in longing. I probably would have killed myself too, had I not met Drew. We were an undying pair – destined for the afterlife, an internal war of the roses, of the sun and the moon vying for time while the other rests. I touched my chest and felt my heartbeat. The sensation of it all would end soon.

I left them both that night. I kissed their foreheads and hoped that they would tell my tale, and whispered to them the sad song of my existence. A tale of desperation and wanting to belong that had led me to my untimely end. I flew to the lighthouse, and I couldn't listen to my own thoughts of retreating. I kept myself numb, as I'd learned to do through all the time spent with Drew. I hugged myself and told myself that this wasn't the end, and that I would live on within the wind. I called to the Earth, and it comforted and supported me throughout my journey to where the lighthouse had once stood.

There was a storm in the distance, watching my every move as I got closer to Drew's home. I could feel the Earth calling to me, asking me to come home. It was dark, the sun and moon hidden from space and time. I felt hidden as well, when I saw Drew. He was shattered, but not unbroken as he lay huddled down on that grassy knoll next to his home that I'd demolished. He was unspeaking and unmoving, and I did the unthinkable. I curled myself in to him, in to the nook of his body and he said nothing. He held me, in a cold and unfeeling way that I didn't understand.

I hated this man.

He hated me.

"Mina," he said to me sounding unlike himself. He sounded desperate and hollow. Of course, he'd always been hollow – a shell of a man that I once believed I loved. He pinched the flesh of my arm and held my hand. The plan was simple. But how could I kill this man? He'd done so much damage, but he was a miserable being. I pitied him still, I don't know how.

"Why have you come here?" Drew pleaded, and I could only cry. I was just a girl. A girl who didn't know the future. I cried and he comforted me. "My love, I'm sorry. I've ruined us both, Mina. What can I do to fix this? I don't know how. I can't change. I don't want to. I want to hurt you. I want to control it all. I want to control you, and if I can't have you... I don't know what to do. I've felt so lost. I can't think. Please, please Mina, tell me what to do. When I first met you, I thought you'd saved my life. I knew what I wanted but saw no way to get it, then when I saw your face I knew I could have it all."

"I love you," I said. "I don't know why. Your cruelty is unspeakable, but you're all the love I've ever known. I can't part with you." I touched his hideous face. I loved Lucas too, I really did, but I wouldn't ever deserve him. I was ruined, and I would ruin him. He deserved so much more than me.

"My eyes Mina, you've stolen my eyes," he cried. "I can't ever see you again. Your beauty... it means nothing now." He buried his face in his hands, and this vulnerability that he was showing me, I knew what it was meant to do. He wanted me to spare him, even without his eyes he will still able to manipulate me. But I was spent. I could take no more of his thinly veiled games.

"Show me the watch Drew," I spoke as a woman, not as a girl. "I can bare you no longer, and you cannot endure me as you once had. You hate me and love me – fear me and desire me, and want me as your own. But I will never be yours, and you were never mine. You know this, you saw it all through the watch. Why?"

"I can't Mina," he spoke with such conviction. "I can't answer your questions, only you hold the answers. You are a pendulum, my love. You've come right back where you belong. Can you deny this?"

"I can't," I whispered in to the night. "But where do you keep the sadness and the broken? What am I to do when you are my destiny? How could your evil be mine?"

"I chose you my love, and you chose me. I know you don't believe it, but it's true. We chose this life. The tale of our lives, intertwined and unbreakable. Your father knew it too. He didn't want this, he wanted to change it so he made the watch. He wanted a different life for you, but he couldn't keep me from you. I had to kill him. Just as you must kill me, my dear sweet girl." He pulled me close and kissed my lips. They burned from his touch.

He reached in to the pocket of his suit and revealed the watch. I grabbed it at once, and held it in my small hand. I kept still, waiting for secrets, waiting for the answer to the end. And what I saw shook me to my core. My name was called. It felt exactly as I knew it would. I pulled Drew to me – grasping him for life. I pinned him down in the grass. I choked him and I choked myself.

The watch flashed us back to the first day we met. I saw myself standing near the river's edge, my park bench stood in the distance. I felt the push and pull of the water. I felt Drew's strength as he watched the memories my mind held. I called to the Earth, fire, water, the wind and the strength of it all killed me, but I watched Drew age as he approached me that day. I watched him wear away with age as he fell, a skeleton of power. And his death was the last thing I saw. His death was my own as the wind swept our souls away forever.

ABOUT THE AUTHOR

Kris Villarreal was born in California, raised in Georgia, and attended college at the University of Georgia, receiving degrees in both journalism and women's studies. With a background in journalism, she held a brief career in technical writing. Her love for words and her passion for social change, led her to pursue a career as a novelist. She wrote her debut novel, *Logost*, as a helping tool for women and girls dealing with depression and abusive relationships. Kris hopes to inspire a generation through words and literature, and plans to address more societal ills through her writing. She enjoys drinking tea, reading, baking, and lifting weights at the gym. Currently, she resides in Atlanta, Georgia with her husband and her two dogs.

www.ingramcontent.com/pod-product-compliance
Lightning Source LLC
Chambersburg PA
CBHW060157260626
47160CB00001B/306